# CARSON STREET CAPER

JAMES M. ZBOZNY

*To "My Franny." Professor Frank Zbozny Phd Duquesne University brother deceased of Pittsburgh and my three sons. Jim,Bill and Steve . Lastly, Mike Rizk from The Paper House Publishing.*

## CONTENTS


Chapter 1 1
Chapter 2 11
Chapter 3 21
Chapter 4 30
Chapter 5 41
Chapter 6 50
Chapter 7 69
Chapter 8 80
Chapter 9 99
Chapter 10 104
Chapter 11 112
Chapter 12 119
Chapter 13 125
Chapter 14 131
Chapter 15 140
Chapter 16 148
Chapter 17 152
Chapter 18 161
Chapter 19 169
Chapter 20 181
Chapter 21 187
Chapter 22 206
Chapter 23 212
Chapter 24 222
Chapter 25 231
Chapter 26 243
Chapter 27 262
Chapter 28 275
Chapter 29 282

Chapter 30 302
Chapter 31 309
Chapter 32 327
Chapter 33 342
Chapter 34 348
Chapter 35 360
Chapter 36 369
Chapter 37 385
Chapter 38 397
Chapter 39 418

*About the Author* 435

# CHAPTER 1

I JUMPED up off the threadbare sofa in my office when my alarm went off. It wasn't the usual wake up alarm. It was the god-awful screeching noise of the hallway door that opened to my outer office. The sound it makes ranks it up with fingernails scratching across a blackboard. It was daylight. I must have passed out sometime after midnight. The noise from a breaking glass half filled with vodka that I just knocked over would alert the intruder to my presence.

"God damn it!" I called out.

I was angry at whoever was on their way in for causing me to spill the vodka. I needed that drink to help quiet the hammers of Hell that were starting to pound in my head. I saw two empty vodka bottles lying on the floor next to a half-eaten ham sandwich from the party I must have held last night.

"Get the hell out of here, whoever you are. You made me knock over a goddamn glass of vodka, and unless you have another bottle with you... FUCK OFF!"

For an instant, it became silent in the outer office. Then I heard footsteps coming toward my inner office door.

"I know you're out there. I have my .38 pointed at the doorway." I warned with my dry, raspy voice common to me after a night of boozing. I had no idea where my .38 was, so I couldn't stop anyone coming through the door who wanted to whack me. Right now, with the hangover I have, I don't care. The footsteps were getting louder.

"Hurry up and come on in, only aim for my head...I won't shoot back... I promise." I'm going to have to remember to lock that fucking hallway door.

I heard the faint sound of knocking on the opaque glass of my inner office door. My gun was nowhere in sight. "C'mon in!" I was anticipating a dark-haired Italian to enter with a .22 caliber pistol aimed in my direction. If he were a good shot, he'd make my hangover go away. The door opened slowly.

"Don't shoot me, Mr. Canyon, I presume! Do you greet everyone this way?"

The intruder spoke in a soft voice. It wasn't a soft, sexy voice. It was the soft, aged, worn voice of an older woman. Standing before me was a five foot five-inch-tall slightly hunched over old lady. When I saw her, I thought it was the cleaning woman. I was about to tell her to get out and come back and clean the office later when I noticed the bottle of vodka in her right hand. This was no ordinary cleaning lady. She walked over to where I stood, balancing myself, and handed me the bottle.

"Sit down somewhere while I find some glasses. You won't mind drinking from a paper cup, will you? Oh, and you can skip cleaning the office today if you're the cleaning lady," I said as I looked into her time worn grey eyes.

I walked slowly over to my desk, where an old coffee cup from Quick Stop was sitting, dumped the three-day-old coffee into the trash can, opened the bottle of vodka she had brought, and poured her a cup full. As I handed her the cup, I raised the bottle to my mouth in anticipation of administering the first stage of the cure for my hangover.

She handed the cup back to me as I was beginning to swallow the vodka and softly said, "No, thank you, Mr. Canyon. I don't drink vodka, and I'm not the cleaning lady."

"If you're not the cleaning lady, then you must be delivering the vodka; I do not remember ordering last night. And why are you delivering booze on Sunday morning anyway?"

"It's one o'clock Monday afternoon, Mr. Canyon. Your ad in the Yellow Pages said you require a bottle of vodka as a part of your retainer. I found that a bit unusual for a private detective, but I brought it anyway." She answered in that quiet, steady voice you would expect from an old lady.

Now, I'm thinking I've been out for a day and a half, and the last I remembered, it was around midnight, Saturday, and I had two broads here with me that I was putting the make on. One of them must have slipped me a mickey and rolled me. I gotta get rid of this old lady. The Mexican army is walking around barefoot in my mouth, and I probably smell like a construction site crapper.

"What do you want, lady?" I asked, trying to be respectful. After all, she paid the initial retainer and deserved to be heard if it was quick.

"I want you to find out who killed my husband, Horst Strump. Your ad said you're the best detective in the city. I've been to five other private detective agencies recently and they have all told me the same thing: save my money. It's doubtful they could solve the case and it would be unethical to take money from me."

"If they all gave you the same answer, then why are you bothering me? Is it because they told you I'm the best detective in Pittsburgh?"

"No, Mr. Canyon. They all said you are the most unethical bastard in the City and that you would take money from a church collection plate. Some also said you were a damn good homicide detective when you were on the City payroll, but that was before you, in their words, "Began hitting the sauce."

I was ready to tell this old broad to go screw, but instead, what came out was, "How much money can you pay me from your social security check?" The words were sticking under the feet of the Mexican army, still walking around in my mouth. I couldn't take this little old woman's money if the others in the trade turned her down. I didn't sink that far into the muck just yet.

"Lady, save your money. Go play bingo. Get a new hearing aid or something." I sarcastically said, hoping to piss her off enough to leave, but I wouldn't give her back her retainer, the vodka.

"Fifty thousand dollars, Mr. Canyon. I'll give you fifty thousand dollars as a retainer to begin working for me."

I almost spit out the swig of vodka I was gulping down. "Did you say fifty thousand fucking dollars, lady?"

"Yes, Mr. Canyon, I did, and would you please refrain from using that salty language around me?" She scolded.

Salty language! The only other time I remember hearing that phrase was with my Annie at an artsy theatre Downtown, showing movies from the 1930's. Marie Dressler used that kind of line on W.C. Fields in the movie 'Yukon Anne.'

"Where are you going to get that kind of money? Did you hit the lottery?"

The expression on her face changed briefly from one of annoyance at the use of my salty language to one of surprise. I would soon know why.

"I find it curious that you would ask me that question, Mr. Canyon, and yes, I did hit the lottery in February of this year. Are you psychic, Mr. Canyon? No, of course, you're not. Never mind! My name is Hilda Strump. Please call me Hilda or Mrs. Strump, whichever you prefer."

"Okay, lady, I mean Hilda, and you can call me by my first name, Red, since I'm going to be working for you," I said in the best business voice that my alcohol burned throat would allow.

If I got fifty grand from Hilda, I could pay my bar bills and the couple of grand I owe the bookie. I was about to get the money from Hilda, when I heard a loud disturbance going on below the second floor windows of my suite. When you rent a two-room office in the dump I'm in they call it a suite.

From my window I could see my cousin Jimmy had some broad by the hair and was dragging her across Carson Street toward the entrance to my building. I heard the bottom door kick open, and the screaming female being dragged up the steps. From the mouth on that broad I knew she wasn't a lady.

Hilda was showing signs of fright. "Relax, Hilda, it's just my cousin Jimmy and his girlfriend," I said, with the intention of keeping her calm.

The outer office door was kicked in and I could hear Jimmy pushing the broad through the doorway.

I guess he shoved her a little too hard toward my inner office. She stumbled forward through the opening, tripped and landed on the wooden floor in front of my desk. Holding on to my desktop, she pulled herself up from the floor. When her face came into my view, I recognized her. She didn't look quite as good now as she did late last Saturday night when I picked her and her girlfriend up and brought them back here.

Hilda had stepped as far back in the corner of my office as she could. I didn't want this pigeon going anywhere. Jimmy was telling the broad to shut the fuck up as I rolled my desk chair over for Hilda to sit on and then closed the inner door so she couldn't run.

Jimmy glanced over at Hilda and said, "Excuse me, Mrs.," and blurted out, "This hooker was just in Max's restaurant trying to pay her bill with your credit card. I was standing on the corner in front of the place when Max called me inside. He handed me your plastic and told me he wouldn't have given it a second look except that your card bounced. They nixed a fifteen-dollar check. He pointed the hooker out and I caught up to her and dragged her over here. I figured she ripped you off."

"Hilda," I said in the least threatening voice I could work up, "I'll be with you as soon as I get my wallet from my associates' friend. She must have accidentally picked it up at the party on Saturday night."

The words hadn't finished coming out of my mouth when the broad handed me my wallet. I told Jimmy to excuse himself for now and take the trash with him; I was having a meeting with a client. All the time this was going on, Hilda was writing on a pad she had pulled out of her purse.

I was sitting on the side of my desk about to ask her for the fifty-grand front money when she got up from the chair and came over to me.

"I've written my phone number and address down for you. Here is a cashier's check for fifty thousand dollars in advance for your services. There will be another five hundred-thousand-dollar bonus payment when you find my husband's killer." With that announcement, she headed for the door, stopped for a moment, turned her head toward me, and said, "With the money I've given you, I expect you to get a new suit, clean yourself up, and be at my home tonight at seven o'clock for dinner. We need to discuss business. Don't be late."

She stopped again when I asked if I could bring Jimmy with me. I was on a thirty-day driving suspension for going over the limit on points, and he needed to drive me everywhere until the suspension was lifted.

"You may bring him if he is your assistant and under the conditions that he shows up in the same manner as I've requested of you. New everything! Otherwise, you may leave him on the street corner where he receives his mail."

WOW! It looks like Hilda has a nasty streak hidden under the soft voice old lady facade.

I needed to know one important piece of information before Hilda left my office: "When did your old man get bumped off?"

"He was murdered on May 30th, 1990… fifteen years ago today," she calmly announced and then walked out.

# CHAPTER 2

The door to the street closed with a thud as Hilda exited my office building. I watched her walk to the curb through the rain-streaked windows of my second-floor suite. As she reached it and stopped, a white stretch limo pulled up in front of her. A dark suit got out, came around, and opened the passenger door. She glanced back up at the window I was sitting in front of as she entered her ride. I waved goodbye to her with the check she had just given me. Now, she could wonder until seven tonight if I was going to skip out on her with the money. If I hadn't shown up at her house for dinner on time, she could have figured on kissing her fifty-grand goodbye.

Thanks to Hilda, I have fifty thousand bucks on a Monday afternoon and my bank is still open. When I add that to the money I have in my bank accounts plus the cash I have in my wallet, I have a total of fifty thousand dollars. I was heading down the stairs and across Carson Street to the Iron and Glass Bank, where I had my account when my cousin Jimmy joined up with me.

"Here's forty-six dollars and thirty-seven cents I nabbed from the hooker's purse. I figured it was all she had left from the cash she stole from your wallet." Jimmy said with a wide smile on his face as he put the money in my hand.

"Thanks, Jimmy." I gratefully said while accepting the money he had just ripped off from the hooker. I think I only had eleven dollars left over from the liquor store on Saturday night. That was all about to change now.

I've been doing business for twenty plus years at my bank and I knew just about everyone that worked there. As we entered the bank the manager approached me with that troubled look on his face that I've seen before.

"Red, I need to see you for a minute. I tried to call you, but your business phone is shut off, and I bet you don't read your mail. I sent you three letters in the last two weeks." Andy, the branch manager complained. "You bounced three checks in the last four weeks and your account is overdrawn eighty-five dollars. I can't keep covering for you, Red. You're gonna get me fired!"

I let him blow off steam and shook off Jimmy's tug on my shirt sleeve. He was trying to get me to leave before Andy hit me with anything else I might have hanging at the bank. This would all go away when Andy sees the cashier's check I'm pulling out of my wallet.

"Andy, deposit this into my account and get me three grand cash in fifties. Make sure you put the check in as cash. Don't try to play that hold back shit with it."

Andy took the check, looked at it and then to me as he headed to the closest cashier. "It looks like you hit the lottery," he mumbled under his breath as he walked away.

What I dumb thing to say, I thought, just because I have a cashier's check for fifty grand.

"Do you think you can scam this guy with that phony check routine?" Jimmy was asking me quietly.

"I got this guy in my pocket. When he hands me the cash, we beat it out the door. Don't look back. We'll head up the block to the Italian Gardens and get us a couple of beers. We have business to take care of, so we only have time for one. You're coming with me the rest of the day and we have to get ready."

I wasn't going to tell Jimmy just yet that I dropped fifty grand in my account. He could believe that I ran a scam on the bank manager and would tell the tale on the street. I'd have to insist that he didn't reveal the party I scammed so no one else would try to work the mark. The legend of the street-smart Red Canyon would begin to grow again. I needed something to jack up my rep. A con job at the bank would gain me some street beat. I was on a big case now, and I needed to have respect on the streets to help get some answers to questions I didn't even know that I was going to ask yet. I've been on the skids recently, but Hilda Strump ended that today.

Me and Jimmy were almost at the entrance door to the Italian Gardens when it flew open and outran a little old man wearing a mix and match outfit from the disco era. John Travolta would have been proud. He was followed by the barmaid in a white uniform hollering at the ejected patron that if she saw him in the bar again, he better not dare grab her ass.

"Hi! Annie," I said as we touched shoulders, squeezing through the doorway into the bar.

"Hi! Red! Hi! Jimmy," Annie said warmly, returning the greeting. "You're early, Red. Where did you find Jimmy? I thought he was at the nut house of the V. A. hospital."

"It ain't a nut house, Annie. It's a rehabilitation facility. That's what they call it. And who's nuts anyway, me or you and little Mike with your grab ass and chase thing with every afternoon?"

"Oh, shut up, Jimmy. You're too damn sensitive. Better check back in. You missed the session on when to shut your fucking mouth." She paused for a moment, looked at Jimmy, and said, "Only kidding!"...and then walked over and gave him a hug.

"Make nice you two. Jimmy's working for me now, Annie," I told her to Jimmy's surprise. He hasn't been able to hold a job since he was discharged from the Army.

He was released from Walter Reed eighteen months ago and is carrying a titanium plate in his head from an injury he received during a Desert Storm operation.

Jimmy always marched to a different drummer. The plate in his head sometimes caused him to stop marching. On those occasions, his brain would take him to a place that none of us knew, including Jimmy.

"Give us a couple of beers and tell me how much my bar tab is. I want to square up with you."

"Red, I quit adding on to your tab last month when it hit nine hundred bucks. I figured that I probably wasn't going to get paid anyway. Are you going to pay me now? What did you do... hit the lottery?"

What a dumb question to ask just because a guy has come into some money.

Annie and I have a thing together. She's been trying to get me to the altar since we were kids. Whenever I've been down on my luck, she's given me a place to stay, a hot meal and reluctantly a bottle of vodka. Annie's special, very special.

"Will a grand cover it? And, no, I didn't hit the lottery. I'm working on a big case now. The other agencies in the city couldn't handle it. They sent the client to me, and you know I don't take on a case without a big retainer."

Anne let me slide on that remark about only taking a case with a big retainer. My usual big retainer was a gallon bottle of vodka.

I dropped the cash on the bar, drank my beer, gave Annie a kiss on the cheek and headed toward the door on my way to the local tailor for some new clothes. Jimmy was close behind.

"You better go upstairs to my apartment first, take a shower and shave before you start your detecting. You smell worse than the dumpster behind the Chinese takeout joint. You have clean clothes in my bedroom closet and new underwear in the second drawer of my dresser."

I looked back at Annie and saw Jimmy shaking his head in agreement. A quick sniff of the suit coat I was wearing caused a change in my direction. I headed upstairs to her second-floor apartment. Jimmy would have time for another beer.

Annie's apartment was first class. It occupied the second and third floors over the bar. I had my first view of it four years ago after she bought the building and opened the bar. She had a spiral staircase installed to the third floor that led up to what she called her media room. The whole place was decorated in what she referred to as eclectic. She asked me at the time what I thought of it. I asked her how many flea markets she had to shop at to collect all this mismatched junk... which promptly got me a knee to the groin. We never talked about the subject again.

When I returned downstairs to the bar, Jimmy was finishing his beer. I said goodbye to Annie again and headed back up Carson Street to Sam Grayson's tailoring, dry cleaning, and rental center. He's been in business since 1935 at the same location here on the Southside. I was counting on Sam to get me and Jimmy hooked up with the new suits, shirts, and ties that we were going to need for the dinner at Hilda's tonight. Sam grew up in the business and had a thimble for a thumb. He continued running the family business after his father died. It was three forty-five and we had less than three- and one-half hours left until dinner.

When we arrived at Sam's I explained to him what I needed for Jimmy and me and waited for him to begin showing us our new threads. "I can't do it. First, I don't have anything on the rack in your sizes. Second, you don't have any credit with me, Red. I've been carrying a $140.00 dry cleaning tab for the last three months."

I reached into my pocket, pulled out my bankroll, and handed him three fifties. "We're square now, Sam. I have a pocket full of fifties to cover the new bill I run up. There's a very important client who lives in Fox Chapel that's expecting me at seven o'clock tonight for dinner wearing new clothes. I'm not leaving without new suits for me and Jimmy. You stop whatever else you're doing and get it done." I threatened in my hoarse voice. Sam knew from my body language he was on the spot and that if he didn't want any trouble, he had an hour to get us suited up.

"I'll get you through your dinner tonight, but you're going to have to work with me on this. You'll come over tomorrow and I'll have something more practical for both of you." Sam spoke half apologizing. "Both of you come into the back where I can get some measurements and get you fitted so you can get your asses out of here on time."

I had my own plan in mind. Sam was about my height and thirty pounds heavier than me. If he didn't' make the deadline I was going to take the suit he was wearing and go with his baggy ass pair of pants on. I wouldn't take off the suit coat so no one would notice.

Once in the back-room Sam handed Jimmy and me each a pair of tuxedo pants to try on. While we were putting on our pants, he approached us carrying two white formal dinner jackets.

"Sam, we're going to dinner at my new client's home, not to a fucking wedding. Where's my gun, Jimmy? I think I'm going to shoot this smart-ass kike in the ass," I said, figuring that threat would get Sam back to reality. I was wondering what the fuck he was trying to pull.

"So, you can tell your client you assumed it was a formal dinner or you can tell her that's how you always dress for dinner, schmuck." Sam sarcastically barked. "Or you could tell the truth that you didn't have enough time to get a new suit, so you rented. You do remember what the truth is, don't you, Red? Now, try on the shoes that go with the clothes so I can get you both the hell out of my store."

"Kristallnacht, Sam. Pay up your window glass insurance."

"You've been breaking my windows since you were a little boy, Red." Sam told me as he came over to me and patted me on the head the way he's been doing as long as I can remember. He used to hand me a lollipop and then pat me on my head every time I came into his cleaning store with my pop. That's some good history I have with Sam.

He reached into his pocket and pulled out two lollipops…handed one to me and one to Jimmy and said, "Let's get this done and stop all the bullshit. I have other customers to take care of."

I knew I could count on Sam. We'll show up in white dinner jackets tonight at Hilda's. That should show her I'm serious about her case.

A fifteen-year-old murder case ain't going to be easy to solve. The cops couldn't do it. She may as well offer me three million for the killer of her husband. The chances are few and none she'll ever have to pay it out.

Where to start... I'll start with Hilda… tonight.

# CHAPTER 3

SAM BAGGED OUR TUXES, and then Jimmy and I headed back down Carson Street to Annie's place for a couple of beers before we changed and headed out to Fox Chapel. I didn't think she would mind if we used her apartment to change in. I looked back at Jimmy as we entered the bar to see why he was falling behind. His eyes told the story. He was in that place again. The one no one knows. I grabbed his arm and led him over to a booth and sat him down. There's no telling when he'll come back to the real world.

"Annie," I called out. "Jimmie's gone to his private place again. If he's not back by six, I need you to go with me to Fox Chapel."

"No thanks, Red. The only time I'm going anywhere with you in a tux is down the aisle at St. Johns."

"You know I can't drive, Annie. I can't fuck this case up," I said, imploring her to reconsider.

"Take a cab. You have lots of the clients' money." She reminded me.

"Oh yeah, you're right. I have money for a cab. Cancel the request."

"I'll take you, Red. You know I would. I was just yanking your chain. Sparks comes in at five to work the night shift. I'll tell him to keep an eye on Jimmy, and then I'll be up to get ready."

"See you upstairs, Annie. Maybe we have enough time for a quickie." I headed to the stairway to her apartment.

"If you got a ring, Red, we have enough time. Why don't you call those hookers you left here with last Saturday night?"

"Nothing happened, believe me."

"I know, Red. I set you up with them. They slipped you a mickey and rolled you. I told them, too. You needed a lesson in how to behave in front of me. You were too drunk Saturday night to make it with your hand let alone two pros. I trust you're done with that kind of behavior."

"Yes, Annie, how about it?"

"No, no, Red. No, no… No sex."

"If Sparks doesn't show up at five, he's getting a beating from me!"

"He'll be here, Red. You go upstairs and figure out what you are going to give me for the Saturday night insult. It better be something expensive." I heard as I headed upstairs.

My first thoughts were to give her a fifty-dollar bill when we got back from Hilda's. I dropped that idea. It would only get me another knee in the groin. That wouldn't be good for later tonight getting laid. I'll buy her jewelry.

Annie came upstairs at five thirty. She told me that Jimmy was back and I wouldn't need her to drive to Fox Chapel. He was changing in the back room. I asked if she wanted to go anyway.

"I'll tell Hilda you're my secretary and I brought you along to take notes. This woman's loaded and has the big address. She will probably feed us prime rib or squab or something that rich people eat. Come on! We can make it like a dinner date." I offered. I guessed it was too late for a jump. I was right. No time now.

"No thanks, Red. You have your dinner party with your new mark, I mean client. Come over when you get back from Fox Chapel. You can tell me about your meeting and the dinner."

"I know why you were late getting back upstairs. That punk Sparks was late. You know I'm going to kick his ass when I get back tonight. I told you what I'd do if he were late today. He messed up the bedroom rumble for us." I headed out the door.

"Why do you always have to behave like a jerk? You know you're not going to kick anybody's ass. Just come over when you're done, Red."

I turned back and walked over to Annie and gave her a kiss and a hug. "I could be a few minutes late, Annie. What do you say?" I hopefully asked her again.

"Don't you mean a few hours late, Red. You're past being a sixty-second man. Get out of here now and go see your client."

I couldn't do any more begging, so I grabbed Jimmy, and we took off for Fox Chapel and Hilda. I was getting hungry. I don't remember eating anything today. From Hilda's accent and first name along with a husband named Horst Strump I'm betting she's a German. I sure hope she doesn't come out with that German sauerkraut stuff. Fifty grand or not I'm not eating any of that shit. I'd rather eat dumpster doughnuts.

We found the address and drove up the typical circular driveway of the rich. The place was about what I expected. It looked big enough to be an apartment building. How large was that lottery hit anyway?

Jimmy parked the car right in front of the entrance and we waited for the valet. The doorway was guarded by some Greek type statues. One of the male statues had sacrificed his manhood and became a fountain. What a stupid statue. Does anyone think daVinci sculpted any of his statues to become pissing ornaments on somebody's front lawn? Come to think of it, he did. Oh well!

After a minute the door opened and an older man in a tux motioned for us to come in. I guessed no one was coming to park the car. I knew I should have had it washed before we left.

"My name is Carl. I'm Hilda's brother. What the fuck are your names?"

"Carl," I said, "I wish you wouldn't use that salty language."

He started to laugh and then said, "I think I like you whoever you are."

"That's great Lerch, but we came to see Hilda and have dinner. We're hungry."

"Follow me!"

We followed the creep and walked past a room on the left that had a grand piano in the center of the floor and no other furniture except a bench. The room to the right was filled with arcade video games. I was starting to get the sense that Hilda's a whacko.

Could we be at the home of the new Adams family? If the check Hilda gave me wasn't a cashier's check, I'd think I was being scammed. When some young blonde comes out and introduces herself as the niece, I'll start looking for the cameras and the host of the candid cam show. I could tell from looking at Jimmy that he was in the same place I was.

We entered the dining room and were told to look for our place cards at the table and take our seats. Hilda would be here in a minute. Lerch said she was overseeing the dinner. I found it interesting that someone made place cards when there were only four place settings at the table. Jimmy was seated across from me with the two end seats going to Hilda and Carl, maybe.

The table was set with gold trimmed dishes, crystal glassware and plastic knives and forks. Carl said the silverware was stolen recently by one of the help and Hilda was waiting for the claim to be paid before she purchased the replacements. With all her money she's waiting for an insurance check!

A woman in a clean maid's uniform entered the dining room through a double hinged swinging door that probably led to the kitchen. Carl announced that dinner was being served as Hilda brought in the first tray of food… fried fucking chicken. It was followed by a couple of bowls of mashed potatoes with side dishes of gravy. I knew what was coming next… biscuits. Now, I know this woman is nuts. Hilda verified my diagnosis by announcing that the darker fried chicken is extra crispy. This old quack is serving us the Colonels take out. I got up from the table and headed to the kitchen to look for the red and white buckets the chicken comes in. Bingo! I was right. There were four empty buckets sitting on one of the counters. I pulled out my .38 and clicked off the safety.

I'm probably wrong, but right now this whole set up reminds me of a scene from the movie 'Arsenic and Old Lace'. If Carl invites me and Jimmy to go to the basement, I'm going to put a slug in his chest.

I busted back through the swinging door and was about to tell Jimmy not to eat the fucking food… it may be poisoned, when I caught a piece of the conversation. Hilda was telling Jimmy why there was a lone piano in such a big room and arcade games in the room across the hall from it. It seems her dead husband played that piano when he was alive, so she set up a sort of shrine for him that she could visit every day.

As for the arcade games, they belonged to her son who was killed some seventeen years earlier. He lived there at the house and that was his game room. Hilda just couldn't bring herself to get rid of his toys.

I listened to the explanations and was somewhat relieved to hear them.

"What about the plastic utensils?" I asked Hilda.

"I thought Carl apologized for them when he seated you."

"Okay, but what about bringing us out here and serving us this fucking fast-food chicken?"

"I do wish you wouldn't be so crude Mr. Canyon. I could have served you beef Wellington, but I thought you would be more at leisure with the comfort food you people generally eat. I'm sorry if I've offended you." Hilda said apologetically.

I was about to tell Hilda to shove the chicken when my thoughts were cut off by my cousin Jimmy.

"Red, what's the problem with the chicken? You and me eat this bird two or three times a week on the Southside."

"Shut the fuck up, Jimmy. Don't you know we've been insulted?"

"Fuck you, Red. I'll eat your share if you're going to be a baby about it."

I looked over at Carl and could see he was laughing his ass off. "Fuck you too, Carl." I was pissed, not at the chicken, but at myself for thinking Hilda was a whacko and for not looking for a simple explanation about the Piano and the Arcade games. I was trying to figure out a way to get out of the situation and save face when Hilda provided the path.

"Everybody, just sit down, shut the fuck up and eat… especially you, Red. We have business to get to."

"Yes, ma'am!" I didn't need to save face now.

# CHAPTER 4

We finished dinner in silence. The table was cleared, and I was ready to get to the reason for my being here, but Hilda wasn't quite done with dinner. Jimmy asked for another beer.

"Would anyone care for dessert? You can have Bananas Foster or German black forest cake. Which would you prefer?"

"The appropriate desert with the meal you served, Hilda, would be Twinkies, cookies or mud pies."

"I'll take that as a no, Mr. Canyon. What about your young man?" she asked, looking at Jimmy.

"I'll have both, but I ain't finishing that banana stuff if it isn't good."

The coffee came out automatically. I drink mine black. I was ready to press Hilda about getting down to business when she got up from the table and asked everyone to join her in the study. That's where dessert would be served. There were some questions I had for Hilda and her brother. I was mostly looking for background information on Horst. I could research the newspapers and police files to get a picture of how he was murdered and where. Most people don't get murdered. Someone that knew him wanted him dead. That would be the track I would follow.

The study was covered with oak from the floor through to the ceiling. It felt like I had entered an expensive wooden box. Like maybe the inside of a coffin. Hilda sat behind a desk and the three of us sat on two leather sofas across from each other. I had to turn to the left to address Hilda. Fuck this I thought.

"Hilda, come from behind your throne and sit with the people."

I wanted to get Hilda on the ground without her scepter. I sized her up as someone that needed to be in control. She would learn, beginning today, that I'm the quarterback and she's just like a team owner. She's got the money, but in the field I'm the boss. My field of play is the streets, backrooms and alleys of the city, any city I play in. She reluctantly moved to the sofa next to Carl. Now we could talk. Me and Jimmy on one side and Hilda and Carl sitting across from us. Let's play!

“Hilda, how was your husband killed and where did it happen?”

“He was shot multiple times in the face and in the chest. It happened in the parking lot at his business in the Lawrenceville section of the city. He entered his car around six thirty to head home for dinner. The police claimed it was a robbery since his wallet was stolen.”

“Was anything else taken from him like rings or watches?”

“Yes, his rings, watch and jewelry were also taken along with his cane. Horst had a hip replacement a few months before and needed the cane to help him get around.”

“Were any of his belongings ever recovered?”

“No. I offered a reward for their return and for information as to who killed Horst, but it brought no success. The police said at the time that it was a random robbery and there were signs of a struggle and that’s why he was killed.”

“You know he was robbed so what other motive do you believe there could have been that would cause someone to want to kill him?” I was asking the standard questions, trying to find a crack in this old broad’s armor.

"Is there something you know, but didn't tell the police at the time?"

"I'm not sure what I told the police. I do know that he was concerned about something that happened before we were married. That was in August of 1965. He mentioned something about his being a loose end that powerful forces wanted to tie up. I asked him then if he should go to the police, but he said he would handle it. I knew he was troubled, but I thought the powerful forces he referred to were business related. A few months before he was murdered, he told me of his plans to write his autobiography. He said he was sure it would be a bestseller. I found that a bit strange."

Carl was waiting to jump into the conversation. Before I could ask him a question, he began telling me something I found surprising.

"He was friends with Vinnie Giganni. You ought to know him; he's a big dago boss from the Southside. They were always sneaking around together. Horst was doing business with the Italians. I could never figure out what business. He didn't manufacture anything the mob could use, and he didn't have a retail business to launder money through. Go talk to Vinnie. He probably killed Horst."

"Horst set up his optical business in Lawrenceville in the building that he bought from Vinnie. That's how they met; I think. For some strange reason, they seemed to form a friendship that lasted until his death. Vinnie assured me then that he would do everything in his power to find the killer or killers of Horst. I didn't see that he had anything to gain from my husbands' death." Hilda quietly said as I interrupted to ask another question.

"Why did you wait so long to begin a new investigation? It seems to me you have had plenty of money to hire private detectives. Is my assumption correct about your financial condition at the time?"

"Yes, Mr. Canyon, you are correct. I was wealthy before I hit the lottery in February and in fact did retain a firm that same year to do just that. One year later after paying them seventy-thousand dollars for nothing, I ended the inquiry."

"What makes you think that anyone can come up with different answers fifteen years later? Do you have any new information?"

"Yes, I believe I do. Yesterday evening, I began looking through the sheet music in the piano bench Horst used from time to time when I came across a page that had been torn out of his diary. It was dated May 29th, 1990. I was never able to find his diary once the police and the FBI searched the house and the business after his murder. When I read my discovery, I decided to open a new investigation," she said as she handed me the page to read myself.

It read,

*I began carrying my pistol again. My life is now in serious jeopardy. I made the mistake of telling Vinnie I was going to write my autobiography but that I would keep his link to my activity out of it. I didn't intend to have it published until after my death anyway. He must have contacted some of the others from the past that we once both dealt with. I've noticed strange people around my office making inquiries about me. I've been followed every day for the last week. It appears that the friendship Vinnie and I have is second to his business. I'm concerned for Hilda. The only thing I can do now is take it to the newspapers. I'll tell Hilda everything in the next day or* so.

"Did you tell anyone else about this page from Horsts' diary that you found?"

"No, I haven't told anyone until just now. It was the diary page that eventually led me to you."

"Let's keep it that way. I don't want that information going out of this room. Do you understand, Carl? The only lead I have to go on is Vinnie and he is a very dangerous man. He is a *made* man and very powerful in the local mob structure. I've known the old bastard since I was a kid and I know what he can do. I've seen his work and busted him on some numbers beef while

I was on the job. Do either of you two have any idea why Horst would fuck around with Vinnie?"

Carl jumped in with, "Horst liked living on the edge. I believed he had two lives: one as a businessman and one as a man in the business. That's why he associated with Vinnie. There was something about him that I believed was evil. He didn't show that face to Hilda, but I saw it frequently while I worked with him in the factory. He had a violent temper and often threatened competitors, employees and even me. I know that he loved Hilda and would never harm her or let her see his other face. Come into the office and ask around. I have employees that worked for him that are still working for the company."

"Pay no attention to my brother. He's still carrying a grudge because Horst only left forty percent of the company to him. I own the balance. Carl felt that because of his work with Horst, he should have received one hundred percent of the business. I could never sell my share. I didn't have to. Horst left me a small fortune when he died. I take nothing from the business. Carl runs it and keeps all the profit. I just can't let it go. I guess it's like the piano to me."

"Carl, why do you think Horst was killed?"

"The dagos killed him. I think he had something on them, something bigger than that grease ball Vinnie. He tried to put the mussel on me right after Horst was murdered. He claimed he had some gambling markers from Horst. I told him to go fuck himself. I wasn't afraid of him. I told him I'd go to the cops if he ever bothered me again. Horst was many things in my view, but he wasn't a gambler. He didn't watch sports, not even soccer. He wouldn't even buy a fifty-fifty ticket from the church. He always told me it was a waste of time to chase luck when he could make his own and earn money, lots of money, in many ways. I asked him what other ways he meant besides the optical lens business. He never answered directly, just that there were exciting and sometimes dangerous ways he knew of. When I said, like hanging out with Vinnie and those dagos, he always became irate and told me that I shouldn't ever bring that up, especially in front of Hilda. He told me that kind of talk could get me killed. I always shrugged it off as I did with all his threats," Carl answered in a quick and believable manner.

It looks like I'm going to have to investigate two men to find out who was murdered. Was the man murdered by the kind, loving husband Hilda knew, or was he the authoritative, threatening, dangerous man that Carl described as having a mobster for an associate?

So, now, I have the first two pieces of the puzzle; Horst the good and Horst the evil. Which one did someone murder? I may not find out until I solve the case or maybe never.

"Hilda and Carl, do either of you have any other information that could help me solve this mystery? Hilda, you didn't tell me about your son before. When was your son killed, and how did he die?"

"He was killed on August second, 1988, during a carjacking. The car was found a week later with the gun used to shoot Trent. They said the black man driving it did the killing. He claimed he was innocent and that someone called and told him to pick up the car and deliver it to the address on the insurance card. He claimed he was told there was a hundred dollars in an envelope waiting for him when he made the delivery. He said he found the car up on the 'Hill,' the black section of the City."

"Was the kid named Delbart Johnson?"

"Yes, he was Red. How did you know? Did you work on the case?" Hilda asked me, although I believe she already knew that I hadn't.

"I didn't work the case, but I knew about the kid. I dealt with his old man on the Hill at different times while I was on the job. His father's name is Wrecker Johnson. He owns a salvage business on the Hill and a nightclub. Somebody killed the kid while he was out on bail. Wrecker called me to see if I could help him find out who popped him. He thought the cops were dirty and covering up for someone on the job who did his kid. I never came up with a lead and neither did Wrecker. As I recall, the case was closed, and his kid took the rap for your son's robbery and murder."

"Why did you want to know about my sons' death? Do you think it has anything to do with Horst's murder?"

"Your son was murdered, Hilda. Why didn't you want to find his killer too? Is it because you believed the police account of what happened and that they had the right guy?" I wanted her to answer so I could get a read on her expressions when she talks about her son. Were they different when she talked about Horst?

"Yes, that's exactly why or I would have pursued it at that time."

I didn't believe her.

"I don't have any reason to believe that the two murders were tied together. I just think the odds of your husband and son both being murdered in robbery attempts two years apart must be astronomical. It's throwing up a red flag for me, Hilda. It may just be a coincidence. I'm going to work on Horst's murder and see where it leads me. If I find a connection between them, you are going to get a twofer… two answers for the price of one."

It was time to get out of Hilda's place and head back to the Southside. I had a lot more questions I'd have to ask. But to whom? They'll have to wait for another time. My instinct was telling me that Carl knows a lot more than he's telling me. He seemed to be a clever guy, but I'll work him over to get everything out of him that he is holding back on me. Red Canyon is on the case… until it's solved. I'm back... MAYBE…

# CHAPTER 5

We said our good-byes to Hilda and Carl with the caveat to Carl that he'd being hearing from me, soon.

Jimmy had been silent through all the conversation that went on in Hilda's study. That's not like Jimmy to be quiet that long. We were five minutes away from Hilda's when he finally opened up.

"What's the chances of the old lady finding one sheet of the dead guys' diary dated the day before he was hit in a piece of music that she probably looked through a thousand times in the last fifteen years?"

"Good job, Jimmy! The answer is it was planted for our benefit. Hilda said she couldn't find his diary after the cops and Feds searched the house and the business and took away all his personal papers. She said they told her that they brought everything back, but I'd bet they never took inventory. That means she had no record of what they took and couldn't possibly know what wasn't returned, like a diary."

"Who wrote up the diary page and planted it where Hilda could find it," Jimmy asked me.

"Carl. He wrote up the phony page of the diary and planted it in the sheet music so Hilda could find it. My bet is Hilda looks through the sheet music on a regular routine. Carl placed it in a piece of sheet music that he knew Hilda would look through that morning of the anniversary of Horsts' death."

"But why wouldn't the old lady know it's a set up since she looked through the sheet music regularly?".

"She knows it's not from Horst's diary, but it provided a reason for her to reopen the case. She knows Carl planted it and she doesn't care. They're both like actors in a play and they're doing a scene from 'Who murdered the Strump Guys?' The question is what is Carl's motive for wanting to open the investigation again? What does he hope to gain? Somehow, I think she feels a re-connect with Horst because the case is alive again. She may have told Carl to write it up so she had something to show me. Maybe they like to play these kinds of games with each other. They are apples off the same tree." I explained to Jimmy as I began to wonder what the real motive was behind Hilda's reopening of the case.

"Are you sure it was Carl who created the bogus diary page?"

"Yeah, Jimmy, I am. Remember Carl telling us he thought Vinnie was the one who murdered Horst. The lost diary page pointed to Vinnie. That's why it had to be Carl's hand in it, too."

"You're pretty fucking smart, Red. Yeah, pretty fucking smart!" Jimmy said before silence rode with us the rest of the way to the Southside.

As we headed down the parkway at seventy miles an hour, I found myself hoping that cousin Jimmy didn't get a call from that place no one knows. After all, I still have to see Annie for some midnight magic. I couldn't disappoint her, not my Annie…

It was almost eleven o'clock by the time we arrived back on the Southside. Jimmy parked close to the Italian Gardens. The bar was located almost in the middle of the block between 17$^{th}$ Street and 18th Street. There were no other bars on that side of Carson Street, but there were three gin mills on the other side. The one good thing about that was there were less drunks sleeping one off in the doorways on Annie's side of the street. The Southside was still a shot and beer section of the City. You wouldn't find too many extended pinky fingers holding and sipping from champagne glasses in most of the joints here on Carson Street, but it was changing. It was a shot of cheap rye and an eight-ounce glass of beer for three bits. Most of the serious drinkers here on the Southside mix a little cheap Muscatel wine in after every four or five shots and beer. It gets the buzz on quicker and for less money than straight shots and beers. The alcoholics on a really tight budget buy a pint at the State Store and sneak in their sips when the bartender isn't looking, or they swill it down in the men's room. These are serious drinkers. You find some of them in most of the bars here on the Southside, even the yuppie joints.

When I solve Horsts' murder and get the five hundred grand from Hilda, I'm going to sponsor a shot, beer and wine drinking contest against the other sections of the City. I'll put up ten thousand for the first prize or a year's free booze at Annie's place. In order to qualify as a contestant, you'll have to have been arrested for being drunk and disorderly at least seven times in your life and prove it. No candy ass, weekend boozing college punks. It'll be for the 'Pros' only… Yeah, that's what I'll do!

Jimmy gave me my car keys and told me he was heading home. He lives with me on Wrights Way right behind Annie's bar. I took Jimmy in with me when he got discharged from the Army some eighteen months ago. I have a row house that I bought from my mom and pop when they moved to Florida five years ago. They hold the mortgage. It's a good thing for me.

Sometimes, I send them a payment when I hit a lucky streak, but they don't expect to get paid anyway.

Jimmy was going to be alone tonight. I was set up with Annie this evening.

The case I'm on now is already giving me bad vibes. I've always talked with Annie about my cases. When I just talk to her and listen to my own voice, I seem to be able to clear out all the bullshit and recognize the important pieces of information.

Sometimes when I've jumped the track, she's been able to get me back on the rails and moving forward. That's my Annie.

I said good night to Jimmy and went into the bar. Sparks saw me and quickly raised his hands in surrender while staring at me.

"Just wait a minute, Red. Annie told me you were going to kick my ass when you got back, but I couldn't help being late. I was on the throne, and I ran out of paper and had to wait for my kid to go to the supermarket and get me a roll ," he said that to me with a big grin on his face.

I have known Sparks for thirty years. We go back to grade school. The first time I kicked his ass we were eleven years old. Now, I'm going to kick his ass again. I considered not doing it when I first came in, but after he makes up a fucked-up story he thinks is funny and tells it to me in front of some of the regular drunks that hang in the bar, I have no choice except to kick his ass.

"Okay, Sparks, now you have to get a beating," I said loud enough so that everyone in the bar heard me.

"Wait a minute, Red, how about I buy you a shot and beer and we call it even?"

"Fuck you! You can't get out of this with a shot and a beer."

"How about I throw in a round for everyone in the bar?"

Most of the bums in the bar were now all telling me that it seems fair, and I should do it. I could see all of them already tasting their next free drink which is always better than the one you pay for. Everybody in the bar, all ten of them, sat drooling while anxiously awaiting my answer.

"No deal Sparks. It's not enough."

"How about if I make it two rounds, Red."

The eight men and two women hanging on the bar suddenly sat up and twisted around to look at me, waiting for the answer that would bring two free drinks, unexpected but well received. One of the older ladies looked me in the eye and said, "Take it you son of a bitch. We're all fucking thirsty."

Well, how in the hell could I now disappoint my ten drooling fans? I didn't want to kick Spark's ass anyway. That would have surely angered Annie and got me sent home tonight. I don't like fighting more than… screwing...

"Okay, Sparks, deal," I said, much to the relief of my new-found team of boozers. I'd bet most of them can qualify for my Southside Drinking Challenge when I hold it.

Now, I would become a legend up and down Carson Street in every bar and coffee shop these ten midnight tippers visited. They would tell of how I threatened the bartender with an ass whipping if he didn't give each of them two, not one, but two free drinks. The real reason for the free drinks would never be known to these newfound 'Red Canyon' promoters. Perhaps this is just the kind of street rap that I need to spread around the Southside streets and sidewalks that I'm now pounding again.

You would think I'd just been responsible for their winning the lottery the way I was being praised and told, "Good job, Red. He's a punk. You sure showed him. And on and on…" Things calmed down and I sat at the end of the bar where Annie usually sits when she's off duty. Sparks set me up with a shot and a beer just as Annie came down from her apartment above the bar.

"What's all the noise down here?" she asked as she looked over at Sparks to assure herself that I didn't carry out my threat.

"My friends at the bar were all applauding me for not kicking Spark's ass."

"Maybe you're growing up, Red. Is that what I'm seeing in you now that you're working again and have an actual client that can pay you?" Annie said with a doubtful look in her eyes.

"That's it, Annie. I'm all grown up now so let's go upstairs so I can practice shaving like the grown-up boys do. Okay?" I sarcastically answered that bullshit she just dumped on me.

"You know. Red…" she started to say when I quickly cut her off.

I jumped off the bar stool and grabbed Annie by the waist, moved her in the direction of the door that leads to her upstairs apartment, and quietly whispered to her, "Thanks for reminding me about the mattress trampoline… Annie. Hurry before you change your mind."

"You didn't let me finish my sentence, Red. That wasn't what I was referring to."

"I know, Annie,"

"You're never going to grow up, Red. Can't you tell that you don't have to hurry me? We have all night. I've missed you, Red. I know you've missed me. Right?"

"Yes, I've missed you probably more than you missed me. I'm not going away again. I promise," I said as I tightened my hold on her and kissed her cheek.

For the last six months, I've been in a place I'm not going back to. I've been in the bottle, so far in, I wasn't sure I could get out. That ended early this afternoon when Hilda Strump walked into my office—no more benders for me. I intend to solve the murders of Horst Strump and her son. Whether or not the two murders are connected won't matter. I'll get to the truth for Hilda. I was once the best homicide detective on the City payroll, as Hilda reminded me. I have the best two people a guy could have standing beside him, Annie and my cousin Jimmy. I'm ready for the streets again: are the streets ready for me? I had a reputation for being able to see the vermin and rats of society that buried themselves in the garbage of the City, and scoop them up and carry them to prison, a cage, or a coffin. I didn't just have excellent night vision; I had infrared vision back then. I can have it again. I'll need Annie to help nurture it. We'll start tonight. I will become like my old self again, and soon.

# CHAPTER 6

It was a little after seven when Annie woke me with a message that Jimmy was on his way over. He was bringing doughnuts from the 'Whole n the Wall bakery.' "He said he knows what you like and asked me my favorite. Do you think he'll be able to remember what I told him?"

"Annie, Jimmy's not retarded. The injury to his head caused him to lose cognitive recognition intermittently, usually without any warning. This is how they explained it to me at the Walter Reed Hospital, where they put the plate in his head. The doctors said all the testing on Jimmy revealed he hadn't had any loss of his brain function. You knew him before he was injured. He always marched to a different drummer. He was never a genius. He was always just an ordinary guy with average intelligence and a mild temperament.

He's just a nice guy, Annie, and I love my little cousin. He needs me and you."

"I'm sorry if I upset you, Red. You know I didn't mean anything by my remarks. I always have fun capping on Jimmy. He likes to play. He doesn't complain and would think I was mad at him if I didn't throw an insult when we saw each other. When did you become a member of the politically correct police anyway? And thanks for the clinical explanation on Jimmy. Now, tell me why you're fucked up!" Annie finished saying as she hurriedly tried to jump out of the bed.

"Too slow, Annie; I need you here to screw my head back on so I can answer your question. Start screwing ," I said to her as I waited for her reaction. She would either think my remarks were funny or I'd get another groin shot. I had no immediate pain in the groin. My way was cleared for me to begin my explanation… later. Jimmy would have to wait to have coffee with us. It would only take a minute, I told Annie, as she looked at me with a smile on her face.

"Call Jimmy and tell him to eat the doughnuts himself. They may be stale by the time you finish."

"We'll see, Annie, we'll see!" I thought to myself as I began my journey to the seventh level of something. She explained that Indian crap to me once, but I can never remember it. Oh well!

It was nine o'clock when I called Jimmy back and told him to bring the doughnuts up and Annie would make the coffee.

"Annie called me before and told me to eat them. She said you were trying to do something, and it was going to take a couple of hours. She said I was to go and get fresh ones for you and her when you called. What kind of doughnuts did she tell me she liked again, Red? I ate them all."

"Get a fucking coffee cake and forget the doughnuts, Jimmy." I hate it when Annie's right.

She walked by me and asked if I was talking to Jimmy. I said yeah, and before I could cover myself in the conversation, she shot out. "I told you he'd forget," she said with that sweet smile on her face that really meant she was right.

The way I'd describe my Annie is beautiful, intelligent, and rich with a sense of humor that's almost equal to mine, I think. It's close, really close.

Jimmy was on his way up the steps when Annie came into the kitchen and announced to me that my mother had just called her.

"She said she hadn't heard from you in over a month. She wants you to call her. I didn't think you wanted to talk to her right now, that's why I didn't put you on the phone with her. She also wanted me to remind you that a mortgage payment was due and it's the twenty-seventh month in row you haven't made a payment, and she loves you."

Jimmy arrived and put the box with the coffee cake on the kitchen table which prompted Annie when she saw it to say, "Coffee cake? Good choice Jimmy. I like coffee cake more than doughnuts anyway." She bent over and whispered in my ear, "Jelly."

I knew it was coming but couldn't hold back my laugh. Maybe she has I better sense of humor than me. Oh well!

"What's funny?"

"Annie just blew in my ear; that's all, Jimmy."

"If you two want to be alone again, just tell me, Red. I thought with you being here all night your tank would be full. I can figure things out with you two. What do you think, I'm retarded?"

"No, Jimmy, we don't think you're retarded, do we, Annie?" I said to my cousin. "You're just fine, Jimmy, just fine," I told him as Annie handed him a big piece of coffee cake.

"That's a special piece I cut just for you, Jimmy. We both love you a lot," Annie said to Jimmy. "And by the way, that's my favorite coffee cake, walnut."

Jimmy had a broad smile on his face knowing that he had brought Annie's favorite coffee cake for her to enjoy.

"See, Red; you should have known that when you told me to get a coffee cake for her. I won't forget it, Annie, and neither should you, Red," Jimmy said proudly.

Then the next thing he said, which stopped Annie and me cold, was…

"Jelly! It's jelly." Jimmy told Annie as he looked into her eyes for the recognition he needed to remember her favorite doughnut.

"Yes, Jimmy," Annie assured him as I looked at her. I thought I saw a tear forming in her left eye.

Jimmy was going to be alright.

We said our goodbyes to Annie and headed down Carson Street to find a computer store. Annie had to get ready to open the bar at eleven o'clock, or she would have come with us. She knew about computers and could have helped. I was going to need one to keep track of Horst, going all the way back to the time he married Hilda. My instinct tells me this guy didn't have much of a past before then.

"Let's go see Bobby Brooks at his appliance store on 16th Street. He sells computers, and maybe he can give me a deal on a used one."

"Ain't he the same Bobby you told me you threw out the window in grade school when you were kids? I've known him all my life, too."

"Yeah, Jimmy, that's him, but that was over thirty years ago. I saved his ass from some pretty big beatings in high school. He was the brain and a lot of punks pushed him around and wanted to put a beating on him because he wouldn't do their fucking homework. I got him in more trouble when I told him one time when one of these tough punks forces their homework on him, like a book report, to fuck it up so they get an 'F.'"

"That must have caused a lot of trouble for him."

"Not just Bobby. I fought every day after school for two fucking weeks until I beat up all the punks that were coming after him. That's how I first broke the knuckle on my right hand. I had to fight with the cast on till it ended."

"That must have hurt, huh, Red?"

"Getting hit with my cast hurt those punks as much as me. I almost ran out of excuses to my mom about how my cast kept getting broken every day. She believed me, but the nurse in the hospital kept telling me my excuses were bullshit. She never told my mom of her suspicion."

We arrived in front of Bobby's store, and when he saw us out front, he walked quickly to the open entrance doors to greet us. Bobby was putting a hug on me, and I was about to shrug him off when he pulled back and said, "Welcome back, Red. Annie just phoned me and said you'd probably be on by and that you're out of the bottle and back on the Street. She said you're working on a big case. Congratulations, Red. C'mon in the store and let's have some coffee together, the three of us. Hi! Jimmy. You okay now? Is the Army taking care of you? Like I told you before, Jimmy, if you ever need anything, anything at all, you can come to me anytime. You're a war hero, Jimmy. The people on the Southside owe you."

"Thanks for that stuff you said, but nobody owes me nothing and I got my cousin, Red, if I need anything." Jimmy told Bobby.

I didn't remember telling Annie I was going to buy a computer and how did she know I would go and to see Bobby? Jimmy must have told her. That's it, Jimmy told her.

We were drinking coffee and remembering old times when Jimmy asked where the computers were in the store and what brand he carried. I began to wonder what it mattered to Jimmy. He couldn't know anything about them, could he? Then, out of center field, he started asking about hard drives and how many gigs and what comes with them, like printers.

"What do you know about computers, Jimmy?"

"In the hospital, I was with a guy that lost his hands, remember? We became friends and I learned to use the keyboard and type for him. He taught me all about computers the year and a half we were together, right up till you picked me up and brought me home. You remember him, Red. You hung out with us all the time you came to see me and Billy; remember, Red. We still talk every week. They're making him new hands now. We didn't play with the computer when you were there with us. We were always bullshitting and getting drunk on the booze you sneaked into the hospital." Jimmy reminded me.

"Jimmy, you and Bobby, go pick out whatever you think we're gonna need."

"We need a desk top and a lap top and we don't want that fruity one cause I don't know if it's compatible with the software we're going to use." Jimmy convincingly told me.

I was concerned about using a computer without Annie next to me. I wasn't sure what I was going to do at my office and considered hiring a secretary who could handle the computer.

That problem is solved.

I said goodbye to Bobby and told him to give the bill to Jimmy, and I'd get him a check from the bank. Jimmy would bring it right back and then he could give him the equipment.

"Red, that's not necessary. Jimmy can take everything with him and I'll send my salesman along to set everything up at your office. That's where it's going, isn't it? You come by when you have some more time so we can bullshit about the old days." Bobby warmly said to me.

"You don't have to worry about getting paid, Bobby," I told him.

He came over to me as I was leaving, grabbed my hand, and we bumped shoulders as men do.

"I'll see you at Annie's later, Jimmy. I'm going over to see Vinnie G."

"Red, you sure you want to go alone?" Jimmy and Bobby both asked me.

"Bobby, what are you going to do if it gets rough over there? Read him a book!"

"You're still a fucking wise guy, Red. I know karate. I can kick someone's balls off them."

"Then why don't you go home and do it to your wife? She took yours when you two got married twenty years ago."

With a broad smile on his face, Bobby waved goodbye to me with his middle finger from the window of his store. I always liked the kid. I just never showed it.

Vinnie's vegetable and fruit store was on the way back toward the Italian Gardens on 16th and Carson. I walked by it every day on my way to grade school. I'd lift an apple or a pear sometimes on my way home from school. Other kids would try but get caught by Vinnie or one of his apron clad dagos. Vinnie would pay special attention when I hung around the corner sidewalk near the fruit and vegetables he had for sale. One day the old bastard was watching me especially close. After what seemed to be a long time, but was probably just minutes, he chased me. He was sure of his victory. I wouldn't steal any fruit from him on that day… so he thought.

What he didn't know was that I had planned for that day. The day the old bastard would come off his orange crate in the back of the store and do security on me himself. No one could get over on old Vinnie. As I walked away after he had grabbed my arm and told me to, "Get the fuck out of here you little punk. You'll never be good enough to get over on me, not on old Vinnie." He announced loudly so all of his gumbas, my friends and anyone else watching could hear.

As soon as I was far enough down the street so that none of the men could catch me, I stopped, turned, reached inside my jacket pocket and pulled out an apple. I quickly took a bite and threw it back in his direction as I ran away. I could hear my friends laughing and cheering as well as some of Vinnie's gumbas while I was running and occasionally raising my arms in victory. I had just ripped Vinnie off right in front of his scruffy face while he was never more than three feet from me.

That story would be told repeatedly in the school, on the street and unfortunately in my home. My folks heard about my escapade at the fruit stand. I had to go back and pay for the apple and say it wouldn't happen again. Vinnie carries a grudge for that apple caper to this day.

Many of my friends that witnessed the event were amazed that I could grab an apple and put it in my pocket with Vinnie watching me and sometimes even holding my coat by the shoulder. It's still talked about in the street in front of his store by people that don't even know who the little boy was that got over on Vinnie on one cold winter afternoon.

I had prepared for that day for weeks. I had to wait for the perfect time. I wanted a crowd of my friends and as many people around the store as possible buying his fruit. I told my friends that this was the day I was going to rip off Vinnie right in front of his eyes. The word spread through my fifth-grade classroom and spilled over to the other classrooms. On my way down Carson Street, I was like the pied piper. I had kids who lived in the opposite direction of Vinnie's, walking behind me to see the biggest event of the school year. I opened my coat and turned toward the doorway so Vinnie, sitting in the back of the store, could see I had nowhere to hide anything. My friend Dickey slipped into the back of the store to tell Vinnie that I was going to steal an apple. He told him I was bragging about it in school. As I reached the first row of pears, I kicked in my plan. Vinnie was just a few feet away from me as I began to touch and handle the fruit. I headed to the apples and lifted as many as I could in a supposed attempt to confuse my stalker. I juggled three at a time when I guess, in Vinnie's opinion, that was enough.

He grabbed my hands and shook free the apples I was holding as his guards that he had posted blocked my exit until I surrendered the prize I was seeking; one red apple. I left without an apple, so everyone believed. The rest is history.

I wanted to embarrass that old bastard for the arrogance and insulting curses he often threw at me and other kids as we passed. That day I shoved all his insults right up his arrogant Italian ass.

What no one knew was that my plan and preparation were far superior to anything an old bastard like Vinnie could ever imagine. I had the crowd I wanted, I had Vinnie on my shoulder, and I had my apple stuffed down in my shorts. I had taken it from my mother's refrigerator before I left for school that morning. Vinnie would never forget my victory over him on that day, and I would never forget the lesson I learned on that cold fall day: some grudges die hard, and some grudges never die.

Vinnie Giganni was at the top of my list of suspects in Horst's murder.

I would go by the fruit store on 16th and Carson Street and renew our mutual dislike for each other. He was past eighty by now. I had him busted a couple times for numbers when I was first on the beat. Another rookie cop just out of the academy wanted to make a name for himself by busting a long-time mobster. I fed him, Vinnie.

There were all kinds of different fruits in his store. One of them was his youngest son, Gino. The older brother was alright. He was about ten years older than me and carrying the curse of the Italian diet. He had a fat gut and a big ass that was out of proportion to the rest of his body. Sal was losing his hair along with his waistline. I never had a beef with Sal even though his old man tried pushing it. He was in the store when I arrived. His father was sitting in the back on a swivel chair that he substituted some years ago for the orange crate he used to sit on.

"Hey, Sal, I just want to talk to your father for a few minutes. There's no problem here."

"Wait a minute. I gotta see if he's busy," he told me even though he could see that his father was sitting on the chair looking at what I'd guess had to be a fifteen-inch black and white TV. Maybe at one time, it had color, but it's just like Vinnie now: it's passed its time. Vinnie signaled to his son that it was okay to have me approach him.

I walked forty feet to the rear of the store and stood beside Vinnie, waiting for him to speak first as was customary. It was a sign of respect for the old man. I'd play his game for now.

"Lost your shield huh, Red" Vinnie said through his brown stained lips. Stained from the decades of hanging one of those smelly Italian stogies from his mouth.

"Yeah, Vinnie, and you lost your teeth, and your clock is about to hit twelve." I flipped back at him.

"What the fuck do you want, Red?" he questioned in a friendly way, friendly for him, considering he disliked me as much as his gay son. Maybe more! I decided to go for the ring on the merry-go-round.

"Why did you have Horst Strump wacked?" I shot at him quickly. Then, before he had a chance to answer, I followed with, "And why his kid two years earlier?"

"Get the fuck out. You're fucking with something that's gonna get you killed if you start digging into the old garbage, you dumb son of a bitch. I don't like you since you were a smart assed punk kid. Consider what I told you as a favor for helping Gino the time he got in trouble with the drugs. The warning I just gave you is the payback, Red. I owed you. Now, we're even. Don't come back here again. The door is closed to you." Vinnie finished saying and then rose from his chair and went into the back room. The meeting was over.

I walked by Sal and told him to go in the back and change his old man's diaper. The tone of Vinnie's voice and the look in his worn-out old eyes told me I scared him with those two questions. He was shit scared. I know that look. I've seen it in the faces of some of the mob guys I've questioned before. They all got that look when I threatened to put the word on the street that they ratted out the big boss. Vinnie was a Don in the local mafia and didn't have to worry about his boss coming at him. Whoever he feared was bigger than the local mafia. What have I gotten myself into?

I didn't get forty feet from the store when Sal called me to come back inside.

Vinnie wanted to talk with me again.

"Red, I don't much like you, but you were always a stand-up guy. That's why my people left you alone. I just want you to know that I ain't going to say anything about what you asked me to anybody. If you go looking into that old business, you're gonna have people coming after you. Look out for the suits. Once you start down that path you can't turn back, and they will keep coming. Maybe even forty years later."

That was it. That was all he'd give me. He wanted to tell me he wasn't bringing on any trouble for me, but it would be coming if I pursued the case. I was going to have to check to see if Hilda employed any other private eyes within the last fifteen years. I'd have to call some of the other agencies to see why they turned down the big bucks. It could be the reason she gave me why other agencies turned her down wasn't the truth.

This time when I left the fruit stand, I picked up an apple, took a bite out of it, pointed at Vinnie, and aimed my finger at him, not the middle one, and gave him the see you sign. I have no idea what the hell he just said to me means. He gave me a warning, but he indicated it wasn't his mafia hoods I should look out for. I should look out for suits. Did he mean suits like in decks of cards? Did clubs mean the clubs I go to in the

City? Is there any danger going to come from there? Maybe he means spades like black people were referred to way back when. What would hearts and diamonds mean? No, it has nothing to do with cards. Then what?

"Hey, Red." I heard from behind me. "It's me, Spooks."

I stopped and turned around to greet the caller. He was a local bum who was always down on his luck. He had slipped into his fifties but looked the same to me as he did twenty years ago. He always wore long sleeved plaid work shirts and sneakers twelve months a year. Spooks lived on the streets of the Southside since he was a kid, the story goes. His mother and dad died when he was thirteen. They had nothing to leave him. An aunt took him in, but she lived out of the City. So, he ran away, back to the Southside, and lived any and everywhere, from dumpsters to church cellars. Everyone knew him, fed him, and gave him tasks like cleaning up, sweeping out the bars and shoveling snow in the winter. He never went back to school. He liked his life on the streets. If anything happened in the Southside, Spooks knew it. He knew every window that wasn't locked and doors that were open and how to hide from the punks that time to time threatened him. Mostly, everyone knew that I protected him when I was sober. Punks that were new to the Southside would learn to leave him alone after a visit from me.

"Hi, Spooks. How you doing? I haven't seen you around lately."

"Yes, you have, Red. You just don't remember. We slept one off in the basement of Saint Marys' church last Thursday night," he told me. Then he said, "I heard you hit the lottery. It's all over the street. Could you spot me ten until I get paid?"

"Spooks, you don't even have a job. How you going to get a paycheck?"

What is this shit about the lottery? That's the second time in less than a day someone asked me that.

"It's just a figure of speech, Red. How about it?" he was asking, knowing I would give him a ten spot and probably more.

"You don't need me to spot you cash anymore. I'm going to give you a job and pay you fifty bucks a week. Your job is to let me know of any strangers, especially strangers wearing suits, come into the Southside asking questions about me. Anything that isn't usual for us here on the Southside you tell me."

"Make it a hundred."

"How about I make it a kick in your ass instead? I'll make it seventy-five. Here's fifty in advance."

"Now, what do you have for me?" I asked, to his surprise.

"I just started working, Red. I need some time to make the rounds. I'll get back to you. I want to check into my office first." Spooks said as he pocketed the fifty and headed toward Annie's bar to spend it. He must be watching TV a lot. That's probably where he picked up that 'I'll get back to you' crap.

# CHAPTER 7

What's my next move? I know… the library. That's where I'll start digging my tunnel, fifteen years down.

I dropped by the I. G. (Italian Gardens) on my way to the library to tell Annie where I'd be for the next couple of hours. Old Mikey was sitting next to Spooks, nursing a beer and talking about the new pizza joint on 15th Street.

"I'm checking with some of my news sources, Red." Spooks called to me.

Anne looked at me and asked, "What's that all about? And, Red, I had your phone turned back on. You need it for the connection to the internet. Jimmy's going over the setup with Bobby's salesman. How about that Jimmy knowing how to use a computer? There still may be hope for you, Red."

"I'm going to the library. If you need me, send Jimmy to get me," I told Annie on my way out the door.

I'd been going to that library since I was in the first grade. The nuns would take us once a month; otherwise, I would have never known what the inside of it looked like. I didn't like to read. Most of the book reports I did while in school were about the movies I had seen. If I needed a report on a particular book, I'd tell Annie and she'd read it and tell me what to write. Annie was two years behind me in school, but she was very smart. All the nuns knew she was like a tutor to me. Starting in the fifth grade, when my teacher saw me falling behind in a subject, she would call Annie in and tell her, and then Annie would bring me to her house and try to get me back on track. It's lucky for me she's still doing it, trying to keep me on track.

The library had a computer I could use to get to the newspaper accounts of Horsts' murder fifteen years ago. I was a beat cop in the downtown part of the City at that time. I hardly remembered it. As I recall it wasn't treated as a high-profile murder. The Lawrenceville section had two precincts in it. My research would tell me which one handled the case. I was going to see how the papers played the story up and for how long it made the front pages. Fifteen years ago, there were three newspapers in the City. Now, there's one morning paper and a late afternoon paper. They're both rags.

I had a librarian get me set up in the newspaper archives. Now, I would have to read for the next hour or so. I was thinking about having the woman in the library who helped me get started call Annie and tell her I need help with a book report, and she should come over.

There were some questions I hoped to get answers to. Who were the cops that answered the call? Who was the coroner? What homicide detectives were assigned to handle the murder investigation? What evidence did the D.A. present? I'd dig the tunnel as far back in time as I could in the next two hours then head to the precinct that had jurisdiction and try to locate the cops involved in the case. There would be a lot of legwork ahead. Any available evidence, if there is any, will be almost impossible to find in the maze of the criminal justice storage facilities. Memories of most of the cops will have been dulled with the passage of fifteen years on an unsolved murder. It's just one of the more than hundreds of unsolved homicides in the City over the last fifteen years.

It was almost four o'clock and I was tired of taking notes and staring at a fucking computer screen. I saw the reflection of a tall broad heading toward me.

"Are you finding what you're looking for, Mr. Canyon?" She asked me.

"Do you work here?" I asked back.

"No, I don't, Mr. Canyon. I'm Hilda's niece, Jackie. You met my father, Carl, last night at her home. The woman in the bar told me you were here. Jimmy sent me over there from your office," she said in a rather arrogant and condescending manner.

She was built, close to beautiful, and snotty. Maybe I can knock her down a few pegs. She knows she's a looker. "Jackie, that's a man's name. What are you, a transvestite?" I asked her, figuring I just knocked her down a little.

"Mr. Canyon, if you look at me and have to question my sex, then I think I'll have to tell my aunt that I don't believe she hired the best private dick in the City; she may have only hired a private little prick. Now, shall we start over?" She just crushed me.

I had no good come back to the spear she just hit me with. I had to come up with something clever, and quickly. My choices were fuck you or back at you. I didn't want to make her a permanent enemy. Back at you would have to do.

"Fuck you bitch!" came out of my mouth. I tried to make it nice, but there was something inside me that just wouldn't let me eat crow. I'd always choose to fight. Oh well!

"How did you know I was the right guy when you approached me?"

"My aunt described you to me. Six foot two or three, sandy colored close-cropped hair and a chiseled, handsome face needing a shave. She was wrong about your weight. She told me you weighed about one eighty. I'd say closer to two hundred, right? Now, Mr. Canyon, are we done sparing or are we going to take this show to a comedy club?" she asked with a smile and a different look in her eyes.

"My aunt said you like to use salty language and, in her words, 'you are a piece of work'."

"What do you want?" She could try that on. I was done with the foreplay.

"The purpose of my visit is to request that you deal through me to my aunt. As you know, she is old and frail and not up to the everyday requirements, and you may find a necessary part of your investigation. I can coordinate your efforts and arrange for you to question the contacts you may want to make at the business. I'm also a director of the company. My aunt has asked me to provide any assistance I can to facilitate the investigative process. I have the checkbook and will set up a business account you can draw on for the expenses relevant to the investigation, such as travel expenses, additional personnel, equipment, and funds you may need to purchase information. All this subject to my authorization, of course."

"Oh, of course," I said, in a tone this bitch should be familiar with. I wanted to shove that of course right down her fucking throat. "So, are you telling me not to call Hilda?"

"On the contrary, Mr. Canyon, she wants to hear from you every day, even if it's only to say hello. She seems to be fond of you, although I can't see why. I'm to handle all the details with you to facilitate the expeditious resolution of the case."

"Are you a fucking lawyer?"

"Why, yes, Mr. Canyon, I am. How could you tell?"

"I didn't like you the moment I first saw your reflection on the computer screen. When I'm not attracted to a good-looking woman, she's either a dike or a lawyer. You didn't set off any vibrations in my pants and I could bet you weren't a dyke from the way you were checking out my package. The 'facilitate the expeditious resolution of the case' language is right out of dopey lawyer talk 101. You should drop all the pretentious language bullshit and learn to talk efficiently like the rest of us."

"You mean like you, Mr. Canyon?" She said in that snotty tone again.

This broad is going to need a saddle put on her. I decided to keep giving her the Red Rough Rider character.

"You're fucking, right," I told her as I reached down and did a Michael Jackson crotch grab for her benefit. "And quit calling me Mr. Canyon. Call me Red."

"Okay, Red, I'll leave you my business card. Contact me when you want to start the interviews at the plant. Bring your assistant with you," she told me as she walked toward the entrance of the library. I could see she had a nice pair of legs and a great ass. I wonder why she wants me to bring Jimmy along. I want him with me anyway.

I'm charging Hilda twenty-five an hour for Jimmy's time and fifty an hour for me. Between me and Jimmy, I'll eat up three grand a week out of the retainer just for hourly time we put in. I'll get Annie to handle the billing. If I do the paperwork, it will never get done.

According to the newspaper accounts the 28$^{th}$ precinct had jurisdiction on Horst's homicide case. I couldn't find any names of any of the officers involved in the investigation. The only referenced officers were the two who made the initial response to a call by an anonymous company employee. I'll start there first thing tomorrow morning. I'll take a bucket of coffee and a dozen doughnuts with me. I know a couple of vice detectives operating out of the 28$^{th}$. The cops could never turn down coffee and doughnuts. Using them as my calling card should get me a little co-operation.

I stopped by the office on my way back from the library. I couldn't get in. The door was locked, and I didn't have a key. I never locked the door when I left. There was no need to. Now, with a new computer, I'll have to learn to carry a key. The problem is I don't have any keys for the fucking lock. Tomorrow morning I'll just break the glass in the hallway door and then call a locksmith and a glass installer. I'll put it on Hilda's bill.

When I walked into the Italian Gardens, I was expecting to see Jimmy and Annie, but not the person in the booth with Jimmy. Hilda's niece was sitting across from Jimmy, drinking a beer from the bottle and talking with him. What's that all about? Is she trying to set up Jimmy to spy on me for her?

Jimmy called me over and asked me to sit down with them.

"No thanks. I'm going to sit with Annie."

"We're just talking about you. She thinks you're an asshole. I said back at you and she's still here. I think she wants to make nice with us."

"She wants me to be her spy. What do you think, Red?"

"What's she willing to do for you?"

"She wants to pay me a couple hundred a week."

"Hold out for sex too. She's a good looking broad. Negotiate, Jimmy. It's okay with me if she wants to pay you to spy on me."

All the time, she sat there and didn't flinch. My guess is she knew Jimmy would tell me about her offer. I took another glance at how Jackie was looking at Jimmy. I know that look. I see that same look in Annie's eyes when I glance at her sometimes. He wouldn't have to negotiate much to sleep with her. I wonder if he knows it. If he doesn't figure it out, she'll do it for him. Pheromones! That must be it.

I went over and sat down by Annie at the end of the bar.

"It looks like Jimmy's not sleeping alone tonight. I saw the way she looked at him. It's like a high school girl looking at her football hero."

"Maybe that's how you look at me, Annie?"

"Or maybe it's how you look at me. Only thing is you also drool."

"Seriously, Annie, how do you figure that match even if it's only for a night."

"I don't know, Red. I still haven't figured us out."

"We're going to Jackie's place so she can change and then we're going to dinner. Don't wait up for me, Red.

See you, Annie." Jimmy called out to us as he left with Hilda's niece.

"Wow! I wouldn't believe it in a million years. Am I wrong, Annie?"

"Now, where are you taking me to dinner? And don't say the Colonels or you'll be sleeping at your home tonight."

"Let's go to the 'Top of the City' up on the mountain. You put on a formal dress, and I'll put on my tux. I didn't return it."

The place was expensive, but nothing is too good for my Annie, and I'm healed.

"That sounds romantic, Red. Are you sure that's where you want to go?"

"I picked it because it is a romantic restaurant, Annie ," I said as I grabbed her around the waist and pulled her toward the entrance to her Apartment.

"You start to get ready, and I'll call ahead for reservations."

Everything was almost too perfect this evening. Jimmy had a date. I was with Annie, and I still had forty-seven grand in the bank and a lead that I could start to follow first thing tomorrow morning.

I began wondering why Jackie showed up at the library when she could have just made a phone call to me. Something is up with that. It will wait until tomorrow. My instinct tells me there's trouble ahead. Does it begin at the 28th Precinct?

# CHAPTER 8

It was seven a.m. when I woke to the sound of the hydraulic crusher from one of the City garbage trucks forcing the weekend trash from the bar to mingle with the Chinese waste that the takeout restaurant halfway down the block had already contributed. The stale cakes from the bakery one stop down the block would be added next to round out the menu.

The regulars at the City dump would be waiting for their three-course meal to arrive. They always ate takeout and had it delivered fresh daily, that is a relative term in this case. I wondered in what order the vultures, pigeons and four legged vermin would eat today. Would it be Chinese appetizers first, then on to an Italian entrée, finished by two-day old doughnuts and rancid cheesecake? The residential trash would have to wait to be picked up until later in the week, as would the patrons of the City dump for their change of menu.

I was brought back to the current time by the soft voice of Annie telling me that the coffee was ready. I wondered if today I would encounter vermin, the two-legged variety. My destination was in some sense a dump. Not the one storing remnants of food waste, but one storing within its cells the vultures and vermin that feed off the unfortunate people they sit in wait for. This dump stored human trash. It was the 28th Precinct.

Jimmy showed at eight and we were off to Grayson's tailoring to return our rentals. I was going to order three suits and a couple of sport coats for me and Jimmy. Sam could pick the shirts and ties out. We'd need ten shirts each to cover the dry-cleaning weekly cycle of shirts. I was going to have us look like well-dressed successful businessmen. If we went undercover on surveillance, we would dress to fit the surroundings and blend in.

We finished with Sam and were wearing the new suits he promised he'd have ready for us today. It was on to the 28th Precinct to begin the search for Horst Strump murderers.

The precinct was in a moderate crime area with a low murder rate. Armed robbery wasn't a major threat in the community. Yet, Horst was murdered in a violent armed robbery at six o'clock in the evening in the parking lot of his factory, with no witnesses. I had the stats for the 28th from 1990 through 2004. I didn't need them. The murder and armed robbery trend were flat lined from 1990 through 2004.

Lawrenceville was an old section of the city. There was an influx of yuppies beginning ten years ago that rejuvenated the community. They bought the old row homes and restored them. New construction was minimal. Restoration was the preference…just like on the Southside.

That theme continued through the business district. Once empty storefronts were now occupied by many upscale tenants offering wish lists for the mixed yuppie residents. The greasy spoon Greek hamburger and coffee shops were replaced with geek Panini sandwiches and lattes. The new shoppers replaced many of the old people that sported black grease-stained hands and fingernails of the mechanic with the polished and manicured nails of the new generation. Fortunately, for this section of the City, time changes everything. The new residents saved it from the wrecking ball of time.

The 28th occupied a turn of the century faded brick building that looked more like a library than a police station. Only the old-style police globes hanging over the entrance door gave it away. I asked Jimmy to sit in the car and wait while I began the journey through what I knew would be one roadblock after another, pursuing a fifteen-year-old case.

Once inside I identified myself to the desk sergeant with my shield and asked for directions to the detective unit. I carried a gold shield for most of the years I was on the job. I only retired four years ago so I was sure I'd know someone in the precinct. While I was waiting, I heard a loud voice from behind calling out to me.

"Red, you son of a bitch… how you doing? You coming back? The city could use you. We only get snot nosed politically correct cops as detectives now." Charlie Cavanaugh was loudly announcing to everyone present.

I have known Charlie for the last eleven years. We never worked together, but he had the reputation of being a solid no nonsense detective. By that, I mean he followed his leads and didn't worry about whose toes he stepped on in the process. He was past retirement age and I wondered why he didn't take his package and walk. It's a break for me to find Charlie still working.

"Charlie, I thought by now you would be sitting on your porch getting fat."

"The department is light on shields, and they asked me to stay on till the end of this year. What are you up to that brings you out here to the 28th? You're still on the Southside aren't you, Red?"

"I'm here looking for some information on a case I'm working. You've been here for the last twenty years and might recall it. Maybe you worked it. It happened in 1990. The victim was a Horst Strump." I waited for his reaction.

"Red, you're probably the fourth or maybe the fifth private dick that's been around here over the last fifteen years digging into that case. Hasn't the wife run out of money yet? That case has been closed for at least thirteen years?"

He hit me with surprise when he told me about four or five other investigators that Hilda had booked over the last fifteen years. She only made me aware of the one that she retained the year that Horst was murdered. Why would she hide that information from me?

Charlie asked me to follow him upstairs to his office where we could talk privately. On the way, he introduced me to some of the other suits that worked for him. He was a captain now. His influence could help me skate through some of the bullshit I was bound to encounter trying to find old records on the case. Wait a second, I thought. Suits! Most of the detectives wear suits. Was Vinnie talking about cops when he warned me? Nah, it couldn't be, could it?

"You handling your demons now, Red?"

"Yeah, Charlie. I put the bottle away. This case is going to put me back on top. I need any help you can give me."

He didn't owe me any favors, but he liked the way I had operated, old school. I was suspended with pay and put on the desk pending internal affairs investigating my shootings over two dozen times in my career with the City. That was more than his score, even though he spotted me more than fifteen years on the job. I saved the City a lot of expense by killing the punks that needed killing and skipping the system.

"You might want to start with the wife. The four or five investigators must have dug up some information you could use to save yourself some time. I can tell you this; one guy got himself killed… gangland style. Ed Franklyn was his name, as I recall. He was shot in the face. Robbery was listed as the motive. No perp was ever found. Sound familiar? I tried to tell the DA at the time that there might be a connection because of the M.O. I was told to stay the fuck out of it. Even my captain was told to warn me to stay out of the case. If I had anything from my snitches I was to give it to him and shut my mouth."

"Are there any files here I could look at or are they all in records storage or maybe in a computer somewhere?"

"It's strange about the records on the case. They all seemed to disappear after that first private investigator began looking into the case back in 1991. The two detectives who handled the investigation told me the fix was in, and it was coming from downtown. Those same two investigating detectives got themselves killed in 1992.

You should remember that Red. Rich Dugan and Tommy Falon were in a high-speed chase when they lost control of their car and hit an oncoming semi. They scraped them up off the street and buried their pieces."

I did remember the incident, but I had no special interest in the accident at that time. The only pressure that came down from the top was to find the stolen car involved in the chase. There was no description of the occupants except that one was a black man, and one was a white man. They were never found, and neither was the car.

I'm only on the case for two days and I've turned up three dead bodies involved in the Horsts murder investigation and two dead kids within three years of Horsts' murder. Hilda's kid and Wreckers kid who took the rap for juniors' murder and robbery.

How many other dead bodies are out there with strings tying them to Horst somehow? The caution light is on. I am going to have to rethink Jimmy's role as my assistant. There may be more danger here than I want him to be exposed to.

"Thanks, Charlie, for the info. If I need some inside push, can I count on you?"

"Sure. I'm retiring at the end of the year. I don't give a damn if I mess someone's hair up. Watch your ass, Red." Charlie cautioned me as I was leaving. "Don't trust anyone downtown to give you a straight answer. Follow Regan's advice when you deal with the department. Trust, but verify."

Back outside I found Jimmy parked illegally in front of the station. He was out of the car talking to a young cop. I was going to pull my ID out and flash it when Jimmy told me the cop was former Army. He saw Jimmy's pass to Walter Reed and asked him if he could help him. He introduced himself to me and told me to call him if he could help Jimmy or me in any way. I'd file that away. It could come in handy in the future.

We were close to the factory where Horst located his business, the same place where he was murdered. I wanted to talk to the people that knew Horst and still worked there. Jackie said she'd arrange it. I didn't want to alert Carl and Jackie because I didn't want them to warn the people I was going to question. I wanted spontaneous responses.

I was starting to feel like my old self again. I had confidence. I was on my way back to being a good street detective. Before the booze and my retirement, some called me the undertaker. The punks on the street hung that handle on me. It stuck with me for a while.

When I arrived at the factory, I had Jimmy drive around the parking lot so I could see where Horst was killed. I was looking for any place the shooter could hide. He had to be out of site or Horst would have noticed a stranger or two in his parking lot. Was Horst carrying at the time? The account in the newspaper said he was shot in the face through the closed driver side window. Someone then pumped a couple more bullets into him that were not needed. A professional mechanic (a professional killer) wouldn't have wasted the slugs unless it was a message being sent to someone Horst was in with on some other deal gone bad. A fifteen-year-old homicide will have many unanswered questions. It's like trying to solve one of those crossword puzzles with letters that need words to fit in all directions to obtain the correct solution. The problem is that I only have the puzzle part of the page. Someone tore the rest of the page from the book that provides the clues to the answers.

"What are we going to do here?"

"We're going to interview some of the employees that knew Horst. We need to get a more complete picture of him. Time often softens the view of the past, so we have to add that factor into the analysis of Horst."

We entered the office area and asked for Jackie. There wasn't much information describing what this company manufactured. The signing on the building and inside the office said Strump Optical, Inc. That was it. There was nothing that gave information about a product. I was going to want to know what they manufactured and sold. Maybe that has something to do with his murder.

Jackie was with us in minutes and escorted us to her office.

"I assume you've come to interview the employees that worked for Horst. There are only three left, Dale Ferguson, the warehouse super, Marie Dixon, his former assistant, and Alice Tremaine the accountant. Who would you like to start with?"

"How long did they work for your uncle?"

"They all started working for him in 1965, the year he started the company. The first facility was over on the Southside of the city. They were part of his first group of employees. I'll let them fill you in."

I wanted to see his assistant first. She could tell me some of the history I needed on Horst. Who were his close business associates? Who were the customers? What was he selling and manufacturing? Where did he travel; only in the U.S., or did he travel outside the country? If he did travel abroad, what were the countries he visited? Did she have any records or notes that go back forty years?

My questions for the accountant would be the same. I would ask for travel vouchers and any corporate tax records that may be available up to 1990. I wanted to know where he traveled to. Who were the customers in those cities? I wanted to know the dates and length of his stay at every place he visited. I was looking for a pattern in his movements to see if there was one. Would any names come up that could be of use to me?

"Bring in his assistant," I told Jackie while wondering what she would tell me about the man with two faces.

"That's Marie Dixon, Red."

She brought her in and introduced me as the private investigator that has reopened Horst's murder. She asked her to cooperate and then left her alone with me in her office while she and Jimmy went on a tour of the plant.

"You've probably been asked these questions before, but I need you to answer them one more time. Do you know why anyone would have wanted to kill Horst?"

"No!" she answered with hesitation in her voice.

"Anything you tell me stays with me; no one else will know anything we discuss. I need you to be honest with me."

I was going to try to loosen her up by feeding her some second party thoughts about Horst.

"Others have told me he had a split personality. Some have said he was a dangerous man. The kind you never cross. Some think he lived two lives. What do you think?"

"He wasn't threatening me. He and his brother-in-law, Carl, had words on occasion. I wouldn't call it threatening. It was business. I guess you'll want the copies of messages that I took for Horst up until his death. I also have my notes from his travel itinerary if I made the reservations. He sometimes made his own arrangements. I had no idea where he traveled on those occasions."

Hilda told me there were no records.

"I was informed that the police and Federal agents took all the files from the office. How is it that you have that you still have that information in your possession?"

"When I was asked to turn over his files, I did. No one ever asked me for mine. I wouldn't have turned them over anyway. They were mine," she calmly said.

"Why didn't you turn them over to the other investigators?"

"They never asked me if I had any files. I guess they all assumed that the police took everything. I can show you where they are stored in the old basements' office supply cage."

"I'll send my associate, Jimmy, with you to retrieve them. Don't tell anyone of their existence and that means Jackie and Carl and especially any law enforcement officials. They could think you were hiding evidence for fifteen years," I warned. I didn't believe that last threat. I just wanted to make sure she told no one of the existence of her files. I don't buy her story. After I go through them, I'll come back to her for the truth on how she came up with the files that didn't exist for fifteen years.

Ferguson and Tremaine had their stories rehearsed. They knew nothing and Horst treated them fairly… blah, blah, blah. They knew of no reason why anyone would want to kill Horst. Tremaine had no other documents socked away. Everything was in police custody except for tax documents on the business. I'd get them also. I didn't know what I'd find in them that could produce a lead.

I decided to take the boxes of detail to Annie's place. The security at my office is non-existent. I get a sense about this investigation that someone is out there that doesn't want the case re-opened. I need to protect what little hard information I have in my possession.

Vinnie gave me a veiled threat. Hilda lied about the role of other investigators, and the three people who knew Horst from his business wouldn't talk, even after fifteen years. Oh well!

I filled the trunk of my Caddy with seven boxes of I didn't know what. I'd get Annie to help me go through the files and notes on Horsts' business life according to Marie Dixon and Alice Tremaine. Somewhere in these boxes could be the half million-dollar clue.

My next stop will be to see Wrecker Johnson up on the Hill. It's not far from the factory. I wanted to get a couple of unregistered guns along with some information about his son's involvement with the murder of Hilda's son. If he didn't have any hot weapons in stock, he could get them for me. I wanted to revisit the murders of both of their sons, Hilda's and Wrecker's. My instinct tells me that they are tied together by some common thread. I'd have to find out what that thread was. The fabric of the quilt I'm beginning to make is going to be made of rope, twine, and silk. When it's finished will it look like a Picasso or Whistlers' Mother. Well, see!

Twenty minutes later, we were at the junkyard looking for Wrecker. His office was in an old trailer a couple of hundred feet from the entrance to the property. I told

Jimmy to be prepared for anything. That meant he was to have his finger on the trigger of the pistol he was carrying. I put a lot of punks away from this part of the city when I began my career with the City PD. I was young and inexperienced and arrested everyone during the first two years on the job.

After a while, you start to get worn down with reports and endless hours in court. Eventually, you learn to measure the level of every crime... Level one is for murder. Level two becomes an assault on another police officer and so on, down to the everyday street hassles.

The door opened as we approached and a dirty looking guy carrying some used parts walked past us heading to his pickup truck. Inside I could see Wrecker in the back of the trailer sitting behind a desk covered with paperwork that matched the boxes of papers and receipts piled all over the inside of the trailer along with used auto parts. I guessed his bookkeeper was out sick…for the last twenty years.

"The rumors are true. They said that Red Canyon was on the street again. What the fuck do you want here? You don't carry a shield anymore and you don't have any friends up here on the Hill," Wrecker warned, but not in his usual manner. He wasn't waving a gun.

"Information! I'm on a homicide case that may be connected to your son's murder."

"Fuck you, Red. I asked for your help seventeen years ago, but you covered up for your dirty boys in blue. You didn't give me help then and now you think I'm going to do something for you? Get the fuck out!"

I needed to give him something that would change his mind.

"I was straight with you then. I didn't connect any cops to your kid's murder, and it wasn't my case to investigate. You told me back then that you believed the Southside mob was in on the murder. You may be right about that connection. If you want to try to help me find the killers, then cut the tough guy bullshit, and let's talk. Otherwise, fuck you. When I do find out who killed your kid, I'll turn them over to the cops and you can visit them on weekends and bring them cigarettes," I warned Wrecker. I didn't know where the investigation was going, but neither did Wrecker. I was betting he wanted the people responsible for killing his kid more than holding a grudge against me for believing I was holding out on him back then. The fact was I didn't have anything to give him.

"There are at least six cons walking the Hill that want to put a cap in your ass for sending them up the river. There's probably more out there I don't know about. These are the ones that come into my club. You show your face around the Hill, and your motherfucking ass is dead. You ain't a cop now so they ain't gonna worry about killing a fucking civilian," he warned again.

"Then you help keep me alive if you want answers. I promise you that when I find out who set your kid up, I'll tell you so you can deal with them. I don't need you, but you just might be able to help me get to the truth a little faster. You know my reputation on the street. The punks feared me."

"You ain't been nothing since they retired you. What I hear is you've been a fucking drunk doing nickel and dime divorce bullshit and security guard crap. Why should I believe you? If it gets around on the Hill that I'm hanging out with you it would be just like putting a bull's eye on my back. The same assholes that want to cap you will want to take me down too."

"I'm your only option if you want your kid's killers. There is nobody else looking for them and you don't have the answers. If you did, you wouldn't be talking to me now. The dance is over! The music stops when I walk out the fucking door," I told Wrecker, believing he wanted his kids' killers more than seeing me get whacked by some black scumbag. I didn't know what he could bring to the table, but every minute that passed, I sensed the instincts of the old Red guiding me again. What would Wrecker decide? I already knew the answer to that question.

Wrecker was kind of like the ad hoc mayor on the Hill. People sought him out for advice about local disputes. The gangs that operated in his hood didn't fuck with him. He fought that war twenty years earlier with them and settled it with a couple of dozen dead bodies floating up on the shore of the rivers that split the City. I was new on the job then, and we had orders to stay out of the war. The City decided to let them kill each other as long as the havoc stayed inside the Hill. They would then deal with the winner. That was Wrecker.

After it got quiet on the Hill the powers in City government gave a tacit authority to him to run it. As long as he kept it under control and kept most of the black crime from spilling over into the other sections of the city he had an ear at City Hall. Just keep sending in the envelopes with cash in them to City Hall every week. That arrangement is still in place. The only rift between the City and Wrecker was the rap they put on his kid. Rumors were they told him to accept it or lose his position of power. That was a battle he couldn't win. It prompted him to come to me privately. I ran into a stone wall at the time, and I didn't have any reason to think the kid was railroaded. He was dead and the case was closed. It was just a black kid killing a white kid in a robbery, or was it?

The interesting thing about Wrecker Johnson's nickname was that it didn't come from the fact that he owned a junkyard and dealt in wrecked cars. He was a boxer and a damn good heavyweight at one time. He had a promising career and had thirty plus professional bouts with twenty-one of them ending in first or second round knock outs. That's how he got the nickname, Wrecker. He wrecked his opponents and sometimes their careers. His boxing future ended when he was shot up on the Hill one night. He got caught screwing someone's bitch. He lost part of a lung and all of his boxing careers, then took his money and started a junkyard, and opened a nightclub up on the Hill.

"I don't want to talk with you right now. If you have an office on the Southside, leave an address and a phone number and I'll call you sometime and set up a meeting at your place. Don't come here again unless I tell you to. Understood, motherfucker?"

I gave him my business card and motioned for Jimmy to head to the car. When I reached the doorway, I turned to Wrecker, "Understood, motherfucker!" and got into my ride and headed back to the Southside and Annie.

# CHAPTER 9

On our way back to the Southside I decided to bring Jackie into the investigation. I would ask her to get a list of all the friends or acquaintances of both Horst and Hilda's son Trent. I'd have Jimmy locate as many as he could on the computer. Then the footwork would begin. I wanted to talk to as many of them as I could find.

I had an important question to ask Jimmy.

"Jimmy, do you still have your permit to carry?"

"Yeah, I don't think it expired. Do you think we are going to have to kill someone?" he asked with a grin on his face. Jimmy had killed the enemy before. He would do it again when the time came.

"Yeah, Jimmy, I think we will probably have to kill someone before this is over. The more we keep digging in the garbage the more likely we are to turn up the vermin hiding in it. Their nest hasn't been disturbed for fourteen years and they are likely to do whatever is necessary to keep from being discovered, even kill."

We arrived back at the Gardens and me and Jimmy unloaded my trunk of the seven boxes of records from the factory. Annie had a back office she said I could use until I set up some security over across the street at my office. I was anxious to begin the search through thousands of pages of unorganized notes, memos and correspondence. I could probably maintain my interest for about twenty minutes. This is the part of the job I like the least. I needed a drink and hadn't had one in over forty-eight hours. I was about to learn if I was in control of the alcohol or if the alcohol was still in control of me. Could I take a drink and then a second and stop, or would I continue and get drunk again?

I sat at the bar and then decided to stay off the booze until I crack the case or Hilda shuts off the spigot that the cash is flowing from. Then I heard those familiar words, "What are you drinking, Red?"

"Seltzer! And until further notice, only soft drinks, Annie," I told her, almost choking on the words I had just spoken. I like booze!

"I'm heading back home, Red. What time do you want me to come over tomorrow morning?" Jimmy asked me.

"Make it ten and bring six salt bagels and your permit to carry so I can make sure it's current," I said, hoping he would remember and would be able to find it.

Jimmy left for the house on Wright's Way, and I went into the back office in the rear of Annie's bar and started digging through the piles of papers in the boxes I just brought in. What would I find?

It took me less than the twenty minutes I gave myself for going through the documents to reinforce that this task was not for me. Annie or Jimmy could sift through the years of miscellaneous paperwork that I believed had some clues to the reason for Horst's murder. Annie would know how to catalog the data on the computer. They could provide the phone numbers that appear frequently as well as the dates and places of his travel. Annie will know how to set the program up when I explain what I'm looking for. What am I looking for?

It was early evening, and I was already tired. I wasn't up to working a full day. My inactivity and bottle busting made me soft and weak. Tomorrow I'll begin to change that. I'm going to buy one of those home gyms and put it in the office next to mine. It's vacant, and until the owner of the building finds out that I'm using it, I'll slide on the rent. I haven't paid my rent in the last five months anyway, and the owner hasn't hassled me about it. Tomorrow I'll send the past due rent money in. I wouldn't want to lose my office. I complain about it all the time, but the truth is I like it where I'm at. I see the streets close up… at least when I'm sober. This is where I grew up and I can see twenty blocks up and down Carson Street from my windows. I can hear the street. I can smell and almost touch the sweet and sometimes foul air that the City belches out.

When it rains, the heavy trucks and busses act like a washing machine agitator, vibrating the soiled asphalt and concrete streets and sidewalks. It helps to wash away the grime deposited by the users and abusers of the City.

The wind that follows the rain acts as a dryer. Everything in the City is clean and dry for a short time as it prepares itself for the next cycle to begin.

Some of the dirt is always missed. That's where I come in. I'm the street cleaner trying to clean up the dirt left behind fifteen years ago on the City streets. Perhaps my next ad in the yellow pages should not list me as a private investigator but as a street cleaner. I could change my retainer from a bottle of vodka to a heavy-duty broom.

I felt a hand on my shoulder pushing me. "Are you having a dream?" I heard Annie saying.

"No, I must have fallen into alcohol recovery sleep whatever that may be. No, that's bullshit. I was having a nightmare. If I start speaking in metaphors, drop me at the psych ward," I told Annie.

"Why would you say that?" she asked me as if the last five years of alcohol bliss hadn't happened.

"I'll tell you why, Annie, but you have to promise to keep it between us. I don't want shit like that getting out on the streets." And then I told her what was going on in my mind before she woke me. I wanted to see if she thought maybe my mind was fucked up from all the booze I'd been drinking in the last five years.

What I got from her was, "Oh, Red, that's a beautiful metaphor."

That's about what I thought she would say. "It's gay, Annie. I don't think like that cause I ain't gay. If I start to think in metaphors, then I fried my fucking brain."

"No, you didn't, Red. You always were able to see things through the different prisms of life. You're just becoming the sober Red. You're getting back to your street wise self… You'll start knocking down some doors and opening others again and soon," Annie told me with a reassuring grin on her face.

Yeah, maybe she is right. Maybe my recovery will be sooner rather than later. After a night's sleep, I'll know better. As I reached to grab Annie's ass, I assured myself of one thing; I wasn't gay.

# CHAPTER 10

I FELT the pressure of Annie pushing on my shoulder and then her voice calling to me to wake up. "It's an emergency! Spooks is at the door. You have to get up. He says it's urgent." I reached for the .38 I kept under my pillow, pulled my pants on and headed to the doorway where Spooks was standing. He was shaking as he began to speak to me.

"I saw them. I saw both of them, Red," he blurted out in a trembling voice.

"Saw who Spooks? Who did you see?"

"They forced the hallway door open and went up to your office. I pretended not to look, but I saw them."

"How do you know anyone went into my office? Maybe whoever you saw went to the old third-floor finance company office."

"No, they're in your office. I saw them close the blinds in the front windows. There are two of them, Red. I saw them!" Spooks kept telling me while standing in front of me, shivering, not from the cold, but from fright.

"Okay, Spooks, you saw them. You did a good job. I knew you would. That's why I hired you to look out for me. Now, I want you to take your time and think before you answer," I told him calmly hoping the tone of my voice would help settle him down.

"How were they dressed? Did you see how they got here? Did someone drop them off in front of my office or did they have their own car?" I was hoping he got a look at how they arrived. If they were dropped off, then there's a third man somewhere out on the street as a backup whose job is to watch for me.

"There's just the two of them. They came in a big black station wagon and parked it in front of your building. I watched them while I was picking up the cans and junk, I sell to the scrap yard. It's my route. The same every day! The same time every day! You know me Red; always the same."

"Yeah, Spooks the same every day. Now, what about the clothes they're wearing?"

"Suits, dark color suits… and short flat hair. They look as big as you and they look mean."

Annie wanted to call the cops. I said no. There was nothing in my office worth anything except the new computers. There's something they want, and they think I have it, whatever it is. I'm only on this case three days and the heat is already turning up.

Maybe Horst was blackmailing somebody, and they think I have the photos or files he used to carry out some scheme. The only thing I have that has anything to do with Horst is the seven boxes of papers I took from the factory. For these guys to have that information, the tip-off had to come from someone who saw me leaving the factory with the boxes or Jackie or Hilda. I need one of the suits alive to get some answers. What to do?

I needed to get Jimmy to give me back up.

I sent Spooks out the back of the bar into the alley to my house to get him. I will wait. I finished getting dressed and sat with Annie. She wanted to know why I don't just call the police.

"I need to know why two pros are in my office; what did they want? Was it me, or was it what I took from the factory, or both? They have the answers. I want to get them."

These two punks are professionals. They planned their arrival just before dawn so they could break into the building in the darkness, so there was little chance for them to be noticed. Then they wait for dawn, so they don't need lights to make their search. They have their getaway car out front just a few steps away from the building. The only thing that doesn't fit is the closing of the blinds on the front windows. They know that it will signal me that someone is waiting inside or has been in my office. Why would they want me to know of their presence? The answer is that they want to guarantee I'll come up to my office. These two punks are sure they can handle anything I can bring. They want me…

Well, they are gonna get what they want. I'm going to go to my office with something they won't be expecting me to bring along.

"Annie, get me the shot gun you keep stashed behind the bar and some shells. I'm going to need my vest too."

"Red, you're not going to try to take these two pros down by yourself, are you?"

"No, Annie, I'm not going to be alone. I'm going to take Winchester with me."

The shotgun Annie was bringing I bought ten years ago at an auction. It was a double barrel 12-gauge Winchester model 24 that was manufactured in 1940. It had a 28-inch length barrel and a modified pistol grip stock. It was a collector's piece worth a couple of grand today. I was sure these two pros were carrying automatic weapons. I wouldn't stand a chance with a .38 or my Glock if we got into a shootout.

The double barrel Winchester would give me the edge I was going to need. With the shotgun at close range a near hit on each of them would bring them down.

At twenty feet or less, I'd put a six-inch hole in them or blow off a limb. No, they wouldn't be expecting me and Winchester. I hoped it would fire. I hadn't serviced it in over a year. Oh, well!

Jimmy and Spooks arrived at the same time Annie got back with the Winchester. I looked it over and checked the action. It would do. I loaded each barrel. I didn't need any other back up. If I didn't get them down with the first two blasts, there wouldn't be any time for a reload anyway.

I brought Jimmy up to speed on what was going to go down in the next ten minutes. Jimmy would keep the Glock and the Makarov. I'd carry my .38 in my pocket holster. I was counting on catching them off guard.

"Spooks, I need you to wrap the shotgun up in crumpled newspapers and put it in your shopping cart. You go to 18th Street and cross Carson Street and head down past my office. Along the way, I want you to set the shotgun down on the step to my office doorway and then continue heading away from my building.

You have to do this without calling any attention to yourself. Can you do this for me?"

"Sure, Red, nobody will see anything except a bum collecting garbage. That's what you want don't you, Red?"

"That's exactly what I want. These guys in my office are watching for me and anything else they might consider out of the ordinary on the street this early in the morning," I told everyone.

"Jimmy, I want you to walk through the alley to 20$^{th}$ street and cross Carson Street to my office side. Then work your way down across from Max's restaurant and just wait there on the corner. When you're in place, I'll leave the bar and head across Carson toward my office. It won't be very long after I'm inside that you'll hear the shotgun. If you don't hear both barrels go off don't come up to my office. Shoot out the tires on the black station wagon parked in front of my office and wait for someone to come out. If it ain't me kill anyone with short hair wearing a dark suit. They won't be expecting you to be waiting outside so the kill should be easy. Just like in the military, follow my orders ," I said to Jimmy as I looked into his eyes to make sure he would do only what I just ordered and nothing else.

"I got it, Red."

"Jimmy, there is the possibility that one of them slipped out of the building or there is a third man Spooks didn't pick up on. They may have a backup. In any case, whoever is heading into the building at five a.m. isn't delivering mail. Take him out." I ordered. I didn't want another shooter ambushing me from the rear. I had enough with two suits to handle.

"What about me?"

"You call the cops if soon after you hear the two blasts of the shotgun, and I don't come to the window and raise the blinds."

"Why can't you just call the cops and let them handle it? Why do you have to confront these guys? Why do you have to risk getting yourself killed and maybe Jimmy too?"

I could see she was troubled contemplating my first serious action in five years.

"Trust me, Annie. I know what these guys want. They want to grab me and find out what I know and what I took from the factory and where it's at. Then they will kill me. Fuck that. They think I have the bottle that holds the genie, and they don't want him to escape."

"None of us are going to get killed today, Annie. My mind is clear and I'm ready to join up with the old Red again… I just need everyone to do exactly as I say. Just follow my directions and everything will go down without a hitch. I'm counting on each of you. You're my team. Right, Spooks?" Surprisingly, they were all calm now.

"Fucking right, Red. We'll learn these fuckers not to mess with you. Nobody messes with you especially here on the Southside," Spooks called out with pride now that he sensed I was back to my old self. Or was I? I'll know soon enough.

## CHAPTER 11

"You're not planning to kill these guys are you Red? You're just going to take them in custody to question them, right?"

"Yeah, Annie, I'm just going to take them in custody to question them. I'm only firing the shotgun to distract them so I can capture them alive. Okay? No more questions now. Does everyone understand their assignment?"

I couldn't believe Annie asked that dumb question. If someone just wanted me off the caper, they would have sent a couple of punks to rough me up. Someone is going to die within the hour. I had to make sure it wasn't Jimmy, Spooks or me or Anne. I had my plan. Now, to make it work.

"Jimmy, I want you and Spooks to start your walk. It's now ten minutes after five. Jimmy, you should be in place by five twenty. When I see you at Max's corner and that Spooks has dropped the shotgun off on the doorstep, I'll leave the bar and start my walk across Carson Street to my office. Now, go!"

I urged my team. What a crew to have to risk my life with: a guy with a plate in his head that drifts off at any time to some other world and a homeless bum from the streets. I'm their leader… a drunk for the past five years and sober for only the last three days. We should be a match for two trained professional assassins. Oh well!

Looking at my office from inside the bar I saw the window blind spread a little at what I would guess was eye level for the intruder. He was looking out on the street and waiting for me to show. I wouldn't disappoint him. How did they know of me and where my office was located? Why would they be looking across the street at the bar for my appearance? How did they know about the bar? If they know about the bar, then they know about Annie and Jimmy. If I didn't take them down now, Jimmy and Annie would be their next targets if they disposed of me.

Spooks pushed his grocery cart across Carson Street to my office side of the block. I watched from the bar to see if the blinds would move again. The noise of the cart scraping along the concrete sidewalk from its locked front wheel must have stirred the lookout. The blind quickly spread open and closed, and when they were satisfied, it was only a homeless man pushing a cart looking for the makings of his next meal. I saw Jimmy crossing over from the corner across from Max's, just four doors away from the entrance that would lead me up the stairway to my office. It was time for me to begin my walk. Annie begged me to just call the cops! I opened the door of the bar and began the short walk across Carson Street to my fate.

The City issue bullet proof vest would offer me some protection in case their plan was to kill me as soon as they identified me. I was counting on them wanting me alive.

As I was walking the thought of an old western movie passed briefly through my mind. 'Gunfight at the O.K. Corral.' I was Wyatt Earp and Spooks, and Jimmy were my two brothers who joined the fight against the Clanton gang. The thought passed quickly and now I had to choose another option in dealing with the hired guns in my office.

Spooks had delivered the newspaper wrapped shotgun and I now freed it so I could use my two best chances to keep breathing: two oo buckshot shells. It was time!

The sun was rising as I approached the building. It gave me a good feeling seeing the sunrise. Maybe my last. I entered my building and started counting the thirteen steps to the second-floor landing that led to my outer office door. I knew that the number thirteen was going to be unlucky for someone this morning.

I remembered that the third window in my front office lined up with the two entrance doors. The lookout used that window to see out on the street. These two had no way of knowing I was coming with a shotgun.

I aimed at the bottom half of the hallway door lined up with the inner office door and the third front window and then I pulled the trigger. If the lookout was still standing in about the same place when I last saw him looking out the window, I'd probably catch a piece of him with the first shot. Even if I missed, I would catch them both by surprise and I could get the second barrel into one of them. If that worked, then it would be a race between me and the second man to see who would get off the next shot. I'd have to drop the shotgun and reach into my pocket holster to get to my .38. The time for thinking was over. Fuck it. I squeezed off the first round.

The blast from the shotgun shattered the glass insert of my hallway door, blew it open and continued through the interior glass panel on its way to the outside through the third window unless it hit an object like a body. I could see clearly through my inner office and the sunlight seeping through the cracks and holes in the blinds the first shotgun blast made. The glass had been shattered and the blind was now swaying on the outside of the window frame. I also saw a silhouette of a man in front of the third window, trying to raise his weapon. The first round got a piece of him that slowed him down. As I stepped into my reception room, I was still aimed at the window he was standing in front of.

I squeezed the trigger that set off the second barrel of the 12 gauge. This time I hit him in the upper abdomen and opened a five-inch hole in his chest. The force of the blast sent the asshole to hell through my front window and down to the sidewalk below.

The surprise was over, and I realized the second man wasn't in front of me. That could only mean he was behind one of the doorways. I hoped it was the front office as I reached in my pocket for my .38. Before I could pull it out, I realized he was behind me. I tried to prepare myself for the initial impact of his shot to my back. If he was using a Teflon bullet, the vest couldn't protect me. I'd almost surely be dead at this range. Jimmy would get him as he left the building, and I would be taking a dirt nap.

The force of the two shots he got off to my back sent me face down on the floor across the room. I guess the shooter must have figured I had on a bullet proof vest because he jumped on me and covered my body. He had I different plan in mind as I soon found out. From behind, he threw his left arm around my neck and locked it in with his right arm. He rolled me over on top of him and began crushing my windpipe. He had a death hold on me. I struggled to get my left hand between his left forearm and my neck. I could hold his grip around my neck only for a few seconds before I'd begin to pass out from lack of oxygen. My body was on top of his and our legs were matched one on top of another.

My right hand was still in my pocket where it had been when I took the two shots in the back. I aimed the .38 as far down to the floor as I could while it was in my holster pressed against my outer thigh, and I prepared for the sting and burning from a bullet through my own leg. It was that or die. I knew the assassin who had me in the choke-out would let go of enough pressure for me to break the hold when the bullet that went through my leg and entered his leg. I fired and never felt the sting of the bullet. I now had that split second to draw out my pistol and move my right arm back far enough to get a couple shots into his lower body. I felt a sting and wondered if I fucked up and shot myself in the fucking gut instead of Hans. Those two shots were all that was needed for him to go limp and release the death grip he had on me.

As I rolled off onto the floor over the now motionless body, I heard Jimmy calling as he rushed into the office and viewed the tableau I had just arranged.

"Red! Red... Are you still alive?"

"Yeah, Jimmy. It worked out just as I planned it."

I managed to get out through my contorted vocal cords.

"I'm just fine," I told him as I tried to stop the bleeding from my upper leg wound.

## CHAPTER 12

I HEARD the blaring of police sirens getting closer. Annie must have called them when the first body went flying through my second-floor front window. Now, I had to get Jimmy away from this mess.

"Jimmy, get out of here. Now! I don't want you around when the police arrive. Now help get me to my desk so I can see the sidewalk and the street."

I had to get a quick look at the dead punk on my office floor. The suit he was wearing looked like it was European made from the cut and feel of the material. The labels were removed. I took his billfold out from inside his coat pocket and found nine hundred in American money along with German currency. He had a New York driver's license and a couple of credit cards with the same name, Curt Vonner. There is no doubt in my mind that when the cops run them along with the driver's license, they will come up counterfeit.

This guy had a tattoo on the inside of his left wrist. It was nothing I recognized or associated with what the cons wear in prison, at least not a prison in the United States. After they check these two bodies into the morgue, I'll get a chance to find out if they carry any other markings that could give me a lead as to where they came from and who they are tied to.

Looking around my office I could see these two were searching for something. They ransacked the file cabinets, desks and smashed my new computer. There was a new roll of duct tape on my desk that wasn't mine. I wanted to look through the clothes of the dead man on the sidewalk and go through their car, but the first squad car pulled up out front and two officers with their guns drawn rushed toward the body lying close to the curb. The second and third police cars arrived in less than a minute. Four more cops got out of the squad cars and headed to the downstairs doorway. It was time to let them know that Red was upstairs and not to start shooting. I only hoped that one of them knew who Red was.

"This is Red Canyon," I called out to the cops coming up the stairs. "If any of you don't know me, call Lieutenant Ruff. I'm unarmed! I took down the perp on the street and there's another one down on my office floor. You need to call a medic. Not for the perp, but for me. I got hit with a slug in the leg."

Then I heard a response to the message I just called out. "Red, this is Danny O. You alright? I'm coming in!"

"All clear, Danny boy! I'm inside my office, sitting at the desk. Tell one of your boys to go across the street to the Gardens and tell Annie I'm okay."

I heard Danny tell someone to go to the bar and get Annie and bring her back upstairs to me. He had his weapon extended in front of him as he approached what was left of the doorway to the outer office. He took a quick peak in, and then the rest of him appeared.

"What happened here, Red? You three boys drinking too much and get into an argument? This shit doesn't usually go on until the weekend. Anyway, I heard you sobered up and were on a big case now. What went down?"

"I don't know. I came over to my office to go on my computer and these guys were waiting for me and jumped me. You see the result."

"The guy lying down on the sidewalk has a hole in him that I could put my fist through. It looks like he got hit with a shotgun blast. Do you always come to the office carrying a shotgun at six in the morning, or do you want to tell me he committed suicide?" Danny asked sarcastically. "And what's wrong with your voice?"

"The guy on the floor was choking me out and almost had me. He was strong and did some damage to my vocal cords. I'll get better, but he won't."

"Jesus, Red, do you know how much paperwork you just laid on me? He shot you in the leg during the fight, right?"

"Something like that, Danny. I'm not going to say anything else till I get to the Southside hospital. I know you're an honest cop, but there are still some people on the job who wouldn't mind railroading me into the pen. Then there is that p.o.s. DA Jeffrey Whitty. He's the one I called witless and locked up for DWI when I was on the job. I'm sure that prick will ask for this case to be taken to the grand jury. Get me to a hospital, Danny." My last words to the cops for now.

I was still sitting on the floor when Annie burst through the cops standing around me. She could see I was bleeding, and when I spoke, my voice was raspy. My right pants leg was blood soaked from the bullet I put through it less than fifteen minutes earlier. I wondered if Sam, the tailor, could get me another pair of suit pants to match the jacket. I only got one day on my new suit. Oh well!

Annie was bending over by me to either give me a hug or a smack. It was a hug. I whispered to her to say that she doesn't know anything and was sleeping when I left her place this morning.

"Help me stand up, Annie, so I can lean against the desk. And take off your blouse and wrap it around my leg where you see the most blood."

"I have a better idea, Red. How about if it's a bullet hole that's bleeding out, I just stick my finger in it? That will plug up the hole and stop the bleeding."

"Just hand me the roll of duct tape on the desk and I'll tape around my leg."

It wouldn't matter anyway. I heard the EMT getting closer and in a few minutes, they would patch me up and take me to the emergency room at Southside General.

I whispered to Annie, "Have Jimmy call Hilda's niece Jackie and tell her what went down. Ask her to come to the hospital. I need her to act as my lawyer. I wouldn't talk to the cops without her present. Remember, you and Jimmy know nothing. Get Spooks and tell him not to shoot his mouth off because these punks have friends and they'll be looking for him if they think he fingered them. That should keep him quiet."

The paramedics showed up and stabilized me, loaded me on a stretcher and began the trip to the hospital. The scene on the street in front of my building looked like there was some kind of giveaway going on and the cops were there to keep order. They were cleaning up the debris I dumped on the sidewalk earlier this morning. The reporters had arrived. I heard a cop answering a question from one of them.

"I'll tell you what happened. Canyon is back in action. This, today is probably only the beginning. He's putting the bad guys on notice. This is his way of saying he's back on the street," the cop was saying.

What did I get myself into? Hilda hands me a fifteen-year-old murder case. She lies to me when I ask her about other investigators she hired. The people that worked for her dead husband are afraid to talk fifteen years later. Two of them find files that no one knew existed including the Feds. And now two shooters have come into the City looking for the files I took less than twenty-four hours ago and wanting to whack me. This isn't just about finding the answer to a fifteen-year-old murder.

I don't know what else I might turn up while I'm looking for the killer of Horst, but someone wants me to stop and they're willing to kill me.

The stakes were raised this morning. There's no turning back now.

# CHAPTER 13

When I arrived at the hospital, the ambulance driver told me there was a crowd beginning to gather at the entrance to the emergency room. As they opened the back door to unload the stretcher, the media jumped at me and began firing questions and shoving microphones and television cameras in my face. I saw a couple of plainclothes cops that I knew pushing the crowd back so that the stretcher could get through the hospital emergency room entrance.

Then I heard a familiar voice in the crowd calling out the words, "Red Canyon is back in town. The Southside is safe again."

I was looking around for Annie, but the voice I recognized in the crowd belonged to Spooks. I needed to get her over to him and tell him to shut the fuck up. There was going to be enough bad publicity about how I iced two innocent men. I didn't need to have the press stoked up by Spooks. Whoever those two dead punks were, they have associates that are going to want payback. That means killing me.

For now, I'm going to clam up until Jackie gets here. Danny O. showed up and told me they were going to leave two beat cops with me. It was orders from the top brass in the department.

"You wanna tell me anything about what happened at your office? You can tell me off the record," Danny said to me, knowing in advance that I wasn't going to give him anything.

I pointed to my throat and told him in a hoarse voice that when I was ready, I would request him to take my statement. A couple of nurses and one doctor rushed into the room. They put me in and began cutting off my pants leg.

"Nurse, get me a unit of plasma going right now, and get the operating room ready. Our patient had an artery nicked from what I can tell."

"Forget the blood. I'll drink lots of water. It's not an artery there in my leg that was nicked. It's a vein. The blood's not dark red enough to be an artery, Doc. I've had pressure on it since it happened. The vein probably knitted together by now. But you already know that. Right, Doc? That's a bullet hole you're looking at. Just pull the skin together where it entered and exited and sew it up. I need cleaned up really good. The scumbag that was bleeding on me might have rabies."

"Look, Doctor Frankenstein, since you've made your own diagnosis, why don't you finish and sew up your own wounds?" The now angry intern shot out.

"Okay, doctor quack. I'll do just that so you can go along and empty your bedpans. I'm Red Canyon. Why don't you come visit me at my office when I get out of here? I can fix the crooked teeth problem you have in your mouth. There's no charge for the visit," I managed to get out through my damaged vocal cords.

"Clean this patient up and call Doctor Frazier to sew him up," an angry boy intern ordered on his way out of the room.

"What about the blood transfusion?"

"Note on the patients' chart that he refused the transfusion and the recommendation to have a surgeon examine his wounds in the O.R." were his last comments as he left my bedside.

"You angered Doctor Bowmann," the nurse said to me.

"That guy is going to wind up working in a nursing home pushing pills on the old people and burying his mistakes."

"I'm going to give you an injection now. It will ease the pain when the doctor stitches you up and by the way you're on the news, Mr. Canyon."

I needed to beef up my reputation on the street anyway. What better way than killing a couple of out-of-town punks. The press and the television will spread the news. The street will know Red Canyon is back. Whoever these punks belonged to would be sending others to find what they were looking for and settle the score with me. Horst must have been into some heavy shit to get two big hitters out after me for some old records from his factory basement. I'm going to have to warn the two women who gave me the boxes of papers. There's fifteen years of unfinished business these two came to settle. I began getting drowsy. The injection wasn't just for pain. She slipped me a mickey.

When I awoke, I was in a private room with an IV hooked up to me and two cops standing near the door to my room. I knew one of them. His first name was Willie, but I couldn't remember his last name. My mind began clearing from the drugs they pumped into me. Why were the cops stationed inside the door instead of outside in the hall? The door opened and in walked a new face in a suit.

He walked over to the side of my bed to see if I was conscious. When he was satisfied, I was awake he spoke.

"I'm Detective Jacinski. You feel like talking, Red? I'm from homicide, as you probably guessed. I'm going to have to ask you some questions, Red. I got one dead punk that we scraped up off the street with two blasts from a twelve gauge and another one on the floor in your office with a slug in the leg and two or three bullets in his lower abdomen. Friends of yours?" he sarcastically questioned.

"What's your first name detective?"

"Walter."

"How about you go to the coffee shop and get me a large black coffee and get one for yourself. Take the twins with you and fix them up too. Just put it on my room tab. We'll talk when you get back." And then I closed my eyes and shut him off.

"I heard about you, Red. They told me at headquarters that you have a sense of humor. You're gonna need it when the DA finishes with you. You remember him, don't you, Red? Jeff Whitty. You almost cost him his career. He's juiced and ready to throw the book at you. I'm told when he got the call before seven this morning and knew you were involved in a shootout; they say his first question was, 'Is the son of a bitch dead, followed with… I hope?'" Walt snickered with a sarcastic chuckle.

"That's straight black, Walt, thanks," I shot back at him. I figured he was one of Whitty's boys. How else would he know what that prick said unless it was him that made the initial call to Whitty? I wasn't going to talk until Jackie showed. I've questioned hundreds of homicide suspects before and I know the drill. I pushed the call button for the nurse. I wanted to know why I didn't have a phone and why Annie wasn't here with me.

When the nurse showed, I asked her those questions.

"Why don't I have a phone, and where is Annie?"

"The police are not letting you have visitors or a phone. You're in lockdown."

"Hey, Walter, am I under arrest?"

"No, Red, but you are under protective custody. You know we can hold you for forty-eight hours without charging you."

I didn't want to continue the back-and-forth bullshit with Walter. There was a TV playing and I could see the moving flash bar at the bottom of the screen recounting the murders on the Southside. I switched to the local channel to see what take they had on the shooting.

# CHAPTER 14

The door to my room opened again and in walked Jackie. She didn't waste any words on an introduction to Walter.

"I'm his lawyer and I want privacy. Whoever you are take your entourage and leave me alone with my client," she ordered Walter.

He started to protest with that bullshit about me being held in protective custody when she cut him off with a move I didn't expect. She handed him a court order.

"This is a court order from Judge Falcon. If you read it, you will see that Mr. Canyon has been released into my custody as of 8:45 a.m. this morning. Now take your men and leave before I charge you with obstruction of a court order," Jackie warned the detective.

I watched as Walter made a call on his cell phone and then motioned for the uniformed cops to follow him out of the room. As he left, he gave me a parting warning. "You're going down on this one, Red. I promise." And as they began to leave I gave him one more parting shot.

"Don't forget my coffee, Walter." Then I turned my attention to Jackie.

"Good fucking move, Jackie. How the hell did you get a judge to get his ass out of bed that early and issue the court order without knowing what went down this morning on the Southside?"

"Judge Falcon is a friend of mine. He owes me. Let's leave it at that," she answered and then asked me what had happened early that morning.

"My street eyes spotted these two tough looking men in suits getting out of a black SUV and breaking into my office building. Then he saw them close the blinds in the front window of my office. It was still dark around five a.m. when this was taking place. From his description I figured they may be professional mechanics. It turned out I was right, and I had to take them down. One of them roughed me up a little. It's that simple."

"Aunt Hilda wants to know if this incident was because of your investigation into Horst's murder. She doesn't want you getting killed over his fifteen-year-old unsolved homicide," Jackie was saying.

"I can't say for sure that this was the reason these two showed up at my office. What I do know is that this is the only case I'm working on. These two shooters that showed up were carrying Soviet made weapons and phony ID's. I found some German marks in one of the shooters' wallet. When the cops run a check on their fingerprints, my bet is they aren't on file in any U.S. data bank. I believe these two hitters were imports already in the States and looking for something before I hooked up with Hilda. For some reason, they took an interest in me.

You can tell Hilda that someone wants to stop the investigation. I don't know what Horst was into, but it must have been big to carry a fifteen-year tail. You can also tell her I'm not pulling out now. The other players in this game have raised the stakes, and I'm all in. I think I have enough to show that Horsts' killer or killers are still out there somewhere."

"Tell me, Red, why did the detective say that you're going to take a hit on the shooting? It was a clean shoot, wasn't it?"

"I have history with the DA, Jeff Whitty. About seventeen years ago, I arrested him for DWI. He hit another vehicle carrying a family with two kids that were injured. He lit up the Breathalyzer with .24. They pressured the family to take part in the blame for the accident. I took a lot of heat to drop the charge to driving while impaired, but I wouldn't cut him a deal. It set his career back. From that point on he became my avowed enemy. He tried to set me up a couple of times, but I was always clean. I didn't run my own book like some of the other badges in the department. He'd like to hang a murder rap on me now and I wouldn't put it past him to rig the evidence. He'll probably try to make those punks the victims," I told Jackie.

"I'll have him removed from the case."

"You have that much muscle?"

"I don't, but Judge Falcon does. Just don't hold out on me. I don't want any surprises at the hearing. You should go see Hilda when you leave the hospital and feel up to it. I'll let you know when we have to go to headquarters to make your statement. I'll deal with the reporters outside. You talk to no one and give the standard answer if you feel the need to respond to some questions, 'on the advice of my council, I cannot answer any questions dealing with my attempted murder.'

Now, I'm going to tell the nurse to let Anne and Jimmy in to see you. If you have any ideas about leaving this hospital today, forget it. Stay in the hospital until at least tomorrow. That will give me enough time to stop any attempt to arrest you. I'll call Whitty when I get to my office and give him the opportunity to recuse himself from the case before the court orders it. I'll have no problem establishing his prejudice. I'll remind him that with an election coming up, it wouldn't do him any good to drag out old skeletons from his closet. Any questions before I go, Red?" Jackie asked.

It looks as if I've underestimated Jackie. She may not be an empty dress. She'll cut Whitty's nuts off, and I won't have to go through a lot of his bullshit. I'll send Jimmy over with some flowers to thank her tonight.

I'm sure he'll know how to show her my appreciation. Now, I'm going to have to get the boxes of files stashed somewhere the cops or whoever can't find them.

There's a very good possibility the two women that gave me the files may be in danger. I'm sure they have no knowledge of any information in the files that could tie someone to Horst's murder.

"You should warn Dixon and Tremaine to lock their doors or go out of town for a few weeks. They may be in some danger."

Jackie said she would talk to both when she arrived at the plant. The files I gathered from the two women have created a new interest for some old enemy of Horst. If the cops find out about them and can tie them to the hit on me, they're going to want them as evidence. Once they get them in their possession, I'll never see them again.

Jackie left and Annie and Jimmy came into the room to see me. I have one important task that I need done soon; pick up the seven boxes I took from the plant and get them stashed in a secure place. I'll send Jimmy over to Bobby's store and have him ask if he can store some things from his mother's house in his warehouse. Maybe I can rent a storage unit outside the city until I can go through them.

"You feel better?" Annie asked as she looked at me propped up in the hospital bed.

"Yeah, but I have to stay here another day while Jackie makes a move on the prosecutor. The DA on the case has a grudge against me going back seventeen years. Jackie is going to get him tossed off the case. Annie, I need you to forget ever seeing those boxes we stored in your office. I'm going to have Jimmy take them to a secure place until I can go through them. As of now, they don't exist. If the cops ask me about them, I going to tell them they were in my office and that the punks must have snatched them before I got there."

"Where do you want me to take them, Red?" Jimmy asked.

"Some place safe. Write down the location on a piece of paper and mail it to me. Then go get some flowers and take them to Jackie with thanks from me. Do it in that order. Take a thousand dollars out of my wallet and keep the receipt for the flowers. Put the other receipt from the storage unit in the envelope you mail to me. Now go! Get it done."

I was hoping he understood how important the assignment is that I just handed him. Annie came over to the bed and started giving me hugs and kisses and asking me if I was okay.

"Yeah, Annie, I'm really okay. Just to make sure you can check under the covers."

"I don't have to Red. Soon as you opened your mouth you answered my question."

"I have to stay another day and I haven't talked to a doctor, but I'm leaving tomorrow no matter what. When you come back over tonight, bring me some clean pants along with a shirt and underwear."

"Who were those two guys you wasted? They weren't mafia, were they?"

"No, they were not mafia. I don't know who they were connected to. These were bad guys of the first order. I think they may be foreigners. They each carried the same tattoo on the inside of their left wrist. I've never seen that brand before. When the cops run everything they have through the FBI system, they'll probably come up with an ID on them. We're just gonna have to wait. I need you to bring me back the Saturday night special I sleep with under my pillow," I told Annie, knowing that I had just upped the danger level in her mind.

"Do you still think your life is in danger in here, and do you think they are going to let you have a gun in the hospital?"

"I'm not going to ask for permission. Stuff it into my shaving kit. It's just for insurance. I'm into something bigger than just a fifteen-year-old unsolved murder. When I get out of here and get squared up with the cops, me and you are going to go on a little vacation. Can you take a couple of days off?"

"Are we talking about a vacation or are we talking about a working vacation?"

"A little of both. I need your help to dig through the papers I took from the plant. There must be something in that mess that somebody doesn't want me to find. Besides, I want to get out of the city until things cool down and we see if anyone else shows up looking for me."

Annie had that worried look on her face. I'd seen it before. I had to reassure her that this was a mistake on the part of the two dead guys. The story would be they fucked up and were sent for the files and not me. She might believe it, at least for a little while.

"Things will cool down now and I'll have the time to put a new plan together once we read through the files. Now, go get me my piece."

I watched Annie as she left the room, and I knew I had to keep her close to me from now on. The way I see it, everyone that's close to me is a target. Someone could grab Annie or Jimmy and use them to get to me. The two dead guys in the City morgue will cause their employers to send three or four men next time to get what they want. They're going to keep coming and the bodies are going to keep piling up. It's the files…the fucking files. Are these the suits that Vinnie warned me about?

## CHAPTER 15

I HAVE to clear out of this hospital tomorrow. I don't want to catch any disease they're spreading around in here. With a fresh wound just healing, I'm a prime candidate for some staph infection. Nobody touches me without clean gloves on their hands.

The door to my room opened, and what looked like a doctor walked in and headed to my bed.

"I'm Jerry Berman. I'm the doctor that patched you up. How's the pain?" He asked.

"It feels like I was shot in the leg."

"They said at the desk that you have a sense of humor, Mr. Canyon. I'm not here to verify that, just to check on your wounds. A nurse is on her way in to change the dressing after I examine your leg. Did you get shot by someone during a struggle? I have to give the police a report on gunshot wounds along with any information I receive from you," he said while waiting for me to tell him how it happened.

He had the bandages off my leg and was looking at his work when I told him, "You have all the information you're gonna get from me for your report." Then he jabbed at my leg, inflicting some major pain on me. I couldn't let him see that he hurt me.

"Get the fucking nurse in here to bandage me back up. You're done here, Berman." I pushed him away from the bed.

"How does it feel to kill another human being, Canyon?" he questioned.

Here's another fucking bleeding heart. Can't we all get along together, asshole?

I had an answer for him. "You ought to know Berman. The difference between us is that I don't kill the people that come to me for help. Not even by mistake. I only kill the bad guys."

The nurse had entered the room and was coming toward me with a tray holding the repair kit for my wounds. I guess I just burned off another doctor. There's plenty more in this chop shop. I'm getting out of here tomorrow anyway. Anne will take care of me.

As the nurse began cleaning the wounds in my leg, she noted, "You're lucky the bullet didn't hit the bone and shatter it."

"Yeah, I'm a good shot. Do you think it will keep me out of the Army?" I asked, knowing that she had no clue about what I just said.

"Are you in the Army?" she asked me.

I had to pass up the line she just fed me and instead asked her to check my back. I wanted to make sure I didn't have any more leaks from the bullets my vest stopped. It was time for me to sleep. My eyes were closing as the nurse was leaving the room. Would I wake up or would someone sneak into my room and off me while I was visiting Jimmy's world?

The next time I opened my eyes, the clock had moved ahead four hours, and I had two new suits sitting in the visitor chairs across from my bed. They weren't on hangers from Sam the Tailor. They were being worn by two guys I could spot in a crowd. They were the Feds, probably FBI.

"I didn't order two bodyguards. I only ordered one. You two can flip to see who goes home," I said in my hoarse voice.

"They said at the precinct that you were a smart ass." The one in the first dark suit blurted out. "In case you haven't guessed, we're FBI! We need to talk. I'm special agent Russell and this is special agent Parker. We're not interested in how or why you killed those two men today. We are looking into why they were here. Those were two really bad guys. They have many dangerous friends. Chances are they'll be sending others after you until they get what they're after. If it's you then you're dead. If it's something you have that is theirs, you're dead. So, either way you're dead." The dark suit told me.

"Why were they waiting for you in your office at six o'clock in the morning? Did you have a meeting set up that turned sour?"

"You tell me what you know about those two and I'll tell you what I know."

"They were both Germans and, on the Interpol most wanted list. We had warrants out on them in case they ever showed up in America. There was reason to believe they were involved in a bombing at our base in Bremerhaven in 2002. These are big fish, too big to be in the city chasing a half-assed former cop turned private eye. You have to have stepped into the international arena."

"You two have first names?"

Russell looked over at me and said his name is Andy and his partners' name is Bryan.

"I'm working on a case that's fifteen years old, but you already know that. I want to know more about these Germans and the people that sent them. You only gave me the press release crap. I'm not asking for all your classified data, but I need a better picture of the two guys I just wacked and the organization they work for."

I knew what the Feds were after. They wanted the files I took from the factory. What could be in the boxes of papers that these two old broads had stuffed away for the last fifteen years? When Horst got himself killed fifteen years ago, the people that hit him were probably looking for something he had in his possession. They didn't get it, whatever it was, but they believe I have it in one of the boxes in my possession. The clue has to be in one of the documents in that pile of papers. The needle in the haystack. Did I, have it?

"Where are the boxes of files you took from the factory?" Russell asked.

"I don't know. When I got to my office this morning it was tossed, and the boxes were not there. They must have had a third man. Find him. He's got them." I'd stick to that story.

"I don't believe you, Red. If there was a third man, you wouldn't be alive. Even if he was outside when he saw one of his team blown out of the front window, he would have been up the stairs and caught you by surprise. These are professional killers you're dealing with, not street punks."

"I told you they were in my office when I showed up there this morning." I insisted and then posed another question to them. "Why are you in on this anyway? This is local and out of your jurisdiction."

"The company does business with the Federal Government. It's a classified operation. The documents you took may have some sensitive information included in them. We need to review them to redact any classified information that is discovered."

"Bull shit! The employees that turned them over to me said they have been in storage for the last fifteen years. The government didn't care about them in all that time. Your snitch inside the factory missed what now looks to be the jack in the box and I popped it open. When I get out of this butcher shop, I'm going after the third man before he gets to me. If I recover anything, I'll let you know." Could I convince them there was a third man?

"I read the Mickey Spillane novels. I'm familiar with all the tough guy bullshit. You didn't convince me. If you don't get me the files, I'll put you under 24/7 surveillance, maybe even lock you up. You won't be able to blink without one of my agents seeing it. I have deep pockets, and right now, you're in one," Russell said in the most threatening tone he had stored in his voice file.

“I’m going to make you an offer. You get me all the current information on the group the two stiffs belonged to. I want dossiers of everyone you have on file that belongs to it including their photos. If I have to prepare for more of their assassins, I want to know what they look like. That could just give me the edge I need to stay alive. When I locate the files, I picked up at the factory I’ll call you and we can make the exchange.”

“How about if I just lock you up for obstruction and let you sit in a cell for the next couple of months?” Russell shot back at me.

“How about if the files mysteriously show up at the New York Post? You could read them on the front page of that rag,” I quickly countered.

“You’ve got seventy-two hours and then I set the dogs loose on you. Understood?” Russell countered.

“I need a month or no deal.”

“One month, no more; and I’m leaving agent Parker in the City to make sure you stay alive until the exchange. That’s not negotiable,” he told me as they both left the room.

What kind of double life did Horst lead? I know he hung around with the local Wops, but now it appears they were small time compared to the international scum interested in some fifteen-year-old documents. The little old lady Strump has been holding out on me. When I clear this place tomorrow, I'll pay a visit to Hilda.

# CHAPTER 16

I WAS GETTING ready to doze off when Anne walked into the room carrying a small suitcase.

"I was stopped at the nurses' station right down the hall from you. They have a hospital security guard assigned to watch your room. I had to turn the suitcase over to him so he could search it."

"Did they find the gun?" I asked her as I prepared to locate the guard, slap him around, and get it back.

"I was expecting the hassle," she said as she raised her skirt exposing the leg holster I had given her on one of her birthdays. I was surprised she saved it. As I recall, she didn't think it was much of a gift for a guy to give his girlfriend. She lightened up when she opened the second package that went along with the holster. It was a snub nose .38. She offered to use it on me as I remember, but I knew she wasn't serious, I think.

"Next time I'm going to get you a panty holster."

Anne just stared over at me with that look I knew too well. I just stuffed my foot in my mouth again.

"You're so thoughtful, Red. While you're shopping for that see if you can get yourself a muzzle," she said as she handed me the .38.

"I saw two men with dark suits and sunglasses leaving the hospital as I was entering. Were they visiting you? And why the FBI?"

"Good pick-up Anne. It seems you've developed great awareness of your environment. You spotted the new players in the hunt. They want the boxes of papers that were taken from my office. I told them when and if I locate them, I'd let them know."

I took the .38 and put it in the top drawer of the night table next to my bed. It fit snugly in the small shaving case Anne brought me. If any more Germans show up before I leave here I'd give them a free admission pass to the morgue downstairs. They could visit with their comrades.

"Anne, I need Jimmy to come back here tonight. Tell him I want him to stay the night in the room with me. There may be unwanted visitors later."

"You told me there was no need to worry. You said it was the files that the two corpses were after, not you." Annie snapped back at me.

"Yeah, that's right. I just don't want to be alone. The nurses look horny. That's why I need Jimmy," I told her, hoping to defuse her concern with my humor.

"I'll send Jimmy back to you. As long as I've known you, Red, you never needed a bodyguard. That tells me you may have become involved in something too big for Red Canyon."

"Good night, Annie, and thanks," I whispered in her ear as she gave me a kiss goodbye.

I flipped the TV on to the local news channel to see if they were still exploiting the shooting on the Southside. It was seven o'clock and past the regular news hour. One channel was running a special report on 'Red Canyon' outlining how many previous shootings I'd been involved in and how many dead men I left on the city streets during my career as a City cop. I already had the answer to their story. They could only report on the stiffs the Department could prove were at the hands of Detective Canyon. The other two dozen I racked up over the years on the job were written up as unsolved and not part of their report. When I retired, the body count dropped in the City, except on the Southside. Strange… hmmm.

The story would hold the headlines until some other event in the city overshadowed it or a national disaster happened. I couldn't cause a flood, but I may be able to put some dirt out on a certain DA. Maybe I could expose the connection between the ex-Mayor and his interest in thanatophilia. I learned that word and its definition one night in a funeral parlor.

I bagged Whitty in his brothers' mortuary while I was checking out an alarm that had been set off. I didn't turn him in at the time. The big brass dumped my report and told me to wait for Whitty to show his gratitude. Three months after that incident, I was given a gold shield and assigned to homicide. It was a payback from Whitty. He would have rather paid me back with lead. I was constantly reminded by my superiors that I was to investigate homicides do not commit them.

I was starting to fade when Jimmy arrived with Spooks. He said Spooks was gonna take the outside grounds while he stayed in my room. I could rest now, but as I began slipping away, I thought for a split second that I saw a huge electric sign in my mind's eye. It said… HILDA! and then it went out, and so did I. Tomorrow, I'll try to clear out of the City till things cool down. Bad idea! The drugs must have kicked in cause I'm not thinking clearly. Oh well!

# CHAPTER 17

THE MORNING LIGHT crossed my eyes and brought me out of the cautious sleep of the last six hours. I wasn't sure if the light woke me or Jimmy's snoring broke the morning in for me. It was time to get the hell out of this hospital. I pulled the IV out of my arm, knowing that I would bring a nurse in to see if the monitor at her station was functioning. I wanted to get my arm patched up where the IV was inserted. When that was done me and Jimmy were leaving.

The door opened, and in came a nurse with no makeup.

"Bandage my arm and clean up the holes in my leg," I told her while pulling back the sheet so she could see that I had ripped off the bandages covering my self-inflicted wounds. She had to clean me up and bandage my right leg. I didn't plan to wait for any doctor.

"Why did you take your IV out of your arm and remove the dressing on your leg wounds?" Nurse hag asked.

"It itched." Would be all that I was going to say. I didn't want to announce that I was leaving when she was done. That would have caused her to panic and alert her supervisor and then probably the die-hard press reporters hanging outside the hospital.

Me and Jimmy slipped out through the delivery entrance. Annie was waiting for us. Jimmy had called her while I was getting dressed. I was going to have to go somewhere these reporters would never think to look for me. I had Annie drop me off at my house. I was betting that Fed Bryan had already been there and searched the place between his naps. He was now back at the hospital waiting for me to make my break.

"What now, Red?" Annie questioned.

"Get a rental car delivered behind the bar as soon as the rental company opens. Make sure you leave the keys in it," I said, knowing there were questions the two of them would want to ask.

Annie asked first, "What do you want me and Jimmy to do? What's the plan?"

"I'll call you as soon as I have one. Just make sure you and Jimmy stay together."

Then I told Jimmy, "Carry the gun I gave you. You're on a mission now. Protect Annie! You'll hear from me in a few hours with the plan."

Annie dropped me off at my house and went on to the bar. It was time for me to go over everything that happened to me since Hilda walked into my office last Monday. There's a foul odor in the air. I either just walked into a firestorm, or I just walked into a shit storm. The heat is on, and I don't smell any wood burning.

I haven't been home for over a week. Nothing seems to have changed. The living room is still dark from the lack of sunlight and the dull floral wallpaper covering the walls. It was the last reminder of my mother's decorating taste. The three front windows had the blinds drawn. My side of the alley never got direct sunlight in the living room. The sun rose behind my house and the three and a half story houses that stood twenty-seven feet across the alley threw shadows that obscured direct sunlight on the first floor.

The neighbors in the alley were the same families I remember since I was a kid. Mrs. Rimsky, across the street from me, was alone now since her husband, Yash, died three years ago. Her children lived out of state, so the neighbors would keep an eye on her. That's how it was in the alley. They even watched out for me. When I was on a bender, they would take turns seeing to it that I got a hot meal once in a while. Katy O'Rourke, the good looking red headed daughter of Mike and Mary, would stop over regularly to see if I needed anything.

She was ten years younger than me and had a crush on me since she was five years old. If Anne wasn't in my life, I would have banged her years ago. Chester Borishenko, two doors over, would get wasted every Friday night and pass out on the sidewalk somewhere close to his house. In the winter his wife, Sophie, would knock on some doors at any hour of the night looking for help getting Chester into the house. During those months, everyone would help pick his big ass up and get him inside. The rest of the year, he'd sleep under the stars on Friday nights. He was a tough old Russian bastard with a ruddy completion and a huge handlebar mustache that matched his six foot, three-hundred-pound frame. Yeah, the Eighteenth Street Alley was still living back in 1965. Neighbors still help each other out. I guess that's why I stay here, or maybe it's because I don't know of any better place to go that's free.

I made my way up to the second-floor bedroom I use when I stay here to look for signs that the room had been searched. There was no need to look for clues. The closets and drawers were all emptied and everything in them had been thrown all over the room. Who tossed the room? The Feds are always neat. The local cops are only sloppy. This mess was made on purpose. Somebody is sending me a message. They're not done with me. When I told the Feds that there was a third man with the punks I killed, it looked as if I wasn't lying.

There's another European suit out there tracking me. Now what... I had the answer to one question. I've walked into a Shit Storm. Now, to find my way out… alive.

The message from the third man has changed everything for now. I have to keep Annie and Jimmy close to me. The last German bad guy may just want to kill them or take them hostage. My priority is no longer to look through the files for clues to Horst's killers. I may already know the people responsible. No, my priority now must be to become the hunter. I have to find and kill the third assassin hiding somewhere in the City.

The advantage is mine. I'll force the last kraut to hunt me in the City, my City, and on the Southside. I grew up here on the streets of the Southside. I know every block, every brick, every alley, and every dead end from the river to the open ground that acts as the border to Center City. Hans, as I'll call him, will have to come to me. I'll build a profile on him as I discover bits and pieces of information. I know he is arrogant and feels superior. The evidence of that is the calling card he left in my bedroom. Hans doesn't consider me to be as dangerous as he is. The fact that I dispatched his two partners didn't make much of an impression on him. He must consider himself several levels above his dead partners. There's going to be more blood on the Southside, and soon.

Jimmy came bursting through the back door and started talking faster than his brain could work.

"Jackie's been trying to reach you for the last hour. She said your phone isn't answering," Jimmy managed to blurt out.

"Slow it down, Jimmy. Just tell me her message. It can't be that urgent," I told Jimmy to try to get him stop and hit the reset button. I had to do that on occasion to get him back to normal which for, Jimmy, was always between gears.

"They're dead! Both, Red," he managed to get out.

"Who's dead, Jimmy, Who?" I asked with no idea of who they could be.

"The old ladies from the factory that gave you the boxes of files, that's who. They were murdered sometime yesterday. Jackie said the cops told her it was sometime late evening. She needs you to call her right away. She said the report of the murders will hit the news any time now. The authorities were calling a news conference for eight thirty this morning here at the Southside Law building. The garbage men found them both in the dumpster behind your office. What the fuck is going on, Red?" Jimmy asked with a worried expression on his unshaven face.

Right now I don't have an answer for Jimmy. An old lady showed up at my office last Monday wanting to find out who murdered her husband fifteen years ago.

Five days later, I got two dead fucking Nazis and two dead women that worked for Hilda's murdered husband. These poor old broads had no idea that they signed their death warrants when they turned over to me some seven boxes of Horsts files that go back thirty years. I need a fucking drink.

"Jimmy, it looks as if I became a target when I took on Hilda's case. Some powerful people don't want me looking into her dead husband's past. Now, they think I have what they want…whoever they is. It's too late now for me to stop. Four bodies too late, Jimmy." I spoke with a clear and measured response. He needed to believe that we were facing serious challenges that would be coming at us twenty-four seven.

"Are they gonna try to fuck up me and Anne too?" Jimmy immediately shot back at me.

"I'm afraid so! They didn't have to kill those two old women. They killed them to let me know that they want the files I have, and they'll stop at nothing to get them, even killing helpless old ladies. So now, Jimmy, I need you to get back over to the bar and stay close to Annie. The three of us are going to be like Siamese Twins from now on. Well, maybe not Siamese Twins, but you know what the fuck I mean."

"You mean triplets, Red, not twins," Jimmy said as he headed out the back door on his way to Annie's.

Now, I'm getting corrected by Jimmy. Is my mind clouded by the drugs they pumped into me at the hospital or am I feeling the effects of five straight years of boozing? It's the drugs from the hospital. It must be that. I handled those two shooters at my office and I can take down Hans and anyone else he brings with him. I need to get an edge, but how?

While Jimmy was closing the back door I heard someone knocking on my front door. I opened it expecting to see the cops, but instead it was Mrs. Hansen from three doors down the alley.

"Red, what's going on? There's been police, FBI, and dozens of reporters knocking on all the neighbors' doors asking all kinds of questions about you. None of us are telling them anything. Are you in trouble for killing those bad people? Do you need help from us?" she was asking me as if she and the other neighbors could do anything to help, like bake a cake or cook me a meal.

"Just keep your eyes out for any strangers with foreign accents showing up in the alley asking questions about me. Don't interfere with them; just answer them and don't worry about me."

With that I ushered her out my door. I could see the worried look on her face as she glanced back at me. She wanted to ask me another question, I thought, but decided not to. I could count on her to tell the other neighbors of our conversation. Mrs. Hansen was the neighborhood gossip.

I needed to get a look at the files from Horst's past. There must be some clue I'm holding that these Germans have been missing for the last fifteen years. Before Horst was wacked his German buddies must have thought they had what they wanted from him, or they would have made sure he stayed alive. Oops! They fucked up… and for fifteen years they've been looking and waiting for a clue. Now, I'm that clue, Red Canyon.

## CHAPTER 18

Annie and Jimmy needed me to protect them while I tried to solve the Horst family murders. I know who killed the old broads. It was time to bring in some tough ex-cops to watch over those two. One eye Eddie was where I would start. He must be close to sixty by now, but he would bring the snarl I wanted in my guard dog. He was retired on disability for the last ten or so years. His eye was lost in a street brawl with four punks from the Southside.

I was the first respondent to the call that an officer was down. When I got to the scene, Eddie had put two guys down on the ground. The other two punks had him down and were beating him with his own pistol. It was four in the morning, and nobody was on the streets, at least nobody who would help out a cop. I killed the one beating Eddie with the pistol and put two slugs in the other punk that eventually caused his death. I found out later that the two on the ground were dead. Eddie had killed them. A witness claimed I didn't give any warning to the two punks beating Eddie, Like I was supposed to read them their rights while they were killing a cop before I acted with force. The disabling injuries to Eddie caused such a public outcry that organizations like the ACLU had to back off and the press dropped the story. I have a plan. Call Eddie.

The Feds are not going to give me a complete package of information on the German connection. They'll feed me just enough to satisfy me. The information they hold out on me is what could get me killed. After Annie and Jimmy are secure, I'll make my own German database. I popped a pain pill and slipped off for a needed rest.

I felt something pushing my right shoulder and a voice urging me to wake up. The voice became louder, but I couldn't open my eyes. I was running down Carson Street with two men and a woman chasing me and shooting at me. I didn't have a weapon and had blood on my clothes. As I approached Grayson's Taylor shop the windows and doorway disappeared. The entrance to the store I was trying to enter for my own safety had turned into a solid wall. Bricks had replaced the glass windows and entrance door. I kept running.

Patko's Café entrance door turned to solid brick as I approached it also. My pursuers kept getting closer to me. I ran and ran, and each time I thought I had reached a place of safety, the entrance filled with brick as I reached for the door handle. Then, I saw the Italian Gardens across the street from me. I kept running in the direction of the entrance I had passed through so many times to see Annie. The door to the tavern opened and a hand reached out to help pull me inside. I was almost close enough to reach the hand when the opening began to close, and the doorway shrunk to a size that only a child could fit through.

The people chasing me were almost on me and I could hear them calling to each other in German. Then I awoke to see Annie standing in front of me holding my hand. I made it. Somehow, Annie pulled me through the disappearing doorway. Annie had rescued me again as she had done so many times since we were children together in grade school.

"Red, are you okay? You were mumbling and shaking all over. Are you having nightmares?"

"No dreams! I had a fever that just broke. That's it. I don't have dreams. I don't have metaphors going on in my head. I must get ready. One eye Eddie is coming to the bar at one."

"What does he have to do with the case?"

"He heard about me getting shot and wanted to know if he could help. He feels he owes me."

"You're beefing up the manpower, huh, Red? There's real danger now isn't there? Jimmy, you and I are targets, aren't we?"

"Nothing I can't handle and the answer to your three questions is…yes. The dead men in the morgue are Germans. They belong to some radical underground group headquartered in Germany. I don't know the name of the organization just yet. The Feds are going to fill me in. I made a deal with them. I give them the files for the dossiers on everyone in their data bank associated with that group. I need to know everything I can about these people."

"Do you really believe they will give you all their information on some radical Germans?"

"No, not everything, but enough so I can get started in the right direction. I have to get dressed now. Stay with me and we'll go back to the bar together. You need to always travel with Jimmy or one of my new detectives. It's time to expand the agency. I have a backer. Hilda! I'm putting three more men on payroll today. You can help me with their paperwork."

Annie looked surprised at my announcement. I was going to need at least three more guys to provide security for Annie, Jackie, and Hilda. They might be on the hit list along with the three of us. The files! I need to investigate the files and then turn them over to the Feds. I need to find the rat that tipped off the Germans about the files. That person is the next link of the chain that I'm going to use to drag him down with. It's almost time to meet one eye Eddie. I'm back. The street-smart Red Canyon has dried out and is focused.

I was sitting in the last booth in the bar when one eye Eddie walked in. He hadn't changed that much since I last saw him five years ago. Eddie was wearing a dark suit and a yellow polo shirt. I could see the outline of the Beretta he was carrying in his shoulder holster. With that patch on his left eye from a distance he almost looked like the guy in the old ad for Hathaway shirts. I was just about to wave him back to where I was sitting when he signaled that he saw me.

"You don't look too bad for a guy that just took I slug. What the fuck was that all about on Carson Street and what's with the two dead old ladies they found in your garbage this morning? I didn't think you killed old ladies, Red."

"Funny Eddie, very funny. I need your help. Five days ago, I took on a fifteen-year-old unsolved murder case. Now, I have four dead bodies on the Southside and more to come. I'm making Carson Street on the Southside of the City the new Deadwood according to some of the news boys. You got a look at all the media hanging out on 19th Street just waiting for the next stiff to show up."

Eddie sat quietly, listening as I began filling him in on the situation as it existed now. I was going to need him and two more retired cops that weren't drunks or at least could stay sober most of the time. The job would now begin for him right here in the Italian Gardens. There would be no way he could remain anonymous with that gang of news people hanging outside the bar. Eddie was alright with that.

"What do you want me to do today?"

"Your job is to keep track of Anne and Jimmy every day. We'll rotate every week so that everybody gets a turn on the dead man shift if we need it. Annie should never be without a bodyguard. Jimmy will be harder to keep an eye on. He's carrying and can take care of himself. Consider anyone with a German accent as hostile. That includes women."

As I was sitting across from one eye Eddie, I recalled the dream I had being chased by two men and a woman down Carson Street. I heard the curses the three were throwing at me filtered through their German accents. I'm going to go see the witch tomorrow morning and tell her about my dream and maybe have her read the cards.

Sophie was a gypsy who worked on the Southside. She was probably close to ninety by now but was still telling fortunes at the same storefront on Carson Street for as long as I can remember. All the women in the alley would get together once every month and have a witch party. Sophie would show up at the designated home at six o'clock and begin her readings, one neighbor at a time. When it was my mother's turn to host her all my aunts and my grandmother would show up to see if good fortune was coming their way. Me and my dad had to get the hell out of the house. No men were allowed in the house on the day the witch showed up.

There were always stories about how she predicted illness, death and good fortune for all those that paid her some small amount for her vision into the future. She didn't have a standard fee. She took what was offered.

The thing I remembered the most was that no one fucked with the witch. The stories of her evil eye and curses she could place on those that angered her could fill the library.

I wondered if she still wore the multicolored house dress with a red sash tied across the waist. She always wore a solid color babushka and black women's boots. When I was young, we were told to never look into the gypsy's eyes. I followed that order when I was a young kid. I didn't want to be turned into a fucking frog.

When I grew older, I quit believing in that gypsy bullshit. Now, I'm going to see her to learn if she can tell me about my dream and maybe tell me something she sees in my future. I probably won't go. I still don't believe in that bullshit. Do I?

Annie sat down next to me in the booth and nudged me back to the present.

"Hi! Eddie."

She didn't use one eye name when she referred to him. It was her opinion that it was insulting. Eddie didn't care; he kind a liked the title.

"You going to be my shadow, Eddie?"

"Yah! For a while, Annie, me or another shadow. Red says there's still a shooter out there after him and he wants to ensure the punk doesn't grab you and use you for leverage to get to him. Don't worry too much; Red will draw him out. It could even be today."

"Yah, Annie, I might end this problem today. I have some leads on where he's holed up and I'm going to set a trap for Hans, one that he won't be able to resist," I told Annie that story, hoping she would believe that Eddie would be around only for a short time or as long as needed. I could end it if I could find the answers in the boxes of files from the factory. Will I be able to stay alive long enough to finish this caper?

# CHAPTER 19

"Oh! Red. I forgot to tell you that you had a call from a Mr. J. He said he was from the Hill, and you'd know who he is. He wants you to call him."

Mr. J. is Wrecker Johnson. Could be he's decided to throw in with me. I could use some additional eyes on the street. He could be those eyes. I excused myself and headed upstairs to Annie's place to make the phone call in private. As I stood up and glanced around the bar I could see that it was almost full. Every booth in the place was occupied and there was standing room only. All the publicity about the shooting on the block has brought out all the creeps looking for a glimpse of Red, the guy who took down two thugs from out of town. To these thrill seekers, I'm the head freak in the circus that the Southside has turned into. Annie should triple the price of the drinks in the IG till the curiosity passes.

I made the phone call to Wrecker. He told me to meet him in front of the 28th Precinct at two thirty. Then, before I could say anything he hung up.

Why would he want to meet me in front of a police station in the Lawrenceville section of the city? Wrecker didn't like cops.

On my way out the back door of the bar, I called Annie over and told her where I was going and to stay close to one eye Eddie, then I jumped into the rental car she had parked behind the bar, grabbed the keys from under the mat and took off down the alley on my way to meet Wrecker. I'd have to lose the van from one of the TV stations that was following me. That would be simple unless the TV station had eyes in the sky. Losing a chopper would take a little more skill.

I arrived at the 28th Precinct forty minutes later and parked in the police parking lot behind the building. My retired City ID gained me access. There were no tails on me. I was back in action. Now, where the hell is Wrecker?

"Red." I heard a voice coming from the front door of the station. I just found Wrecker. He was waving to me from inside the doorway.

"What's with you and this police station?"

"I hope you brought some of that big roll you got. You need to bail out one of the guys that works for me."

Before he went any further, I cut him with my response.

"Fuck You! Why would I want to spot you bail money for one of your fuck ups? I can't believe you brought me out here for that. If you needed a loan, you should have just asked me."

"If you shut the fuck up for a minute I'll finish what I was saying before you started talking your shit. Delmons got busted driving my tow truck late this morning. They busted him on open warrants, mostly unpaid parking tickets. He asked me for three hundred ninety-five bucks so I could bail him out. I told him to stay in the fucking jail and that I wasn't going to give him shit, just a beating for getting my tow truck impounded. Then, he said he saw you at the yard the other day and he had some information that should be worth at least the bail money to you. He said it was about foreign guys. You bail him out and he'll tell you."

I wondered if Wrecker was running a scam on me, but for three hundred and ninety-five bucks I'd take a shot.

"You said three hundred and ninety-five didn't you Wrecker?" I asked him as I headed to the desk sergeant to tell him to get this guy Demons paperwork started; I was reluctantly going to post his bail.

"Tell me and the desk sergeant Delmons last name so they can bring him up front."

"You gotta also give me a hundred and thirty-five bucks to cover the impound charge."

"Why don't just wait till it gets dark and break in and steal your fucking tow truck?" I asked him sarcastically as I handed him the cash. I was betting he wouldn't waste my time or money on bullshit. If Delmons came up empty, he'd have to deal with Wrecker who would consider his actions as disrespecting him. Delmons would choose jail before wanting to face his wrath. I told Wrecker to take him back to his junkyard when he clears the bail. He asked me to wear some sort of a disguise when I came to the junkyard so that I wouldn't be recognized; then we could both hear what Delmons had to say that was worth three hundred ninety-five dollars.

On my way over to the junkyard I drove through what could reasonably be called the slums. Buildings that once stood proudly showing off the quality of the neighborhood now drooped from the years of abuse and neglect. Some of the street corners had the usual gangs of unemployed bums disguised as homeless people drinking booze and hailing invectives to the passing motorists that obviously didn't belong to their lifestyle. A quick glance up the block showed a lookout leaning on a parking meter waiting for the out of Up-

Towner's to drive by looking to score some drugs. Debris was scattered everywhere; empty booze bottles were randomly spread on sidewalks and roadways, along with the week's empty food containers and papers. I knew that the liquor bottles were empty otherwise they would have still been in the hands of the winos. Food containers that held the skeletons of the fowl that were served in them joined the other trash from the fast-food chicken restaurants that seemed to be spotted on every corner of 'Dump City'.

As I pulled into 'Wreckers Junkyard,' I realized that his property had become the showcase property of Dump City. The local residents didn't realize it. Wreckers Junk Yard was cleaner than the neighborhood that surrounded it. As I entered the office I called out, "When are you going to clean this place up?"

"This is a fucking junkyard. It's supposed to look like this motherfucker."

"I wasn't talking about the junk yard. I was talking about the neighborhood surrounding it."

He ignored my comments.

"You were supposed to be in disguise. You know that I don't want to be seen with you."

"I am in disguise. That's not my car, I drove in here today."

"Let's get this done so you can get the hell out of here." Wrecker barked out like the junkyard dog he is.

"Delmons, give the man what he paid for."

"I was walking through the hood last night when a black SUV pulled up to me and asked me if I was Raheem Mohamed. This honkey talked with a foreign accent. It sounded like the German guys I seen on TV. Then he asked me again if I knew where he could find Ali Shabaz and Raheem Mohamed. I told him I didn't know where they was, but to go check out the Double Deuce Club on Fisher Avenue. He headed one way, and I headed the other way. Those two brothers are some badass motherfuckers. I went over to the Deuces later and heard that the honkey got hooked up with them. The bartender told me that he overheard that somebody was gonna get killed. He said the guy in the suit passed them a bundle of money and a piece of paper and told them he'd see them later."

I was staring down Wrecker, showing anger cause he brought me over to the Hill and beat me out of over four hundred dollars to listen to bullshit.

"Before I start slapping your ass around, Delmons, I got some questions for you. Why should I believe that the bartender at the club would tell you anything about some bad ass punks and some white guy?"

"He's my brother, man. He's my real brother."

"So, how do you connect me to these three punks?"

"My brother said he heard a name. It was a Red somebody, he said. I figured it was you cause you been in the papers and on the news and you capped two foreign guys. I wouldn't have told you shit, but when Wrecker punked me on the bail I figured you'd pay to get me out."

I didn't recognize his face, but I probably put some of his boys from the hood in the slammer when I was still on the city payroll. Maybe I even locked him up. The last couple of years on the job were fuzzy for me.

I turned to look at Wrecker and was about to say something to him when he took the play away from me as he told Delmons to get to fuck to work.

"That warning just might keep you back on the streets and out of the morgue, but there's more. The two brothers that Delmons named are using their Muslim names. The names you'll recognize are Willy Gaston and Raymond Carpenter. Ring a bell? You put those two punks in Danora for a ten timer when you were a badass street cop. They just hit the streets about six months ago. When they got out, they reported to me to tell me they were back on the Hill and they weren't going to step on any of my actions. They both asked me for the obligatory job cause they needed to show their parole officer they were looking for work."

"There's more scum on the streets of the Hill that have a beef with me. Why did the Kraut search out these two punks?" I asked rhetorically. I got an answer from Wrecker before I could answer my own question.

"Someone inside the law enforcement community wants your ass capped. How else would the man get the names of the two punks just put out on the streets?"

He came up with the same conclusion I was coming up with. FBI, City police department, could even be DA Whitty or some of his flunkies. Could be a dirty cop that was involved in the Strump murders is still on the job.

"That was a good observation on your part, Wrecker. The tip had to be from inside, but inside what? That would mean these three Germans were operating with the blessing of any or all the policing agencies. How else could the third punk be reached unless he has a direct contact on the City police department or there's a rat inside one of the federal law enforcement agencies working with the Germans. Either way there is a leak. That means I go dark."

"What the hell are you talking about, Red? What's this go dark bullshit about? You talking about me?" Wrecker wanted to know. He knew what I meant. He just wanted to hear me say it.

"It has nothing to do with your color and you know it. It has everything to do with tightening up everything I do and who hears what. It looks like you threw in with me after you talked with Delmons. You didn't just call me for a hundred and thirty-five bucks to get your truck out of the impound. You wanted to see me face to face to work something out. Right?"

"I want the killer of my son. I want everyone that had anything to do with it; that means cops too. I figure you're my best shot. So now, I got a reason to keep you alive. I'm in."

I don't trust Wrecker. The history of him is that he never does anything unless he makes a profit and has control. I don't see him making a profit unless he buys an insurance policy on me. He knows that he can't control the action.

"What do you want, Wrecker? You don't care if I get wacked. You can't even be sure I can find the people that killed your son seventeen years ago. When the word gets out on the Hill you're doing business with me you're going to create new enemies for yourself. You may even get some heat from down at City Hall. Put your cards out on the table."

"The rumor is that the 'undertaker' is back and sober. Now, I believe it myself. I wanted to make sure you were out of the bottle and had your brains out of your ass before I said I'd help you. You need my help cause without it, you are gonna get yourself capped, and besides, I want in on some of the action. I want to fuck up some of you honkeys and make a profit from it. So, you put me on your payroll at a hundred a week as a private eye. I get an ID and a license to carry a concealed weapon legally and you get more eyes on the street. It's sorta like the early warning system that the government has on the Ruskies. I'll be like your bounty hunter. You pay me, say, five grand for each punk I cap."

He must have rehearsed that speech. It almost sounded logical which is not Wreckers' style. He's more of a freewheeling asshole.

"I'll give you five hundred bucks a week, but there is no guarantee you can get the permit to carry or the private eye license. I'll have Annie fill out the paperwork and fax it to you to sign and then she'll send in the application to City Hall. Right now, I'm not a favorite son Downtown. We'll see what happens and I'll give you a lawyer to keep you out on the street if you have to blow anyone away on my clock. No bounty. Deal?"

"I got all the paperwork on my desk. All you gotta do is sign on the dotted line and I'll be a legal private eye working for your agency before the business day is over. Man up motherfucker."

He pushed some papers over in front of me and handed me a pen.

"Sign all four copies every place you see a checkmark. One of my runners will take it to City Hall and be back here before you leave. I want you to stick around for the buffet I have coming to celebrate the alliance between the junkyard dog and the nearly famous Red Canyon. I got ribs and fried chicken, mashed potatoes, gravy and biscuits coming from your favorite spot on the Hill… Mammas Kitchen. You look like you need a good meal you skinny ass honkey. All that booze dried you up."

He was right about needing a good meal and Mommas made the best chicken in the City. I'd stay to see if Wrecker was just shooting his mouth off about having the fix in Downtown.

"Call me Red. I don't like the nicknames you might make up right now."

"Fuck you! I'll call you any name I want, including whitey, honkey, and bitch. Right now, I like the undertaker. It has a more threatening meaning to the brothers on the Hill. If I call you by that name, you'll get more respect. You need it here on the Hill. I'm trying to kick you up. You don't have to thank me, Red. That's okay."

The delivery boy showed up in the trailer with the food and gave Wrecker the bill. He quickly handed it back to him and pointed to me.

"Pay the bill and give the kid a twenty-dollar tip. Make sure you tell Momma that Red, the Undertaker, is back."

Wrecker told the kid knowing that the word would be all over the Hill that Red Canyon and Wrecker are having chicken and ribs together. Eating the meal together was a sign that there was peace between us; no old grudges carrying forward. It would cause worry for the two parolees that just took a contract on me.

What's Wreckers' real motive? I'll have to think about it awhile before I can be sure. It was time to eat Momma's cooking.

Wrecker hasn't been out of my site since we met at the Police Station. That means he had the food ordered in advance with a scheduled delivery time. This was a set up. Was Delmons a set up too? Maybe!

# CHAPTER 20

The chicken and ribs from 'Mammas' just didn't seem to taste the same as I remembered. Maybe it's because most of the nights I stopped there to eat was after the bars were closed. She could have served barbecued spare tires and fried chicken beaks. I wouldn't have known it most of the time. Was this our first dinner together or was it the last supper?

It looks as if Wrecker has joined my gang. I got a glimpse inside his head today. His first order of business is to get the killers of his son. The second is to fulfill one of the items on his wish list. He probably had the desire, since he was a kid, to be a cop. That wish couldn't be fulfilled. He could have become a rent-a-cop, a security guard, but that would have been too low on the scale of one to ten. So, he seized the opportunity I presented when I first walked into his office this week. He could have his badge, a license to carry a gun legally and be as close to being a cop as he could ever get. The advantage of being with me is that I don't follow the rules; a cop has to. This will work out… maybe! I'm tired of eating fucking chicken. It was time to go.

On my way back to the Southside, coming down off the Hill, I looked at the view of Downtown from the top of Fifth Avenue. In the distance stood new skyscrapers mixed among the older buildings that once housed department stores and offices. The near view on the Hill displayed the same scene as before; worn out buildings, broken cobblestone streets and the usual garbage of liquor bottles, soda cans, fast food bags, paper, beer bottles, and an occasional drunk passed out on the sidewalk. The debris seemed to grow like weeds in the slums. As soon as the yuppies get the courage to visit the Hill the slum will be replaced by townhomes and condos facing the heart of the City. That transfusion is the only prescription that can cure this part of the city of the disease of slum.

I hadn't received any calls from the Southside, so I figured that everyone was okay. Hans was setting up the attack on me with his newfound comrades, the jailbirds. Wrecker was on the prowl, and I was counting on him spotting these punks and getting a tail on them. They would have to come to my playground, the Southside, to continue the game. It's my home field and nobody wins there, but me.

There were no parking spaces close to the IG with all the reporters and sightseers clogging up Carson Street. I had to ride down three blocks in the direction of the river to Bennett Street before I found a spot without a meter. When I was a kid, I broke at least a half dozen windows on this block. I remembered the alleyways and rooftops I used to escape from being caught in the street version of hide and seek or what we sometimes referred to as you bet your life. That escape route may be needed again by me before this case is solved. Could I still climb a roof? Motivation and fear would eventually answer that question, but would it be caused by Hans?

The three blocks to the IG somehow didn't seem as long as I remembered as a kid. I guessed it's because I take bigger steps. With a few exceptions the view was the same, only the people have changed.

I entered the IG through the alley entrance. The press had a stakeout hanging out in a van in the alley. There would be no privacy for a while until another major event moved me off the front pages.

One eye Eddie was still sitting in the booth where I left him. Annie was working at the bar with Harry, the extra bartender. I heard Annie telling two of the gawkers sitting at the bar that they had to buy drinks to keep sitting there. Annie had kept the backroom closed to the public. I gave her a hug and headed to my usual booth in the back room and motioned to one eye Eddie to follow me. We couldn't have a private conversation in the bar area with the news people listening in along with some of the geeks.

"Nothing happened since you been away. Annie's been selling a lot of booze, though."

"You remember Wrecker Johnson from the Hill, don't you?"

"Yeah! Is he mixed up in this, too?"

I explained how Wrecker fit into the picture and that he just threw in with me. His network on the Hill might produce some leads that could tip me off on the movement of the German. I would make him come to the Southside to get to me, and just maybe Wrecker could tell me when. I was counting on it.

"Why don't you just give him what he wants? It's the papers from the factory, isn't it?"

"I don't have them in my possession at this time, Eddie."

"He doesn't believe that."

"That was probably true until I killed his two pals. Now, this guy wants me and the files. That's my edge. He's going to try to take me alive so he can get the files and give me lots of pain, Eddie."

"You just told me you didn't have the files."

"No, what I said was that they were not in my possession. I don't want you to know anything about them. The Feds are after the files, and they can bring a lot of heat down on you."

"Red, you can do what you want with this case, but my advice is to give the Feds the files; keep the retainer and go public that you are off the case."

"Even if I did that, I still have a German and the boys in the hood coming after me. I have to settle that matter before I can consider your option."

"Yeah, I just threw it out to you, Red. I knew you wouldn't drop this hot potato. You always did like to stir up the shit. This time you're standing in it."

Eddie was right. I was in the big leagues now and I wasn't quite prepared for it. I took on a fifteen-year-old unsolved murder from a seventy-year-old wife. How much trouble could that cause me? When I took the fifty 'G' retainer, I thought the only problem would be how to burn up the fifty grand. Now, everyone close to me has a target on their back and I only know three of the hunters; Hans and his two gun bearers from the Hill.

I gave Eddie the bail receipt for Delmons and asked him to run him through the police computer. I wanted to see if he had a rap sheet. This guy couldn't be clean.

He smells like a con. Eddie was also to get me the visitor records at Donora, where Willie Gaston and Raymond Carpenter spent the last ten years. The only visitors scum like these two would have might be a mother and some other street punks. I wanted to know what gang they belonged to in prison, where it operated in the city and who was the local head of it. While Hans was playing Hitler, I was playing MI 5.

# CHAPTER 21

Anne came into the back room and sat down with me and Eddie. Sparks had just showed up for the night shift. Harry was working on the grill in the kitchen and more people were coming into the bar.

"I'm opening the dining room. It's going to be a very busy night thanks to you, Red. If you help at the bar I can get sparks to help wait on tables if I need him. Okay?" Anne asked, knowing the answer I'd give her.

"I'll work the bar and maybe sign some autographs too. One eye Eddie can put on a show. Ask him, Annie, to do his impression of Sammy Davis Jr. Can you still tap dance you fat bastard?" I asked as I was looking at both of them and waiting for their answers.

My answer came from both at almost the same time.

"Very funny, Red," from Anne and "Fuck you… You piece of shit!" from one eye Eddie.

"Me and you are good then Annie and I'll take that as a no from you one eye on the Sammy Davis thing," I said it with a grin on my face. It was time for everyone to lighten up.

Hans wouldn't be coming after me with all the exposure he'd have here on the Southside tonight. He's a Pro. He'll wait. But where is Cousin Jimmy? Is he still with Jackie?

I stepped behind the bar to begin banging out drinks for the mixed crowd of curiosity seekers and news hawks. Then that asshole Sparks did something that's gonna get him a beating after the bar closes. He made an announcement.

"Hey! Everybody! Meet Southside's most famous private eye, Red, aka the Undertaker, Canyon. He's the guest bartender tonight," he announced loudly as he pointed to me.

There was a mixed reaction from the crowd in the bar, some clapping and some booing. The bleeding-heart liberals, I guessed, sang the blues because I exercised the death penalty on some street scum. The others that applauded wanted the final solution exercised on the street by the good guys… with a bullet. The others standing and just looking were like the Independents. They couldn't make up their fucking minds on which way to go until the last minute, a bullet or handcuffs. On the streets, their independence would cost someone their fucking life. You drive down the middle of a highway, and you get run off the road by the driver in the right lane or the driver in the left lane. Pick a lane with the fewest potholes and ride it. I'm daydreaming again. I usually give that speech when I'm bombed.

This was going to be fun for me tonight. I didn't have the slightest idea of the price for any mixed drink here at t, and except for rum and coke or scotch on the rocks, I couldn't make a proper mixed drink. I was going to cause chaos at the bar. I'd try to save my best insults for just before the bar closed. They would be for the last big mouth on the other side of the bar. My leg was still painful from the gunshot, but I wanted to have a fight. I needed to kick someone's ass and who better than a big mouth punk. Yeah, this was gonna be fun for me tonight at the IG.

I heard a group of drinkers down at the end of the bar calling to me and almost begging me to come down and serve them drinks. After a few more shout outs I headed the thirty feet to my fans.

Most of them were shouting a chorus of "Red! Red!" and reaching across the bar to shake my hand. I slapped some hands but didn't shake them. I reserved the handshake for the as needed situations. There were a couple of broads with this crowd that had assess I wouldn't have minded slapping. They ordered four bottles of Rock and a couple of Captain Morgan's. I gave them six beers and told them we were out of Captain Morgan's.

"The fucking ship sailed with the Captain on it," and then charged them thirty dollars. The duke that put the two twenties on the bar wanted to question the price for a split second, but changed his mind as he took a quick look into my eyes. That was the 'suck it up' look I was giving him.

It was almost like everyone in the place wanted Red to serve them a beer. An hour later I had to call on Sparks to get the beer coolers filled again on both ends of the bar. Beer was flying out of there like an open bar at an Elks Club picnic. The word had been passed around that I was only serving beer and not making mixed drinks. The women that wanted my attention ordered beer. There were a lot of them drinking beer tonight.

The comments I was getting from the crowd were varied. Most of the females I overheard were saying how tall and handsome I was. I had a half a dozen phone numbers slipped to me by some good-looking broads and a couple of gay guys. After the last gay guy hit on me, I decided to grab some broads' ass in the crowd to let the left handers see I'm not a switch hitter. Everyone in the place, all night long, wanted to buy me drinks. I was a celebrity and liked it, but I turned them down, saying I didn't drink while I was working. I didn't want my fans to think that I wouldn't drink with them.

The air handlers Annie had installed in the bar couldn't scrub the volume of cigarette smoke the puffers in the crowd were creating. Branded cigarettes smoke was mixed with the sweet flavored smoke of weed. I wasn't a cop anymore and didn't care if some of the crowd wanted to pass a joint around. Strange, no one offered me a hit.

This bar was always busy on Friday night, but nothing like this night. When I wasn't serving beer, I circulated through the crowded bar all night long, bumping elbows with the curious drinkers and repeating, "I can't talk about the incident cause I'm gonna have to go to court" crap. I was having fun. I can't count the number of times some broad grabbed my ass that night. That was something I was usually accused of doing and rightly so.

Around midnight I took a break and went outside to get some fresh air. There was a crowd waiting to get into the IG that I had to push my way through. Someone must have recognized me and called out 'there's, Red!' and the push was on to get close to me to meet the gunslinger of the Southside. The questions being called out to me had become monotonous. Why did you kill those men? What about the two women in your garbage and so on and so on? There were plenty of autograph hounds pressing me with paper and pens in hand. I worked myself over close to the curb and leaned on the parking meter. Spooks pushed his way through the crowd to stand in front of me as a shield.

"Everybody back the fuck up! He's gonna talk to everyone in a couple of minutes, just give him some room or you're gonna piss him off."

Someone in the crowd called out, "What's he gonna do, shoot us?"

"No, he's not gonna shoot you, but I'm gonna come over there and kick your fucking ass."

Spooks was earning his pay. I hadn't asked for his help, but he took it upon himself to quiet the crowd. That makes twice in the last couple of days that he has done more than I thought he was capable of doing. Maybe it's time to give him a raise.

As I was taking in the cool night air and looking at the weekend mass of bodies crowding both sides of Carson Street, I recalled how this block looked when I was a kid.

Southside was in decline thirty years ago. It was never in danger of becoming a slum, just an undesirable section of a City in transition; manufacturing to hi-tech. I remembered two bars on 18$^{th}$ Street being closed and half dozen storefronts with soaped up front windows and "for rent" signs taped to the glass. A couple of decades later, they were replaced with nail salons run by the Asians that seemed to own that skill. Posh boutiques displayed the most elegant of their fashions. Coffee houses replaced two of the bars. It was hippie *light* on the Southside.

I was almost done crowd watching when across the street out of the corner of my eye I saw a dark suit moving in the middle of a group of street walkers. The suit stood out in a crowd that was dressed in the uniform of the night fashioned out the Good Will box. It had to be either a Fed left behind to track me or Hans. No one else would be dumb enough to wear a dark suit after midnight on a Friday night here on the Southside. He was almost directly across the street from me when he turned his head and looked toward the Italian Gardens.

This guy had to be Hans and not some dopey Fed. He had close cropped sandy colored hair and was wearing a white shirt with a narrow tie not seen in America since the fifties. I couldn't exactly tell the color of the suit he had on; maybe dark grey or dark blue. He looked to be about six feet tall with a medium build. So now I know what Hans looks like. I have to kill him, but how can I while he's in the crowd of people?

As he was looking across to the IG, he must have finally picked me up standing right behind a parking meter dead center in front of the bar. Our eyes locked on each other for a few seconds. I couldn't tell what color his were, but he never blinked. The crowd he was mixed in with was moving toward the corner of 19th street with him in the center keeping pace. While we were still locked in a death stare I raised my hand, clenched my last three fingers into a fist and extended my index finger to point the mock barrel of a gun in his direction as I lowered my thumb in the familiar shooting motion. I was pushing my way across the grid locked street in an attempt to get closer for a shot when I picked up another dark suit on the same side of the street about a hundred feet off to my right.

Now, I was in deep trouble. Something I hadn't figured on was taking place. I began to realize that Red Canyon wasn't back all the way. Just a sobering up drunk that was once a good cop was standing in my shoes pretending to be the street-smart detective. Fortunately for me, I'm the only one with that information.

Hans had brought a twin with him that was walking a couple hundred feet behind giving him cover just in case an opportunity presented itself; the opportunity to kill me. They had sandwiched me in between them. The fucking German had out foxed me and lured me into the middle of a trap in the center of my own playground on Carson Street.

Where was my pistol? I had taken it out of my pants pocket holster when I started tending to the bar earlier in the evening. Now what? There I was, stuck in the middle of Carson Street traffic without my thirty-eight. Hans' backup had stepped off the curb and was closing the distance between us. I was fucked. He took a couple of steps closer and reached into his suit coat for the weapon that was going to make me the guest of honor at a Requiem high mass at St. Johns.

I didn't want to run back toward the sidewalk through the crowd that was watching me. I didn't doubt that the German wouldn't hesitate to empty his clip into the crowd while he attempted to take me out. So, I just stood there waiting for my guardian angel to come up with a plan. Instead, my cousin Jimmy showed up and was pushing his way through the crowd, calling for me to look up. Turning back to where I heard Jimmy's voice, I looked up to see my .38 flying over top of the crowd toward me. They began scattering in panic from seeing a pistol being thrown in the air in the middle of Carson Street. I had it in my hand and turned to face Hans's twin, but what I saw flashing at me was a gold shield reflecting off the headlights of the cars crawling along down Carson Street. Hans's backup was a cop not a German; probably the Fed that was assigned to tail me.

Hans had slipped away somewhere in the crowd while I was distracted with trying to come up with a plan to stay alive.

The middle of the street where I was standing was just about clear of all civilians. I still had my .38 pointed in the direction of the shield carrier. People were running and some were screaming. I had to stop the panic.

"That's it for the show tonight folks! Show's over!" I kept yelling out. Jimmy picked up on what I was doing and echoed my words. As the word spread through the crowd the panic ended.

The cop and some Friday nighters reached me at the same time. The onlookers were telling me how realistic the scene I just acted out was.

"Great job! You scared the shit out of a lot of us. You gonna do something tomorrow night, too?" I was being asked.

"Yeah! I'm gonna do something different tomorrow at midnight. Tell your friends," I said hoping this incident would be swallowed by the Press as just an act. I didn't need more cops and another incident tagged on me.

"What's with aiming a gun at me?" the cop in the suit was asking.

"C'mon in the bar and I'll explain." I turned and pushed my way back through the crowd and into the bar.

I navigated through the crowded bar toward the office in the back of the dining room. The bad part about the office was its location next to the restrooms. It never mattered before cause there were no crowds using them and you only had to tolerate some loud conversation and the occasional stinker when someone laid out a bomb in the crapper. With all the people coming in and out of the restrooms the office had now become the toilet annex catching the winds of recycled pickled eggs and booze.

"Where's the other agent I met in the hospital? You know you came close to getting yourself killed out there on the street. The third German, the one that killed the old ladies and left them in my dumpster, was walking a hundred feet in front of you. They wear dark suits like you, Feds. I had you pegged as his accomplice. It's a good thing for you that I have good night vision or you'd be leaving the City in a wooden box."

"If you knew this guy was wanted for those murders, why didn't you stop him? And by the way my name is Al Lewis and I'm your shadow till you turn over the files you took from the factory."

I wasn't about to tell him I was out on the street without my piece.

"When you get back to your room tonight look up in your handbook *agent 101 things you do and don't do*. It says don't kill innocent civilians in pursuit of a perp. You must have missed that crowd walking in front of you," I sarcastically said to Al.

"They told me you were a smart ass when I was assigned to tail you. Maybe I ought to bust you for assault with a deadly weapon. I'd bet there's a lot of punks in the system that would like you in the lock up with them."

"Al, you and your boss can go fuck yourselves! As long as you guys think I have what you want you have to suck it up. You aren't going to do anything except hang out and hope I can come up with the goods. You better make sure that the German doesn't kill me before you get what you came for or your next assignment will be guarding Hoover's grave in Arlington," I arrogantly told the suit. I wasn't trying to make friends. It was alright if he was pissed off at me. He'd keep a tight watch on me and when I needed him around he'd be close. I'd use him as a bodyguard. I could dump his tail on me whenever I wanted.

"Let's go back out to the bar and I'll buy you a drink. There are a lot of broads in there. Maybe you'll get lucky."

Al had a puzzled look on his face. I had just told him to go fuck himself, and now I offered to buy him a drink.

He was angry at me and now he wasn't sure if I deserved that level of anger he showed. I gave him a quick glance and said, "Business, just business, Al." Maybe he'd get it.

"I'm on duty, Red, but thanks anyway. Why don't you just give me the files and I'll get out of your way."

"Watch your ass Al. The German dresses just like all you agency guys. He has short, sandy hair and stands about six feet tall. File that away. It could save your life." I didn't want to see a Fed killed if they ran into Hans and mistook him for one of their own.

The bar was still packed. Jimmy had jumped behind it and was handing out beers and pointing my way as he picked up money for the drinks. My fame hadn't worn off just yet. I started to sweat. Out on the street, I had just dodged a bullet and wondered who else might be coming at me. I had to discover who Horst Strump really was and what he was hiding. It was time for me to look at his past through the boxes of papers I had on ice.

Annie came over to me and wanted to know if I was still going to work behind the bar. I told her not to worry, but I was sending Jimmy and one eye Eddie home. I'd finish up behind the bar for the next two hours.

I wasn't sending the two of them home. But I was sending them to run an errand for me. They were going to get the files that the two old ladies died for. They could bring them back to Annie's. That's where I'd go through them. Annie could help me if I needed it. I wanted to get this part of the investigation completed for two reasons. The first was to try and find some clues to solve the Horst murder. The second was to get the Feds off my back.

The news that the Feds had recovered the missing files could stop anyone else that had an interest in them from looking to me. Hans would keep coming after me. He was clever enough to assume I went through everything and found what he was sent to get. I hope he's right. There was also the matter of my killing two of his comrades that he had to settle the score on with me. I'm going to make killing Hans and the two jailbirds he hired my weekend project. He was too dangerous to live on the streets any longer. Tomorrow morning I'd pressure Wrecker to find him. I'll tell him to spread some money around and promise another payoff if the lead takes me to Hans.

The next couple of hours blew by for me. I liked playing as a celebrity. That night I coulda banged more broads than I did in all my high school years. Every time I started to slip a piece of paper with a phone number from a good looking broad into my pocket I caught a glimpse of Annie mouthing the words 'no more fucking around. I passed the numbers to Sparks.

A couple cops came in right before closing and wanted to know what the hell happened in the street around midnight. I told them to read the morning newspapers. I knew the older cop and he was good with my explanation, but the young one with him wanted more from me. Should I make another enemy of a local cop or should I make nice? Before I could decide, Annie stepped in between us and told Junior it was a show to promote the bar, nothing else. I was about to give him one of my favorite declaratory sentences when Annie reached over and covered my mouth with her hand and softly said to me, "Red, shut up!".

She was right, of course. Annie always seemed to be right. I didn't want to have to go back to my place tonight, so I listened. I'd see this young cop again on the street and let him meet the street Red Canyon. It could wait, for now.

One eye Eddie and Jimmy showed up a little after three. They wanted to know what I wanted them to do with the files. I had them back the car up close to the rear door and then lock it. Right before dawn, I'd unload the records into the first-floor office and begin my search through thirty years of what?

Before the weekend is over I hope to add three more bodies to the pile of stiffs that Horst Strump could claim responsibility for.

At daylight, I'd begin to look for the strand that I can pull to unravel the cloak that Horst Strumps' murder is wrapped in.

After Jimmy pulled Annie's car up tight to the back door of the bar he gave me the keys and left with one eye Eddie for the greasy spoon to get some breakfast. Nick the Greek had run the all night restaurant up on 21st street as long as I can remember. He was old now but still had most of his hair. It was now salt and pepper colored from the passing of time. The age lines on his face were carved deeply into his olive skin and partially hidden by his scruffy beard and a nose that could have come from a Toucan.

Over the years he had spotted me a burger or a roast beef special when I was little short or loaded. I wasn't the only one on the Southside that Nick sometimes carried on the cuff. These days he has his two sons, George and Minoli, working the grill and the kitchen. Some things stay the same on the Southside. Nick's Restaurant was one of them.

Annie's tug on my hand brought me back from reminiscing in the dining room of the bar. She motioned for me to follow her upstairs to her apartment. I always liked to follow Annie up the stairs.

It gave me a good look at her ass and a chance to grab it a couple times on the way up. She always told me to stop, but I knew she didn't mean it except when she was angry with me.

"Are you going to be able to hang behind the bar tomorrow tonight?"

"Sure Annie. My fans would be disappointed if I wasn't there," I said on my way to the bedroom. I was tired and had to get up in three hours to begin the file project.

"Red, was that really the third German on the street tonight or were you just adding to your reputation?"

"It was Hans. He looked like a clone of the other two in the morgue. I underestimated him. In my mind I didn't see any way that he'd show up here on the Southside tonight. I'd bet he thought about coming into the bar and having me serve him a beer. This guy is very clever and bold. I have to find him and kill him before he gets me. I thought I could set him up and lure him to the Southside where I'm the home team. His visit changed that. I'll have to take him down on a neutral field and soon."

"Can't the cops and the Feds capture him?"

"Maybe, but I have to get to him first. If he was in custody, I'd have to worry about him being released on bond or escaping. I don't want to have to look over my shoulder the rest of my life. That's why I have to find him first and kill him. That's the only way."

"If you kill him won't his group of thugs send others to kill you?"

"Good question, Annie. The answer is maybe, but probably not after I turn over the files to the Feds and solve the case. They'd have their answer whatever it is. My bet is they wouldn't want to risk losing any more of their soldiers if the reason for their coming here is answered."

"What if you're wrong about the Germans? Then what?"

"Then I become the most famous Nazi killer of the 21st century."

"How do you know for sure that they are Nazis?"

I didn't want to answer any more of Annie's questions. I didn't want to kill the rest of the night either, but I had to stop her questioning. I knew her continued questions were caused by her nervous concern for me. I needed a closing for the night with her. I considered the phrase shut the fuck up, but instead chose to say I know they're Nazis because Hitler told me they were.

"Okay, Red, I get it. No more questions tonight. How about some sex instead?"

"See you in bed." But before I could finish my sentence I heard; "I thought you didn't want any more questions tonight, Red. I'm going to sleep."

I might have just as well said shut the fuck up. Instead, I was nice and wound up with the same result. What's up with that? The lesson to be learned is just to be "Red" and fuck it.Then I heard from the bed.

"Red, I have a question I want to ask you, but I don't want to upset you."

"They may not be Nazis," I quickly shot back counting on that answer to patch things up. "I just like to call them Nazis 'cause they're evil, and they're German. Okay?"

"Come to bed. I'll ask you my question tomorrow, Red?"

She suspended asking questions again. If I answer with the truth, I'm in trouble, and if I lie, she'll know it. Either way, I lose.

"I'm taking the fifth the rest of the night," I said as I crawled under the covers and grabbed some skin. Annie had accepted my apology.

# CHAPTER 22

It was just after six when I awoke. Annie was already up and doing something in the kitchen. I had a hangover, but for a change, it wasn't from just boozing. It was from all the cigarette smoke I had to eat last night in the bar. I'd change that tonight. I'd make the place a nonsmoking bar for the night. Annie would go along with it. After all, I was the main attraction and the curious customers wouldn't let a cigarette keep them from having a beer with the famous Red Canyon.

Annie came into the bedroom as I was heading for the bathroom.

"Annie, I want to make the bar a no smoking place for the night. I'm hungover from the smoke last night," I told her and waited for her to tell me she agreed.

"No way! I'll buy you a painter's mask to wear. Now let's go someplace and have breakfast. I'm starved from the workout I had last night."

I stopped dead, stared at Annie and was about to bring out my dictionary of curse words to throw at her when I saw the smile on her face as she looked at the expression of disbelief I was wearing. Before the first expletive left my lips she said, "Only kidding. Of course, we can go nonsmoking tonight. Gotcha!"

That's how the morning began for me… with a gotcha.

We went to have breakfast at one of the newer morning cafés. No greasy eggs fried in bacon grease or cardboard fried bacon and boiled coffee. No, this café served lattes, whole grain muffins and a butter substitute. I usually just walk by this place, but never stop in. It was Annie's choice. I would have rather had some eggs fried in lard, greasy bacon and a cup of black coffee from a coffee urn that hadn't been cleaned out since Regan was president and served in a chipped restaurant grade white cup with the green ring a half inch below the rim. That was Nick's greasy spoon on 21$^{st}$. Instead, I was sitting in Buns and Roses all-natural café choking down a house blend of natural bean coffee and eating a whole grain muffin with all-natural watery jelly made from what I refer to as The Grapes of Wrath. It sucked.

“Thanks for taking me here for breakfast. I know this isn’t a place you would normally go. I like the pastry and lattes they serve. How’s your coffee and muffin, Red?” Annie actually asked me that.

My answer should have been that the only drink that could taste worse was sewer juice and as to the loaded with fiber muffin…I think they used the fiber from an old toilet scrub brush, but instead I answered, “The coffee has a robust flavor and the muffin tastes like it was made with love.”

“Why Red, that’s so sweet to hear you say such nice things to me.”

“Gotcha!” I proclaimed to Annie as I slammed my hand down on the table and began to laugh. I just restarted my day and now I stared at Annie for her reaction. I could see the slightest grin begin to form on her face.

“You always must be a smart ass don’t you, Red? That was a rhetorical question so don’t answer. Throw your coffee and muffin in the garbage, leave a five-dollar tip on the table and let’s go to Nick’s.”

I couldn’t believe what I was hearing from Annie. It had to be a set up.

“This is a gotcha back at me, right?”

"No, I could use some greasy food. I'll just skip the fish oil pill today."

It began to rain lightly as we walked up Carson Street to Nick's restaurant. Most of the Friday night trash had been picked up by the city sanitation workers. The local merchants were gathering up the debris that was missed. Saturday is a busy day in town. Everyone that recognized me either just stared or called out to me by name. Occasionally I'd hear someone whispering, "That's Red Canyon the famous detective. He's a Southside guy."

We arrived at Nick's and entered through the same door I'd been using for the last thirty years. I could still see some of the scratches I put on it one night when I tried to carve my name in the glass.

"Red, Annie, it's good to see you both again. It's been a while. I heard you got shot in the ass, Red," Nick announced that loud enough for everyone in the place to hear.

"Not in the ass; in the right leg," I answered back in an equally loud voice.

"Come over to my booth. The padding is thicker. It will be easier on your ass, Red," Nick told me that, as he reached for my arm, he would lead Annie and me to the booth, which he used for himself and his family.

This was an honor of some sorts since no one ever uses his booth, even when they're busy.

"Nick, the bullet went through my right leg. Not in the ass," I told him again. I didn't want any rumors on the street that Red Canyon got shot in the ass. That would be humiliating.

"Okay, Red, but Jimmy and one eye Eddie told me last night when they came in for breakfast that you took one in the ass. Can you show me where you got hit in the leg?"

Annie had laughed enough and finally told Nick that the guys were just having fun and that I really did take one in the leg. She assured Nick that she had seen the wound herself.

"Nick, if I hear you spreading that story around town I'm gonna come back and put my foot up your ass."

He knew I was getting annoyed and told me he was just having fun. The boys put him up to it last night. Jimmy and Eddie have one coming to them. Nick said he'd make my usual breakfast and throw in some pancakes with it. Annie was getting the same whether she wanted it or not. His son Minoli saw me and came out of the kitchen to shake my hand and ask me how my ass is. Annie told him I was fine rather than go through the explanation again.

We finished some of the food and when I went to pay Nick, he wouldn't take the money. Instead, he wanted to know if he could make the breakfast he just served us into a special in his restaurant. He would call it the Red Canyon Special. That's a unique name. I told him it was alright with me and he could use my name if he thought he could make money with it and then Nick told me I could have breakfast for free three days a week. With that we left and headed back down Carson.

Sam, the tailor, stopped me on the way back to the IG to ask how I was feeling. He reminded me that I had a couple of dozen shirts and ties ready to pick up at the store. Maybe he could make me another pair of suit pants to replace the pair I put the bullet holes in.

For some reason I smelled death in the city this morning. The stench of death is unmistakable. I read somewhere that the mind could reproduce a scent for our senses if the emotion was strong enough. It looks as if my emotions and death are in the zone together. My subconscious was telling me to find and kill Hans and the punks he hired on. How many were there? This guy is too well trained to come after me with just two undisciplined street punks. I need to contact Wrecker.

My mind was jumping all over the place. I needed to focus on finding some clues to break this case. It's the files… gotta be.

# CHAPTER 23

THERE WAS a knock on the office door and then the sound of Annie's voice woke me. I must have fallen asleep sometime after two this afternoon. That was the last time I looked at my watch. After five hours of sifting through travel records, visitor logs, and expense vouchers, I didn't know any more now than when I started. I decided to approach all the paperwork in the files as pieces to a big puzzle. The picture wouldn't be complete until the last piece was in place. With the Feds and Hans after me, there wasn't enough time to put all the pieces together. I had to find that last piece, or there were going to be more dead bodies showing up on Carson Street. I didn't want to be one of them.

"I left you alone for the last five hours. Did you find anything that you could consider a lead?"

"No! I didn't find anything unusual. I started my dig with his travel vouchers. I wanted to see where he started his traveling when he founded the business. When that's completed, I'd check to see the companies he did business with to see if they match up with his travel. I had to have a starting point. That's as good as any place to begin. I'd just keep eliminating the dead ends until I run out of files or find a lead." I wanted to finish this part of my search so I could move on to his expenses and purchases. The Feds and the German are still looking fifteen years after his murder for something Horst had in his possession. The key to its location, whatever it is, must be in my possession… maybe.

"Red, do you want to go have dinner at the Southside Steak House on 20th Street? Diana called me before and said she had a table for us in the alcove so we'd be alone or as alone as you could get in her place. What do you say? What should I tell her?"

"Tell her yes. I could use a good steak and some of that fried zucchini. I don't eat the stuff except at her place. Six is a good time."

I locked the office and went upstairs to shower and clean up for the night ahead. Annie had an elaborate state of the art shower. When the glass doors closed, music would begin to play. The box, as I called it, was twelve feet square with seating for two on opposite walls. When you started pushing buttons, water sprayed in from all directions, including the floor. The temperature was set around 100 degrees, but it was adjustable along with the water pressure. My temperature was always cold.

I woke up on the floor of the box more times than I can count. Somehow, I'd make it up to Annie's, and she'd get me into the box, clothes and all. I'd get doused with cold water at full pressure until I got on my knees and pulled myself up on my feet, opened the door and stumble out onto the floor of the bathroom. That ended the water torture. Most of the time I'd pass back out on the floor next to the shower while wearing all my soaked clothes and sleep the deep sleep that beer, wine and vodka administer to a drunk. That was just a bad memory now.

I had to be prepared for a long night. Annie kept the bar open till three A.M. on Saturday nights. She was ready for a busy night and told me that she hired another waitress and two additional bartenders for tonight and tomorrow. All I had to do was stroll behind the bar and talk it up. Besides, I might just announce that I was going to use the IG as the official home for my Southside drinking contest.

I was considering having a couple more beers tonight. I wanted to clear my head of the thought that I couldn't control the booze. I'm Red Canyon not a candy assed geek. We'll see tonight who's in charge; me or Mr.Lager? I'm betting on me.

I was uncomfortable in Annie's shower box. I finished getting ready and headed down to the bar to meet her.

She was waiting for me downstairs and ready for a Saturday night on the Southside. Annie looked great. If she stayed in that dress at the bar tonight, the men and lesbos would be hitting on her. Maybe that's why she got decked out. Maybe she was telling me that I'm not the only one in the bar tonight who's getting hit on. Yeah, maybe!

We held hands as we walked the three blocks to the steak house. I wasn't a big fan of holding hands, but Annie liked it. I had one of my new suits on and a new shirt from Sam's. My Glock was tucked in its holster under my left arm and my .38 in my right pants pocket. Tonight, I was properly dressed for company like Hans, if he showed up.

Diana was waiting for us when we entered her restaurant. I hadn't been in the place in a couple of years. Recently, most of my dinners have been liquid. She had redecorated during that time in a theme from the early Southside. A new big oak bar and a stained-glass mirror lined the back bar. An authentic looking trough had been installed that ran the length of the foot rail that echoed the 1900's. In those days, women weren't allowed to be at bars. Back then, the drunks at the bar used it for spit and urinating. That saved them from making a trip out back to the outhouse. The slop boy, every so often, would throw a couple of buckets of water in from the high end of the trough, and it would drain into the slop bucket at the low end. The better taverns would even empty the filled bucket before it overflowed or the stench from it caused the bar bums to complain. Maybe she's trying to revive that history. I'll have to ask her.

Diana gave Annie and me a hug and talked the usual chatter like… you look great... did you lose weight... blah... blah... blah.

I had her tuned out. I was thinking about the places Horst traveled to over the nine years I had tracked. Chicago was a frequent city on the list. Houston was a repeated name in the early years. Most of his travels though were in the East. It makes sense to build your business as close to the factory as you can. Why is all the travel so far out west? Which city was part of the last piece of the puzzle? Was it a city?

Annie ordered dinner for us. I'm not a salad guy, but I'll eat a made fresh at the table Caesar salad if anybody working in the restaurant knows how to make one.

While Annie returned to the chatter with Diana, I was checking out the people in the bar and dining room. I didn't notice any European style suits or short haired white guys attached to them. But I did see a kid I grew up with on the Southside…Joey Kay. He showed up on the Southside when I was in the eighth grade. Joey was four years older than me and didn't speak much English back then. He was a German kid and lived up in the hollow with a younger sister, his mother, and his dad.

Since Joey was born in Germany I wondered if I should consider him one of my enemies. He wasn't wearing a suit so I could 86 that for now. He must have seen me enter with Annie and was heading toward me.

"Red, how are you feeling? The papers said you took a couple of slugs from one of my countrymen ," he said as he extended his right hand to shake with me.

"Do you still pick your nose, Joey? If you do, I'm not shaking hands."

"You're still a wise guy aren't you Red?"

"Yeah, Joey and you're still fat."

Joey put his hand down and reached my left shoulder and gave me a half assed man hug. We were good friends while I was in high school, but that was some time back. He didn't attend school, so I took him with me to any of the good dances or parties in those days. He had a car. That made him valuable to me back then. After I graduated and went into the Army, we drifted apart like many of the early friendships did. Why did he suddenly show up at Diana's at this time of the day? The answer is that it isn't a coincidence.

Was that half assed hug so he could check to see if I was packing?

"Hi, Annie!" Joey said, acknowledging her. "I need to borrow Red for a couple of minutes. I have a guy at my table that wants to see him. It's not trouble. It's a courtesy call."

While Joey was talking with Annie, I looked over at the table where he was sitting. I thought I recognized the guy as the bartender that used to let us into the German Club when I was seventeen. He looked much older, and I probably would never have recognized him except for the one feature on his head. His right ear stuck out about an inch further than his left, almost like the handle of a water pitcher. I never knew his real name. Everyone called him Wolf, as I recalled. I called him Dumbo.

"Go! You just make sure you get back before our dinner gets here."

"You remember Wolf don't you Red? He's the one that use to let us into the German Club twenty years ago. His name is Wolfgang Berne. He has a message for you. It's from the third man. The German you didn't kill on Carson Street last week."

I stopped for just a moment to absorb what Joey had just told me. Who is this guy Hans that has reached back that far in my life to a German kid I first met when I was fourteen? Is it just a coincidence, or is there more like him over in Germantown?

Wolf stood up as I approached the table and extended his hand to me. I ignored the gesture. If this guy was close enough to get a message from Hans, then he's on my short list of punks that need killing.

"What the fuck do you want?" I asked as I looked into this guy's eyes. I didn't like what I saw. He had the cold eyes of a killer. I'd seen that same cold look many times in the eyes of the murderers in the cells and courtrooms I'd been in over the last twenty years.

"I want you to know I'm not with this guy. I only bring you a message from him because I don't want him to kill me. He told me to tell you he is going to kill you and your girlfriend and your retarded relative if he doesn't get what he wants by tomorrow noon. You are to leave everything with me at the German Club along with a hundred thousand dollars. That's the message."

I was staring coldly at him and Joey. If I wasn't in this restaurant, Wolf would be eating the butt of my Glock, and Joey would become a singing soprano in the German Club choir. I couldn't smack these guys around right now… I'll do it later at Wreckers' yard. The story that Wolf told me is bullshit. The truth will come out in the earlier hours of the morning.

"Joey, you two meet me tonight at Wreckers Junk Yard up on the Hill at two A.M. Bring the German bastards with you. I'll have the goods with me."

"What about the money?" Joey spit out at me.

"No money, just the goods. That's what the Kraut really wants, isn't it? If you two aren't there, then I'll know you were trying to run a scam on me. That would be bad for your health. Verstehen you two Nazi assholes? Now, get the fuck out of this place!"

I knew enough German from watching Hogan's Heroes to translate the word understand into German. Neither one of them had a response, but before I headed back to my table, I had one more question for them.

"How did you two know I was here at Diana's'?"

"I called the bar and whoever answered the phone told me you were having dinner here at six," Joey answered as I turned my back to him.

He started to tell me he was only here with Wolf because he was friends with both of us, but he didn't want his buddy Wolf killed.

I stopped, turned, and took a few steps back to where he was standing so I could get in his face.

"Fuck you, Joey! We're not friends. It's all business between us now. All fucking business! Blow out of here now before I take care of business with the two of you right here."

I was angry and troubled. This fucking guy, Hans, must have some powerful friends in high places in some government agencies. He has, too! He knows too much about me for it to be a coincidence. He knew about my office, Annie, Jimmy and his condition, the two cons I put away that were recently paroled and are back out on the street, and now a German kid I hung out with when I was in high school and an obscure bartender from a club I got bombed in when I was underage. Who the hell am I up against?

I need to take a link out of this chain that's tightening around my neck. I have to kill Hans. I must break the chain.

# CHAPTER 24

The dinner at Diana's' was uneventful after the two goons left. She asked if I'd sign a few menus and wave to some of her curious patrons. For that little inconvenience, she ate the tab. I like the notoriety I'm receiving, I think.

Back at the IG, before I excused myself and went upstairs to make a couple of phone calls, I told Annie never to leave word with the help of where we were going. You can always call in if you're concerned about something back at the bar.

One Eye Eddie was my first call on the list. It was almost eight, and I wanted to catch him before he left his place. I needed him to bring some heavy-duty hardware with him. We'd need more firepower tonight at Wrecker's junkyard.

Then, I called Wrecker to set up the meet at his place tonight. His first reaction was to tell me to take my party somewhere else, but not exactly in those words. I changed his mind when I reminded him that he owes me for setting him up as a private eye on my payroll. I needed his help on this case. When I told him I intended to kill some bad guys, it seemed to turn him around. He couldn't resist the opportunity to kill some honkeys.

Annie was giving me a cold stare.

"Red, you're going out late tonight, aren't you? You're in no condition to start a fight with Hans. You're limping from the bullet wound in your leg. It hasn't had enough time to heal properly. Do you want to get yourself killed?"

I ignored her and worked at the bar. It was almost ten o'clock when one eye Eddie walked in. I headed toward the kitchen and motioned for him to follow. I wanted to get an inventory of the weapons he brought with him. My shotgun was still impounded, but I bought another one on the street a couple of days ago. I'll find out tonight if it will fire. Eddie was just beginning to tell me what he had in his trunk when Wrecker walked in the open back door of the kitchen.

"You can use the front door now, Wrecker. Lincoln fixed that."

"Fuck you… you honkey mothafucker. I didn't use the front door 'cause I didn't want anyone that might know me to see me coming into this honkey shit hole."

I could see one eye, Eddie, looking at Wrecker and getting ready to hammer him.

"You have any more shines with you? Red needs two porters to work tonight with you," Eddie blurted out while looking right at Wrecker through the only visual portal he had left feeding his brain.

"Fuck you too, Cyclops. I remember you when you were on the beat up on the Hill. A couple of brothers from there fucked you up. They put you on pension and you lost your free doughnut pass. You here in the kitchen lookin for a handout?" Wrecker fired back at Eddie.

I had to stop the chatter between these two before one of them started reaching for hardware.

"Both of you shut the fuck up! We're all on the same side. You can pick it up again later if you make it off the Hill later tonight. The people showing up at the junkyard are led by a professional. This German guy is well trained in handing out death."

Before I could get out my next sentence One Eye Eddie jumped in with the info he captured for me off the visitor records at Danora for the two cons that

Hans hired to replace the two I wacked on Carson Street.

"That name you gave me, Delmons Edwards, was a visitor to Gaston and Carpenter eleven times in the last five years. In the last six months before they were paroled, he was there six times. His last visit was three days before they were released. I'd say there is a relationship with them."

"That puts your yardman with Hans and the two brothers. He is working in your yard and planning to knock you off. The three of them are probably looking for a big payday and grabbing power on the Hill. They would get that power on the Hill from knocking you off," I said, looking at Wrecker and waiting for his take on my read.

"That could be, Red. The three of them could have been looking to put a hit on me. Then, this foreign guy shows up with cash, looking for an army. Somehow, he finds Willie and Raymond, who have Delmons inside my yard. And now that I'm running with you, they get a chance at some fast cash from the foreigner to cap you, and I'm just a bonus. I don't buy it. Those fucking punks are too stupid to make a plan. The three of them dumb motherfuckers still think the earth is flat. Shit just happens sometimes, Red, like the case you're on."

"In the end it doesn't matter. All that matters tonight is that Hans gets taken down. He has five men with him that I'm sure of. There may be more."

"I got three M-16s and six four hundred and fifty round magazines," Eddie blurted out.

I looked at one eye Eddie and Wrecker Johnson and the blood stain on my right pants leg and I thought of what Annie had said to me earlier about not being in good enough physical condition to tackle Hans. She was right! I wasn't physically ready to have a two A.M. shootout at Wrecker's junkyard with Hans. He would have to wait. A fifty-five-year-old one-eyed retired cop an undisciplined street fighter and a wounded Red Canyon would be no match for Hans tonight. I wanted him on my turf anyway, the Southside, so I'd send a surrogate… the cops. I'd drop a dime on him.

"Let's go out to the bar and have some drinks while I figure out how we handle this situation."

"I know how to handle tonight. I take one of those three machine guns with me and shoot the shit out of them," was Wrecker's solution.

It was simple and would probably work if all I wanted was five dead punks and a dead German. I wanted Hans alive, but I'd have to leave that up to the cops and Hans. Eddie and Wrecker didn't know that my plan for us had changed. We would be spectators tonight. How was I going to keep Wrecker from going back to his junkyard tonight?

When we walked into the barroom, I could see there were no empty stools at the bar. I started to head to the dining room and an empty booth when Wrecker grabbed my arm.

"I ain't sittin in no fucking back room. I ride in the front of the bus," Wrecker announced loud enough for most of the crowd in the bar to hear.

I tapped the guy on the shoulder closest to me, "Move! You and the two bums sitting next to you are in our seats," I said it loud enough so the three of them could hear me.

They all turned to look at the guy who had just punked them. The look in the middle guys' eyes spelled trouble. He probably had enough juice in him to want to fight. Just then, Sparks told the three of them that I was Red Canyon, and they better move. He told them he'd set them up with a couple of free drinks and they reluctantly got their asses up off the bar stools and were moving. Everything was working out until the one walking closest to Wrecker gave him the bad eyes.

"What you looking at motherfucker?" I heard Wrecker say.

That was the tipping point for the one in the middle. The one I thought could be trouble. Five minutes later after a ripped shirt, a couple of broken tables and glasses, order was restored. One eye Eddie had seen enough of me and Wrecker trading punches with a dozen or so tough guys that wanted a piece of the notorious Red Canyon. He flashed a badge and pulled out his service revolver and the fight broke up.

Eddie, Sparks, and Spooks grabbed a half dozen punks and began pushing them out the door with a warning from Eddie not to come back, or he'd lock them up.

"You owe me nine hundred for damages," I heard Annie call out to me.

"Make it a thousand and get some better tables next time, the kind that don't break too easy."

"You're always a smart ass, Red, always!"

"There are two things I like about you, Red. That's one of them, and I don't remember the other. Now, is anybody gonna put some drinks in front of us or do we start some more shit in here, Red?" Wrecker was telling me through the swollen lower lip he must have gotten in the fight.

"Tell Annie what you want to drink, but she doesn't have any grape or green pop to make you any of those mixed drinks like you people fix up on the Hill."

"Now, there's only one thing I like about you Red. Just bring me a bottle of scotch and a beer in the bottle. I don't want to drink out of any glasses that the dirty finger nailed bartender washed. Just give me some paper cups."

Annie looked at me and Wrecker with the look I know that means she had had enough from both of us.

"The two of you can take your asses down the block to Kupka's gin mill. That's a good place for your fight club. You can pick up there where you left off here, but if you two want to stay here, knock off the verbal brawl."

I looked at her and nodded. Wrecker mumbled something, but the only word I heard clearly was bitch.

Now, I had to jump in and tell Annie we were both good with that before she responded to the bitch thing from Wrecker.

Eddie came back in from escorting the troublemakers outside the bar. The stool next to me was open and Eddie sat down and began to recap what went down out on the sidewalk.

"I don't know which of you hit the guy with a broken jaw. He's heading to the hospital. The guy with the busted-up face said to tell Annie she'd be hearing from their lawyers and you too, Red."

I didn't give a fuck. I felt good, good. It was Saturday night on the Southside, and I just had a fight in a bar. It was like the old days; me having a bar fight on a Saturday night. Yeah, I really felt good. That was just what I needed to kick my ass back in gear… We'll dance with Hans tonight.

# CHAPTER 25

After a few drinks at the bar, I managed to get Wrecker and Eddie to a booth in the rear dining room. A strategy was developing in my mind. The snag was manpower. I didn't know where Jimmy was or when he'd show up. He may be on one of his mind trips. Maybe!

"I want to take the German alive. We kill him only if it's him or us. Is everyone clear about how to deal with Hans?"

"Why did you set this up tonight if not to kill these punks? They're out to kill you! Do you really think this guy Hans will surrender? I'm going to shoot to kill any punk that's shooting at me."

"I'm not saying don't kill these punks, Eddie; I'm just saying if any of us get the drop on the German, don't kill him. He has a piece of the puzzle for the case I'm working on. Once I've had a chance to question him, then I'll off him myself for his murder of those two old ladies he left in a dumpster in the alley behind my office."

Annie came in the back and told me Jimmy called from my house and said he'd be right over.

"He said to tell you he was at Walter Reed visiting his buddy and brought him back home with him. He needs a place to stay for a while."

I needed Jimmy tonight, but not with the kid who lost his hands. When he gets here, I'll let him decide if he's in or out.

"Wrecker, what kind of lighting do you have in the yard? Do you have perimeter lighting and are there any spotlights around the inside of the yard?"

"Yeah, I got spots on a dozen poles inside my fence and some scattered around the yard where I needed them. What's up with that?"

"Do you leave them on all night?"

"No! Only the yard lights stay on all night. The perimeter lighting is timed to go off at midnight."

"Can you control them from the trailer?"

"Yeah! The control box is in my office in the trailer."

"What are you thinking, Red?" Eddie asked.

"I'm thinking about getting an edge on Hans and his punks."

Wrecker jumped in with, "If any of them punks show up at the yard before we get there, my dogs will chew their asses up. The two of them run free in the yard when we lock up."

"What about your man, Delmons? He has the key to the gate and knows the dogs, doesn't he? That means he can get in and chain the dogs up and then let everyone inside to set up an ambush. Am I right?"

"You're right about that, Red. I didn't count on that walking dead mutherfucker, Delmons, being with them. So, what do we do?"

"We wait for Jimmy and have another drink."

The plan I had in mind needed another man I could trust. Jimmy was the only one that fit. He knew how to handle an M-16 and was trained as a sniper. That part of his military career was flushed down the toilet when he was wounded. If his brain didn't short circuit tonight, the plan could work.

I was about to dump a bottle of Rock down when Jimmy walked in the back door with Billy, the wounded vet from Walter Reed. Now, he had two new hands that looked pretty good. They were certainly better than those fucked up hooks they use to stick onto the stumps.

"Where you been at for the last four days Jimmy?"

"I took a bus to Walter Reed to get Billy signed out so I could bring him back to the City with me. I figured he could help you with that paperwork you have. He's a computer ace," Jimmy bragged.

Yeah, I could use his help setting the paperwork into an organized data file, but right now I need Jimmy. I need a shooter.

"This is Billy. He's one of our wounded war heroes," I said as I introduced him to Wrecker and one eye Eddie.

"Billy knows about the case we're on. I've been filling him in the last couple of days. He likes taking out bad guys as much as us."

"We have a date with Hans tonight. Are you up to it, Jimmy?"

"Yeah, Red, we both are."

Now, I begin thinking. There's me, Wrecker, one eye Eddie, Jimmy with a plate in his head and Billy without any hands Maybe I should go out on Carson Street and look for someone in a fucking wheelchair and Ray Charles.I'm fucked! Maybe………

"Wrecker, do you have a tow truck running tonight?"

"I tow for the City so the business is on call 24/7."

"Can you get your tow truck over to the Southside to pick up your car between twelve thirty and one o'clock?"

"Yeah, I could, but why the fuck would I wanna do that?"

"I'll explain later. Just do it!"

Hans will have men inside the yard well before two o'clock so they can set their ambush before we arrive. I need to get Jimmy into the yard unnoticed. I figured he could take his Glock and an M-16 and ride into the yard in the trunk of Wreckers' car. When the car is dropped close to the trailer, Jimmy can climb from the trunk into the passenger compartment. Wrecker will tell his driver where he wants his car dropped. Eddie will follow close behind us and block the gates after we are inside the trailer with instructions to kill anyone trying to get out. When me and Wrecker get into the trailer, he'll go to the control box for the lights and turn them off for thirty seconds, just enough time for Jimmy to exit the vehicle and take up a position with his aim at the three black guys with Hans if he can. If they're not together… Oh, well!

That will be his target. I'll turn this ambush into a trap for Hans and his scumbag pals.

I explained the plan to everyone and asked if they had any questions, but I already knew the answer. They all had the usual what ifs questions which could only be answered with just 'follow the plan, and if it breakdowns, protect yourself.

"Remember, I want all the white guys alive. The three black guys are expendable."

Wrecker started to humorously spout that racist crap. The white guys would have their chance to catch up. I looked at Wrecker.

"Make those four black guys that are expendable."

"I'm taking Billy with me too!" Jimmy announced. He would usually ask me first, especially on something this big. He was telling me that's how it's going to be. There was no time for me to negotiate.

"Billy is in! Eddie, give him your extra gun and an M-16." I reluctantly agreed to Jimmy's demand. Wrecker and Eddie didn't care. They both told me they wouldn't babysit either one of them. The team was complete. There was no time to find a guy in a wheelchair.

Annie came into the dining room and asked to see me upstairs in her apartment. I knew what was coming. It didn't matter what she wanted when it came to this case. I had three career criminals from the Hill, two locals, Wolf and Joey, and a Pro, Hans, to neutralize. His army gets wiped out tonight, and I solve the mystery of Horst Strumps murder.

"What suit do you want me to have you laid out in?" Annie asked without any emotion in her voice.

"I'll tell you when I get back in later tonight."

"Do you really think you're going to make it back here, Red?"

"This is just a meeting with Hans to discuss the peace terms."

"That's why you're taking a group that belongs in a supervised home for the mentally and physically challenged?"

"Don't give me that politically correct bullshit. Say it! You mean mentally retarded and freaks, don't you? I'm only taking them with me tonight to bring my dead body back to the Southside. Remember, you think I'm getting wacked tonight. Anything else, Annie?"

"Don't do it, Red! Dump this case. Walk away. I'll back you till you get yourself set up again. I have plenty of money. You walked into a whirlwind, and it's going to suck both of us up into it."

"I'm going to make sure you're clear tonight. I'm going to put Hans in Dirtland next to his comrades and under the two old ladies he killed. That's unfinished business; I can't let go. I owe it to those two old broads. You know me better than anyone, Annie. You know I have to make the payback to the German."

"Yes, I do know you, Red, and I know you believe that you have to do this, but do you have to risk Jimmy and his friend with no hands?"

"They'll be safe. Only me and Wrecker are taking part in the meeting. The other three will be under cover and out of harm's way. I promise you! I can handle it!" I said confidently because I can handle the action tonight. Maybe…

Annie came over and put her arms around me and gave me a kiss, the kind she'd given me before when she thought I wasn't coming back to her. I couldn't change her feelings. To do that, I'd have to cancel the meeting tonight. So, Annie will have to ride it out again.

Jimmy came upstairs to Annie's to tell me the tow truck had arrived. I hugged Annie and returned downstairs to the dining room to begin the junkyard phase of the Strump case.

"Jimmy, do you understand what you and Billy are to do? I want you to listen to my instructions one last time. When the tow truck drops the car and unhooks it, you wait till you're sure the driver is gone, then you climb into the passenger compartment and wait till you see me and Wrecker go into the trailer, and the yard lights go out. When the yard goes dark you both exit the vehicle and hide yourselves among the wrecks all the time scanning the yard to locate six of the Hans gang. You are not to take anyone out. I'll do that. I expect two or three of the bad guys to come to the trailer. If I go down, kill everyone you see except Wrecker, and then head to the main gate. Eddie will be waiting. The three of you head to the bar. Wrecker will get me out of there."

Of course, I'd probably be dead if Jimmy had to kill the rest of the bad guys.

Wrecker had the driver come into the bar and have a drink while Jimmy and Billy secured themselves in the trunk. When One Eye gave the all clear, Wrecker sent his driver on his way back to his junk yard. There was no stopping now.

I took Wrecker with me. Eddie was right behind us as we tailed the tow truck. I'd stop far back enough from the yard so we wouldn't be seen but close enough so I could observe the drop. I watched as the driver opened the locks on the two chains that provided security on the gates of the chain link fence. From where we were parked, I could see the trailer and the open spot Wreckers' car was being positioned in. From that location, Jimmy and Billy would be able to move to cover and have a line of sight on the trailer when the lights were turned back on. Maybe they might locate the Hill boys. Wolf and Joey would eventually be coming to the trailer after we entered it carrying the empty liquor boxes I brought from the bar. They would serve as a decoy for the files I was to bring tonight.

I knew that some bad guys were going to be killed tonight. My plan was to do all the killing. Well, maybe me and Wrecker. Delmons would be dead tonight by Wreckers' hand. The street code he lived by would demand it. The two cons and Hans would be my targets. I didn't want Jimmy and Billy getting into any legal mess if four more dead bodies showed up on the city streets.

"You have been down on all fours for the last five years doing punk ass security and divorce bullshit. How do you jump from there to the big time?"

"My reputation brought the client to me. The bigger agencies told the client that I was the only one in the City that could solve the fifteen-year-old homicide and they sent her to me."

"In plain language, Red, nobody else wanted the fucking job. That's the truth, isn't it, Red?"

That conversation was over. I had to move on to the meeting, it was one forty-five. Wrecker was most likely right.

"You don't have to go in with me, Wrecker. It's my problem. I can handle it alone."

"You set this deal up in my junkyard. That puts me in."

"If there's any killing, you stay out of it. I'll pull the trigger when the time comes." They were words most likely wasted on this hardheaded son-of-a-bitch.

"If some bitches that need killing are in my yard tonight, I ain't letting you have all the action. You cap who you want, and I'll cap who I want. These punks are here to get what they think is in the empty boxes. Whether they are full or empty, you're gonna be dead, and me with you. That's their plan. Ain't it, Red?" Wrecker figured it out and was making his own plan. Maybe…!

"Yeah, that's the plan the German has. I don't think the others have a plan. He won't want to kill me when he finds out I brought empty boxes."

"I don't know what those white boys want to do to you, but I know that the three brothers are gonna kill you regardless of what that foreign motherfucker wants."

"I want you to hold off killing anyone unless I say to. Give me your word."

"Yeah, Red, you got my word," he told me as he turned away. Probably had his fingers crossed.

I knew Wrecker was blowing smoke up my ass, but in the end, it won't matter if he kills Hans before I get what I want from him.

What did I really want to happen tonight? I had to ask myself that question again. Did I just want to kill some street punks that got tied in with Hans?

I needed to eliminate Hans. That's the reason. He made a threat to Annie and Jimmy. Joey and Wolf will stay away from me after Hans is dead. Without Hans there's no payoff. If they're smart, they won't show tonight. If they do show, then they're still on Han's payroll and I'll have to deal with them as a serious threat. Too bad for them.

I made a call to Eddie and told him not to close the gates until he hears the first shot. He knows the sound of a bullet being fired.

I gave a quick look at Wrecker and pulled out on the street on my way to the junkyard trailer. That's where it will all come down. I should have dropped a dime on them… Maybe…

# CHAPTER 26

I PULLED up to the front gates and stopped while Wrecker got out and opened the two locks that held the security chains together. The tow truck driver had been gone for almost five minutes. He pushed one gate open and waited until I entered the yard before he walked back to the car. We drove the hundred yards to the trailer as I tightened my police issued vest. I offered one to Wrecker, but he refused.

"Don't you start the shooting, but when it breaks out, you have to get to the control panel and turn off all the lights in and around the yard. We're easy targets in the trailer."

"You turn off the lights. I'm going to be busy killing some honky motherfuckers and some Hill niggers."

"Just don't kill the German. I want him to be alive. That means you don't shoot any white guys because you don't know what the two white assholes working for Hans look like. That means all white guys look like Hans to you. Got it?"

"What are you gonna do? You gonna shoot me if take a shot at a honky?"

"Yeah, Wrecker, I'm gonna shoot you if I have to. That's how important it is to me to take Hans alive. We don't have to go there unless you push it there. The two white punks that got mixed up with Hans are small time bums and haven't done anything yet to earn a dead card. They know better than to be carrying when they show up. What they did earn was a beating. That's something you can do, but not until they lead us to Hans. Maybe…"

"I'll play it your way to a certain extent. I ain't making any more promises, Red."

The only thing I was trying to do with Wrecker was to restrain him from killing the white guys. At some point tonight he was going to cap Delmons for trying to set him up. I was going to try to take Hans down before that happened. I was ready for about anything.

We entered the trailer and walked the twenty feet to his office through the path of used auto parts and boxes of unfiled papers. The windows in the trailer were boarded up except for the two that were opposite each other in his office. He had a view through those windows of the front area and the rear area of the junkyard.

"Turn off all the lighting," I said to Wrecker as I took a quick look out both windows, searching for anything that could give me an edge tonight if this became a street fight.

The yard went dark. The streetlights on the blocks surrounding the junkyard provided the only hint of light around the perimeter and into the yard. I told Wrecker to turn them back on after thirty seconds. Jimmy and Billy should be in place somewhere close to the trailer. Now, we wait for Hans to play his hand.

Wrecker and I sat in silence for what seemed like an hour. It was only five minutes. The headlights of a slow-moving vehicle broke through the shadows created by the irregular shapes of the skeletons of old and wrecked American, Japanese, and even German vehicles. Maybe I'd use a VW for Hans's casket. It slowed down and stopped for an instant and then continued its way. They probably picked up one of the snipers that arrived at the yard before me and Wrecker, or they were dropping someone off.

"Wrecker, I don't recall you having to chain up the dogs when we entered the yard. You didn't have to, did you?"

"No! Delmons is usually in the yard before me and he puts them in their pen. I heard them bark when we came in, but I didn't think about it."

"Delmons was here inside the yard before we got here. Those other two punks are with him and maybe some others like Hans. We didn't bring in the empty boxes that we brought for show and tell either. Let's go meet the guys parking the car out front. Remember, no shooting until I say so."

I didn't like the blind spot created by the boarded-up windows in the rest of the trailer. From what I could briefly see it looked like three men were in the car. It probably was Delmons, Wolf and Joey. I heard two car doors open and close and footsteps coming up the four steps that lead to the platform in front of the entrance door. I was still feeling uneasy not being able to observe what was coming at me. Then a familiar voice to Wrecker broke the silence.

"Wrecker, it's me, Delmons. I'm coming in!"

I looked over at Wrecker and was about to give him another warning about gun play, but I was too late. He had his .45 out and pointed at the door; fired three rounds through it just as the handle began to turn. Whoever had the handle in their grip on the other side of the door, probably Delmons, was now a ghost. I could only hope it wasn't Hans.

"You dumb son of a bitch! You just blew up any chance to capture Hans. Get to the lights and shut them off in the yard."

I knew this was now going to be a shootout. I flipped the lights out in the part of the trailer we were using and headed to the door to finish what Wrecker started.

I heard the angry sounds of someone cursing as they fell back off the platform and down the steps to the ground. The impact of a body flying backwards carrying Wreckers two a.m. greeting would have caught the other unsuspecting punks off guard and caused their dilemma. I heard the crack of gunfire as bullets started flying through the thin trailer walls. I quickly opened the door and dove to the wooden platform decking, not knowing what I might encounter there. It was clear, but I saw movement on the ground at the bottom of the steps as two men were pushing a body off them. I began scanning the darkness looking for the flash of gunfire so I could line up a shot. It got quiet. No more incoming fire. I wondered where Wrecker was. It didn't matter. There were headlights speeding up the carved-out entrance road. I told Eddie to block the fucking gate. Is he down, too?

"You, assholes on the ground! Don't fucking move or I'll kill you."

"Don't shoot, Red, it's me and Wolf. We ain't carrying. We ain't moving, just don't shoot!"

I had a major problem. I have a car racing up the driveway that could be carrying more of Hans's men. I have some other shooters out in the darkness of the junkyard and Wrecker hiding out in the trailer. It looks like Jimmy and Billy decided to sit this one out. No, that would never happen. They must be in trouble. If they're not dead, What! Was Annie right about me not being up to taking on Hans tonight? This junkyard war just started. They have one down, and I don't know about us, but I'm betting on Jimmy and Billy. These two are hardened war veterans and know how to fight dirty. They're alright. They have to be.

The speeding vehicle was almost at the entrance to the trailer parking lot when it stopped. I saw the driver's door open and lined it up with my Glock. Whoever was behind the door was about to catch some hollow point slugs out of my weapon. The interior passenger light and the headlights gave me an easy to find target. Hans would have one less shooter in the yard. Then I heard the fucking elevator music from the station that one eye Eddie always plays too loudly on his car radio.

"Red! Red! Are you okay? It's Eddie. Answer me if you're out there. I'm about to M-16 the whole fucking junkyard. Where are you?" I heard one eye, Eddie, calling out to me.

"Stay where you are, Eddie. Take a bead on the two scumbags lying at the bottom of the stairs in front of the trailer. If either one of them moves, drill them both… and turn off the fucking radio and your headlights. There are still a couple of shooters hiding in the yard."

I pulled myself up off the deck and searched for a sign of Jimmy or the cons from the Hill. I crouched and moved from the deck down the steps and over Delmons dead body and past Wolf and Joey.

I had some advice for them as I passed by. "Don't move till I tell you to move. You better hope I get back because if I don't, you're both dead." I wanted them to be scared. If they had more fear of me than Hans, then I could use them to draw him into me. If I didn't accomplish that tonight, then they might both join Delmons.

"Red, it's Jimmy. Walk straight back from the trailer to the blue Chevy pick-up with the hood and motor missing. I'm in between the Chevy and the wreck on the left," Jimmy called out in his usual calm manner.

"Keep talking Jimmy. I'll head toward your voice. I can't tell one wreck from another with the clouds blocking the moonlight."

Where were Gaston and Carpenter? After the initial rounds fired into the trailer, the shooters must have beat it. How did they get past Eddie? Oh yeah, that wouldn't be too difficult since Eddie abandoned the gate and headed to the trailer. The plan was working fine if chaos was the plan.

Jimmy kept calling to me until I met up with him standing in a narrow space between a blue Chevy pickup and a rusty something.

"I heard the rounds coming from this part of the yard, but I never considered that you took one of the bullets. I heard you tell One Eye Eddie that you had one down and two on the ground."

"Wrecker capped that punk Delmons through the closed door of the trailer. The guys on the ground are Joey from the Southside Hollow and a bartender from the German Club he brought with him. They're two dumb losers trying to make a buck that picked the wrong game to get into. The shooters that fired into the trailer could still be in the yard. We need to find them and take them out." I was waiting for more incoming fire from what was left of Hans's gang.

"The two shooters are still in the yard."

"How do you know that, Jimmy?"

"Follow me, Red, and I'll show you how I know."

Jimmy began snaking his way through stacks of junks separated by aisles just wide enough to get through to remove the valuable parts for resale. The paths were strewn with broken glass and scraps of what was once a bracket or fastener that held the parts of the wrecks in place. The kind of junk you would expect to find here in an automobile junkyard. He stopped abruptly and pointed in the direction of an intersecting aisle. I guessed that he wanted me to look at something. After I refocused my eyes in the dim light, I saw what he was pointing at. There on the ground was the body of one of the shooters or some poor unlucky bastard who was grabbing what he thought was a safe night of sleep away from the dangerous streets of the Hill.

"Roll him over for me. I want to see his face."

I bent down close to the body as Jimmy turned it over. There was a massive blood stain on the lower back area of the body and a puddle of blood on the ground under it.

"I did him just like I did the others in Iraq. He never made a sound as I disrupted his central nervous system with my boot knife."

That last sentence was right out of a training manual describing what happens to an enemy combatant when you shove an eight-inch razor sharp steel boot knife into the lower region of the spine.

I recognized the stiff as Ali Shabaz, alias Willie Gaston.

"Where's Billy? Is he safe?"

"Follow me, Red."

I was behind Jimmy walking through more of this maze of junk vehicles that brought thoughts to me of the maze puzzles in the newspapers.

Jimmy stopped at the second cross aisle and pointed to his right. There, standing next to another body was Billy. I was relieved to see he was alive.

I could guess at the identity of the corpse on the ground near Billy's feet.

"Move out of the light so I can see the face. How'd he get it?"

The face belonged to Raymond Carpenter, the other half of the cons on Hans's payroll.

"Billy choked him out with his new hands. You should have seen it, Red. After we took out the first punk, we went looking for this one. We watched as these two fired some rounds into the trailer and then scattered. We saw them head into junkyard city near a pickup, and we circled them. We were standing between these wrecks when this one walked by, and as he crossed us, Billy grabbed him around the neck and choked him out. You should have seen it. He squeezed his neck so fucking hard that he almost popped his eyeballs out of his head. He's got bionic hands like in that TV show."

I didn't want the two of them to kill anyone. How would you handle it… the killing again.

"Are you two okay with taking out these two punks, or are you both going to need counseling?" I asked in my smart-ass way.

"I'm good, but maybe you should get Billy some counseling from your two hooker friends. He's gonna need a couple of treatments. Ain't that right, Billy?"

I had my answer.

These two just wacked a couples of low lives that needed killing. Who knows how many future robberies and murders they stopped by eliminating these sewer scums? I wasn't serious about the counseling, but I'd get Billy set up for a session with those hookers. There's nothing too good for our military.

"Let's go back to the trailer. I have two guys on the ground with Eddie watching them and I have to find out what happened to Wrecker. He may have taken some slugs when these two fired into the trailer."

As we walked back to the trailer, I began thinking about how I was going to clean up the mess. I had to get rid of three bodies and keep the cops out of it. Right now, the only leaks could come from Wolf and Joey. They only know about Delmons being capped. Would they be too big a risk for me to let go? Maybe!

When I reached the steps of the trailer, I told Eddie to stand down and ordered Joey and Wolf to get on their feet and get inside. I didn't know what to expect inside it. Wrecker never followed me out. Could be that Hans or another one of his minions is inside waiting. If that's the case, then Joey or Wolf will catch the slugs meant for me.

Joey was in front of Wolf and opened the door to the darkness inside. There was no sound from Wrecker or shots being fired.

"There's a light switch on the wall to the right of the door. Turn it on and back out onto the deck and freeze."

As they backed out, I pushed my way past them and entered the trailer looking for Wrecker. I found him sprawled out on the floor some five feet from his office door with blood still dripping from the wound I could see on his head. He wasn't moving. My first thoughts were that he was dead and must have caught one of the incoming bullets fired from the two dead punks in the yard, the unlucky bastard.

My police training took over, and I went to the body to feel a pulse at the neck, just as I had done so many times before in the last twenty years.

"Eddie, come in here! Let Jimmy keep a gun on the two on the deck. I need your help. Wrecker's still alive, but he's not moving."

Eddie had seen more emergency personnel work on half dead individuals over his career than me. The bodies I left on the street didn't need the EMT. They usually needed the coroner.

"Take a look at Wrecker and see if you can help him or tell me if he's finished. It looks like he took a shot to the head."

Eddie knelt next to Wrecker, pulled out his handkerchief and wiped the blood from the wound in his head.

"He ain't been shot, Red. It looks like he's been hit in the head by something. He's just knocked out. When he comes around, he's gonna have one hell of a headache. You know that you can't kill one of these shines with a single blow to the head. Think of how many times you had to bounce a billy club off their heads to get them down on the ground."

"What would the EMT guys do, Eddie?"

"They'd patch him up, load him on a stretcher, and take him to the emergency room."

"So, maybe we should call them?"

"No, maybe we should go outside and put a couple of slugs in the two fags on the deck; come back inside and put the gun in Wreckers' hand… turn the lights off in the trailer and go back to the IG and have some fucking drinks."

"I was thinking the same thing. It would be payback for him fucking up everything when he shot the punk, Delmons, through the door."

Not too far from where Wrecker was stretched out was a pile of old starters some of which had fresh blood on them. Wrecker must have walked toward his office, tripped, hit his head on the pile of starters, and knocked himself out. He had just turned all the yard lights off and I put the trailer lights off seconds after he threw the switch to the outside lighting. Didn't he tell me earlier that sometimes shit just happens? I'll remind him of that when he comes to and starts bitching.

"Eddie, let's find some water so I can pour it on his face and try to wake him."

Looking around the trailer, I could see he didn't have a water cooler. There was just the inside of the outside. I did see a bottle that said grape nectar on it sitting on some boxes marked save. That would have to do for now. If he wouldn't come around, I'd have to dump him in my ride and take him to the Mercy emergency room less than a mile from here. I'd try the grape pop first. Eddie stopped looking when he saw me with the pop bottle.

"If there ain't enough in the bottle, I could piss on his head. I don't mind helping out."

I ignored Eddie and got the bottle and poured it on Wreckers head and watched as the grape liquid mixed with his blood and turned black as it trickled down the side of his face. Did the colors mix and turn black because Wrecker was black, or would it have changed to black if a white guy's blood mixed with the bottle of grape nectar? I'll have to try it one day and see: maybe on Hans.

He slowly opened his eyes and tried to focus on me. The first words he mumbled were, "I knew God was white! I'm dead; right?"

"You're not dead, Wrecker. You fell when you were on your way into your office and hit your head. You've been unconscious for the last half hour."

I helped him sit up while he tried to pull himself together. He's been knocked out before in his fight career and he knows how to recover. It may take a little longer tonight.

"Now I remember. You shut the lights off in the trailer, and I had to stumble through the door in the dark. That's why I tripped. As soon as I stop seeing double of one of you in front of me, I'm gonna put a cap in your ass. Who poured some grape shit on me? I can smell it!"

"I did. You don't have a water cooler in this dumpster and the only thing I saw was a half full bottle of grape nectar sitting on a box marked save. I didn't think that the save was meant for the stuff in the bottle."

"You always have to be a smart ass, don't you, Red? I can't stand up just yet or I'd go into my office and get a beer from my refrigerator. You do it for me, Red. Get me a beer so I can wash this shit off my head. That bottle had spit and cigarette butts in it. You probably just poured AIDS into the gash on my fucking head."

"Do you have a first aid kit?" I asked him, expecting a no answer.

"Yeah, I got a first aid kit. I run a business, and you have to have one for the insurance company. It's on the shelf over the refrigerator. You bring it in here and I'll fix myself up. Get me a mirror so I can see what I'm doing."

"Where am I going to find you a mirror?"

"Try out in the yard. There are a thousand of them in the cars piled up out there. Pick one."

I sent Eddie to go outside and rip a mirror of one of the junks stored in the yard. That was an easy enough assignment. It took him only minutes until he returned with a mirror in his hand that he said he got from the driver's side door of a wreck out front. I handed it to Wrecker along with the first aid kit. He could begin his repair. It was obvious he was feeling better. Things were strangely quiet in the trailer, and it looked like Eddie and Wrecker decided to call a truce from the bullshit they're always exchanging. I called it too soon.

"You, motherfucker! You, mother-motherfucker!" Wrecker screamed out at Eddie with the angriest voice he could manage.

I stared at Wrecker, wondering what prompted his sudden and angry outburst. "What the hell are you pissed off about? He got you what you asked for. A mirror, so you could see the gash in your head to patch it up."

"Ask that motherfucker where he got it from."

I looked at Eddie and noticed just the hint of a smile. It was the kind of a smile you want someone to notice that you're making but can still deny that you're making it.

"Where did you get the mirror, Eddie?"

"I did like you told me, Red. I went outside in the junkyard and found a pile of shit to rip the mirror from and brought it in for him. That's it."

"Ask him again where he got it."

"Where was the car you got it off of?"

"It was across from the trailer. What's it matter?"

"Okay, Wrecker, what's it matter? You got a lot of junkers across from the trailer."

"Yeah, Red, there are a lot of junkers across from the trailer. Do you remember where you had my Caddy towed and dropped in my yard? It was across from the trailer. That one eyed fat old bastard ripped the driver's side mirror off my fucking Caddy and I'm gonna rip the ear off that Quasimodo look alike."

"Eddie, why the hell did you rip his mirror off? Tell me it wasn't on purpose," I told him to answer me even though I was sure he knew exactly what he was doing; getting under Wreckers' skin.

"Red, it's fucking dark out there, and I went to the closest junk that had the biggest mirror on it. That's it!"

Wrecker started to get up off the floor without saying anything. I could read what he was about to do.

"Eddie, get outside and keep a gun on the punks on the deck and have Jimmy and Billy take the body at the bottom of the steps and dump it in back where the other two stiffs are laying."

Wrecker dragged himself back into his office and sat down behind his desk as Eddie closed the door on his way out. I followed Wrecker.

"There are three stiffs out in the yard. I need to get rid of them. You got any ideas?"

"You got any aspirins? I got a big motherfucking headache."

I grabbed the first aid kit off the floor and threw it on the desk close to Wrecker.

"There… in the kit. Take a handful."

"What about the two outside the door? Are they taking a trip, too?" Wrecker asked in anticipation of having the pleasure of offing the two white boys standing on the deck outside the door.

"It all depends."

"I got a place to dump the bodies, but it'll cost you?"

"How much and how soon?"

"I have to make a call. It's two grand each for the three brothers. Honkeys are free."

"Make the call." I wanted to get this place cleaned up quickly and before his tow truck operator could pick up a tow and return to the yard.

# CHAPTER 27

I NOW HAVE two punks waiting outside on the deck that need to be questioned and disposed of. This guy Wolf is more than he pretends to be. The Joey I remembered as a kid didn't exist anymore. This Joey is a street wise con man angling for a buck. I don't want to put him down, but if Wolf goes so does Joey.

The story that Wolf tried to pass off on me about Hans coming into the club and forcing him to get to me through Joey is bullshit. There is someone else from the German Club who has ties to Hans or his organization. Wolf pulled the strings tonight. Joey may not know who that other person is. It's Wolf that I must work over. Joey is just a pawn, just a throwaway.

"Wrecker, are you done for the night, or do you want to help me persuade these bums to give up the guy that will lead me to Hans?"

"I got a large knot on my head and a huge headache because of those two punks outside. If you're just gonna push them around and hope they talk then count me out and take them back to the Southside with you. If you want to work them over and I can give them pain, then I'm in. Are these two real tough guys or are they just players?"

"The tall one, Joey, is a player. The other one, Wolf, is a tough guy. He's the one with the answers. I don't care if we mark him up, but I only want to scratch Joey up a little. I'll tell you why later. Which one do you want?" I knew his answer.

"You take Wolf, and Eddie can rough up Joey. Whenever you hear me say the wrong answer… that's your cue to bang him. I want them both to be more afraid of me than of their boss and Hans. I'll tell you when to begin to persuade him."

While Wrecker was preparing to feast on Wolf, I walked out of the trailer to tell everyone what I needed them to do. Eddie was going to come into the trailer and guide Joey through his interrogation. He had a rep for being overzealous in his questioning techniques while he was on the job. It would serve me well tonight.

I sent Jimmy and Billy to chain up the gate in case there were any curious night people passing by. The dogs were barking far too often so I asked Wrecker, who was now standing outside on the deck, how we could quiet them.

"Send someone out to their pen and have him wave a handgun and tell them to shut the fuck up and ask them if they want to die or you could feed them with the five pounds of hamburger I have in the refrigerator. It's your choice."

"Eddie, do me a favor and feed the dogs."

I pushed Joey and Wolf through the trailer door into what could become the entrance to hell for them. Joey moved forward without defiance, but Wolf pushed back when he felt my hand on his shoulder. He would be defiant, but not for too long. Wolf would respond to Wrecker's questioning technique, or he would open the gates of Hell for himself.

One Eye Eddie returned from feeding the dogs and I took him aside and explained how I wanted him to handle Joey. It was now time.

"Wolf, your story about how you were contacted by Hans at the German Club doesn't hold up for me. I want to know the name of who contacted you and where I can find him."

Wolf began telling me that Hans came to the club and gave him a phone number to call if they got the files he wanted.

“Let me introduce you to Wrecker and One Eye Eddie. Wrecker, say hello to Wolf.” With that, Wrecker stood arm’s length from Wolf and threw a left hook that connected somewhere on the side of his head. He went down like I’d seen others drop from a knockout blow to the head in a boxing match. At the same time, Eddie gave Joey an uppercut to the jaw. They were both caught off guard and dropped to the floor and onto the junk auto parts that were everywhere around the trailer. Wolf appeared to be unconscious, and Joey bewildered. He looked like he wanted to cry.

“What have you got for me, Joey? Eddie here doesn’t like it if you lie to me, but he does like to beat the hell out of people. Don’t worry about Wolf hearing you. Right now, he’s out cold.”

Joey pulled himself up off the floor while rubbing his jaw. Eddie started to make another move on him till I waved him off.

“Red, it’s like I told you at the bar. Wolf called me cause he knew we were friends, and I could help him keep the guy that hit those old ladies outside your office from killing him. He gave me five hundred to come with him to the restaurant to see you. He didn’t tell me nothing else. On the way over to meet you, we came up with the idea of getting the money from you. Wolf said you were working for some rich old lady, and she’d pay for it. That’s the truth, Red! I never saw no Hans’s guy," Joey answered me in a shaky voice. His story matched up with my take on his part in today's action. Wolf knew he couldn't resist a chance at making a run at a big money scam.

"Joey, go get Wolf back on his feet and don't talk unless I tell you to, and that means do not answer Wolf, or Wrecker will introduce himself to you too. Understand?"

I watched as Joey bent over Wolf to snap him out of his coma. He wasn't having much success. Maybe Wrecker killed him. Eddie offered to piss on his face if that would help. I ignored his remark. What's up with Eddie and pissing on someone's face anyway? Maybe he is a pissamaniac, the sick bastard.

I grabbed a beer out of the fridge in Wrecker's office and handed it to Joey.

"Dump it on Wolf's head and face. See if he comes around."

If that didn't get Wolf moving again, then he was seriously fucked up and needed a hospital or headshot. His life was marginal since he set me up tonight for Hans. I wasn't going to take Wolf to a hospital. If Wolf threw snake eyes tonight, Joey's luck would run out too.

I heard a groan from where Joey was working on Wolf. I told Joey to get him back on his feet. He had some questions to answer. It took him a couple of minutes to bring Wolf around and get him on his feet. Wolf was looking through glassy eyes as he tried to focus on where he was.

"What the fuck happened?" he asked Joey. He had to lean on him to keep his balance.

"The big Black guy hooked you. Get your shit together and fast. Reds got some questions you need to answer."

"Joey, Didn't I tell you not to speak even if Wolf talked to you?" I was looking at Eddie and then called his name. Eddie picked up my meaning and moved close to Joey and hit him with a gut shot that doubled him over and sent him to the trailer floor again. Wolf needed to take a couple of wobbly steps to get near enough to the trailer wall to lean on it.

"Wolf, I want you to listen carefully to what I'm about to tell you. Right now, I don't know where Hans is holed up or who is helping him. You may have that answer. You need to give me the name of the person or persons that came to see you with that proposition you brought to me earlier. If you hand me that bullshit you fed me at the restaurant about Hans coming to the club, then Wrecker is going to hand out more punishment to you. He'd just as soon see you dead. He'll beat on you till you give up your contact and where I can find him. If you choose to take the beating and the pain that comes with it, then it will continue as long as you can take it."

"It's Freddie Bohn the butcher from the old Germantown section of the city. He belongs to the same group of Germans as Hans. That's what he bragged about to me. That's how he knows him, but he ain't staying with him. Freddie says he's smart and that he doesn't trust anyone and says he would take care of me with the money end. That's all I know."

Wolf coughed up Freddie too easy for me. Joey and Wolf could walk. We did enough killing for tonight.

"Now, you can talk Joey. Do you know this guy Freddie the butcher?" I asked as I was reminded of the Nazis from the Second World War and some of their titles. The name Freddie the Butcher would fit in well. Is that who Hans and his comrades are, Nazi too late or Nazi light? Maybe!

Joey told me this guy was a big deal at the club and acted like the Godfather when he was there. He always traveled with two stooges: Never alone. He said he knew he was into illegal activities besides loan sharking but never heard anyone talk about it at the club.

I had to get this place cleaned up before I let these two walk. I needed to talk with Wrecker privately in his office.

"When's the cleaner going to get here?"

"He'll be here within the hour. What about these two out front? Are they gonna take the ride with him?"

"No, they walk."

"Red, they saw Delmons get capped. You trust them not to talk."

"They'll button up. There's no profit in it to squeal, and they know if they did, it wouldn't be long before they joined him. It may resolve itself after this guy Freddie finds out that not only are they coming back blanked, but they gave him up to me. If he's the German version of the godfather, he's going to have them both whacked. They don't know that the other two shooters they came with are on the ground out in the yard. They probably figured it out, but they don't know it for sure right now. We're not going to set them loose until we get cleaned up. You better put the usual night lights back on in the yard. We don't need the cops coming around to check your place out."

I laid it out to Wrecker. He may be the junkyard dog, but I'm the pit bull tonight. He's going to learn that when he's in any action with me it's always my way.

I went outside to see Jimmy and Billy to tell them to go sit in my car and wait until I needed the gate opened. They could go back to my place after the cleaner arrived. Their job was done. I'd ride back with Eddie. They handled the two cons just as they would some enemy Muslim in Iraq. Come to think of it the cons had both converted to Islam while in prison. I'd say that fact to Jimmy in the future if it were necessary.

Back in the trailer, Wrecker had dealt with his head wound. It wasn't a bad job considering he had only the outside mirror from his Caddy to see with.

"You owe me for a tow and a new mirror for my caddy plus six grand for the cleaner. I need it by Monday."

"I'll throw in another four G's so you can get another trailer. We don't want to have to explain the bullet holes in this one just in case. You think maybe you need to see a doctor?"

"No, what I need is ice," Wrecker told me and was about to say something else when he was cut off by the ringing of his cellphone.

"Red, send someone to open the gate. The cleaner is here. You better come with me and show me where the garbage is." And with that announcement he moved from behind the desk and went to meet the answer to the problem on the ground outside.

I sent Jimmy to drive down to open the gate and then take Billy home.

I hadn't given any thought to how the cleaner was going to transport three stiffs. It wasn't that I had a preference; it's just that I didn't expect a flatbed car carrier from another junkyard. Not a bad way to move that type of baggage. I watched as Wrecker pointed out to the driver of the flatbed the two junks that were to be the caskets for the recently deceased brothers.

They were lined with velour and vinyl and attended by some of the vermin that claim the interiors of the wrecks that sit in the graveyard for dead autos. I would hold a service for them… silently. Ashes to ashes…dust to dust… vermin to vermin. The City is a slightly better place now.

The driver moved with ease through the task. He was no novice at this body removal business, and judging from his familiarity with Wrecker, I'd guess this is a regular stop for him. I watched as the cleaner shoveled up the blood-stained ground where the bodies were lying and used a garden sprayer to saturate the area with what smelled like bleach. Not bad, I thought. I'd almost bet this guy knows where some of the missing bodies of unsolved crimes in the City are buried.

Back at the trailer, Joey and Wolf were waiting to tell me some other information. They said they never saw or talked to the person I call 'Hans,' but they remembered what Freddie told them, "Dieter would be close enough to observe them.' So that's the German's name, Dieter." These two were so scared they would sell out their mother to get out of the jam they were in. They weren't sure that I was going to let them get out of this with only a mild beating. Joey said he'd try to find out where Hans was hiding and call me as soon as he knew. Like as if I believed that bullshit.

"You give Freddie a message from me for Hans. You tell him I'm looking for him. When he comes out of his hole, I'll be there. This is my City, and he'll never get out of it alive. You can also tell Freddie I'm coming to pay him a visit," I told the two of them as I grabbed Wolf tightly around the collar of his bloodstained shirt and choked him.

"Do you know who I am?" I demanded from Wolf, with my face six inches from his.

"Yeah, you're Red."

"Red, who?"

"You're Red Canyon," Wolf managed to answer in a high-pitched trembling voice. He was shaking as I squeezed the shirt he was wearing tightly around his neck.

"The shadow of death is over the two of you and everyone else involved with you. Nevermore!" was my last warning to them as I released Wolf and pointed to the door of the trailer. Without hesitation, they both left as quickly as they could. Their fate had been sealed earlier that night. Poetic justice, maybe!

Wrecker was giving me that look that said, 'what the fuck!' then he blurted out, "What the fuck! What's all that shadow of death bullshit about? You turn gay on me motherfucker?"

"That's my college education coming out. Now that you terminated your yard man, you're going to need a replacement. I have someone in mind who may need a job and could help you get out of the dark ages and into the modern world of computers and cell phones. I'm sure you heard of those inventions."

"I got plenty of young brothers looking for a job up here on the Hill."

"You should hire Billy. He's a VET and a computer master. He also knows how to kill someone at least twenty different ways. He could watch your back for you. You are going to need someone you can trust until I find Hans and eliminate him. Think about it."

"I ain't hiring nobody that has can openers for hands and I don't like honkeys anyway."

"You pay him twenty bucks an hour and I'll give you half of that back, so it only costs you ten bucks an hour. That's a bargain, isn't it? He can start in a couple of weeks if he needs it. I have a job for him right now. Maybe he'll even teach you English. Deal?"

"Yeah, Red, deal! You make sure he understands who the boss is, a Black man."

"He's done that before in the Army. There are a lot of black NCOs and Officers he served with. It's time for you to knock off that racial crap. He may have saved your life when he took down one of the punks pumping lead into the trailer."

Wrecker had a chip on his shoulder that one day I would have to knock off, but not today.

"Get rid of this trailer and get a new one before the cops come around looking for Delmons and his two friends. You have until Tuesday before they show up. Come over to the bar tonight around six and I'll take you to dinner at The Angel up on Mt Washington." With that announcement, I called Eddie, and we left the Hill.

Daylight was starting to break as we drove through the valley that was once lined with the buildings of dreams that time and neglect had turned into the present-day nightmare pit of the street people.

My gang of misfits had escaped any harm, and I had a lead to Hans, or Dieter. Freddie The Butcher, was now the one I would focus on to get to Hans.

It's Annie time today, and it's time I should keep drinking again. Maybe! I took care of enough business for the weekend.

# CHAPTER 28

By the time we pulled in behind the IG it was daybreak, and a light drizzle was starting to fall. The rain wouldn't wash away the sins of Saturday night on the Southside, but it would feed the weeds that grew in the cracks of the sidewalks and the streets of the City.

When Annie bought the IG, one of the first things she did was to remodel the second and third floors, which included new windows. I never really looked at them before, I mean really looked. It was evident the window installer wasn't a brick mason. The windowsills and the brick fillers he used didn't match up in color or size with the rest of the building. I don't know why it bothered me, but today it did. I was going to tell Annie about it and get her to make it right. The back of this building is fucking up the neighborhood.

I pointed out the flaws to Eddie to get his opinion. He answered with his usual thoughtful and learned opinion, which I was sure matched mine.

"Who gives a fuck? That's what Annie is going to tell you. You need to go and grab some boobs and then get some sleep. Trust me," was the advice of One Eye Eddie. He could be right. Maybe!

Annie opened the back door wearing an all-black funeral type dress. Eddie tugged at my sleeve and quickly warned, "Forget the boob grab. Go directly to sleep. I'm going to sack out in one of the booths in the dining room after I knock down a brew."

I decided not to tell Annie about the windows just yet. My sudden obsession with the fucking windows on the rear of the building must be my brain going on pause so I can clean out most of the distractions flying around in it. Yeah, that's it. I'm on pause.

Me and Eddie walked through the rear doorway that Annie had just been standing in. I followed behind her as Eddie headed to the beer cooler behind the bar. Annie had made herself into another barricade at the first-floor entrance stairway to her upstairs apartment. She was probably signaling to me to go back to my home.

"Do you want me to go back to my place, or am I staying here?" I softly asked Annie, believing I knew the answer.

"Come on to bed. Jimmy stopped by before and told me everything worked out and that you and One Eye Eddie were waiting for the cleaner to finish before you came back to the Southside."

"Yeah, something like that. It all worked out. I'll tell you about everything after I get some sleep."

"Sure, Red, after you get some sleep." I heard in that tone of voice she gives me when she's walking back her anger. I didn't want to deal with her right now. I just wanted to go to sleep. I had pain in my leg from my self-inflicted gunshot wound and I was getting a pain in my ass from Annie. I considered going back to my place, but dumped the idea when she put her arms around me and hugged me. The pain would go away. Annie always made the pain go away. I was home.

I awoke a little after two. I hit the shower, got dressed and joined the voices in the kitchen. Jimmy and Eddie were drinking beers with Annie and talking about politics. I'd stay out of that conversation. Me and Annie have disagreements in that area. She told me she had just made a fresh pot of coffee when she heard the shower. I patted Jimmy and Eddie on the shoulder and gave Annie a hug and kiss on the cheek before I asked my first question. "Where's Billy?"

Jimmy had the answer.

"He's in the downstairs office scanning all the documents in the boxes into the computer. Annie found your paperwork right where you hid it on the desktop."

"That was good thinking, Jimmy. When Billy's done, I can dump the files on the Feds."

Jimmy looked over at me from across Annie's new old fashioned Formica kitchen table that resembled the set up at Disney's kitchens of the future 1950's era and told me it was Annie's idea. I gave her a salute with my coffee cup.

"Those fucking files are going to get us all killed or doing time. You can't get rid of them too fast for me." Eddie spoke out, followed by Annie's second. Jimmy stayed neutral.

"Jimmy, stop Billy right now from handling them without medical type gloves on."

"He's way ahead of you, Red. He got hair coloring gloves from Annie before he started, but what about the paperwork you handled? Did you have your protection on?" Jimmy asked me with a grin on his face as the other two snickered.

"As a matter of fact, I wasn't wearing any protection. The files I handled are pregnant. Abort them. Get a shredder from Bobby's store tomorrow. Get the kind that makes confetti out of paper."

The only other people who may have known what the boxes of papers contained besides me are dead, with the possible exception of one other. It doesn't matter what paperwork turns up, the Feds are going to question whether or not they have everything anyway. Hans is still going to come after me. If he gives up on finding whatever Strump had taken from his organization, he still must try to kill me for converting his comrades into dust. It's a matter of honor to him and the people he works for.

Annie left to open the bar and get the evening set up since we were going to the Angel up on Mt Washington tonight.

"Eddie, you heard what Wolf told us about the German being too smart to use Freddie The Butchers' place for a hideout. I figure if I'm him, I'd hide out with people like me, Germans. That puts him in Germantown. Now, unless Freddie, the godfather has somebody above him that he answers to then Hans-Dieter is with him. I need you to get surveillance on the butcher shop early in the morning tomorrow and stay with it all day. Cover the front and the back entrances. Get an instant picture camera. I want pictures of flat topped, sandy haired, six-foot-tall white men entering the store. You do the legwork in

Germantown and find out if Freddie reports to an over boss. If he does, I need to know who he is and how to find him. I may want to pay a visit to the butcher at closing time tomorrow."

I gave Eddie five hundred walking around money. He might have to flip a twenty to a few bums on the street for some of the local rap on Freddie. I wanted to get him to roll over on Hans. Maybe Eddie will come up with something that I can use to open him up. If not, then one of his meat grinders will have to do.

Annie came back to the kitchen and invited everyone to come upstairs and watch what was left of the Pirate game. She said they were winning for once. Eddie passed. He said he was going home to clean up and get ready to meet us up at The Angel on the mountain. Jimmy told us he was going to hang out with Billy and help if he could. I reminded him to be back here by five thirty so he could ride with us. He passed on the ride. He said Jackie was picking him and Billy up.

That would be great if Jackie came along. I wouldn't have to do any paperwork for her to cover the tab for tonight. She could put the bill on her expense account.

Wrecker called me to say he'd be a little late and he would meet us at the restaurant. He said that he went shopping for a trailer earlier in the day and found a good deal on a construction site and that he was setting it up. What he really was saying is that he found a construction site without any security, hooked up their trailer, and pulled it to his yard. He told me he had already jammed the old trailer in the crusher. I think I just beat myself out of four grand. Hilda can afford it.

Annie was back upstairs and getting ready for our dinner party. I wondered if she was going to wear the same black funeral dress she greeted me with earlier this morning. It didn't matter. She always looked good to me. I was checking out my closet and looking for the two remaining suits that I could wear tonight. I picked the blue pinstripe. I liked the tie Sam matched up with it. I was going to make this a real party tonight with my gang of misfits. Maybe this mixture of oddball people could blend into something where the whole is greater than the sum of its parts. That was the case early this Sunday morning. Maybe! Just maybe!

## CHAPTER 29

I ALWAYS LIKED the drive to the restaurants up on Mt Washington. The higher up you drove, the more the view of the city opened itself up like a flower. At night, looking over the Three Rivers, the miles of buildings and homes turn into fireflies blinking their lights along with the thousands of two eyed bugs moving along on paths that head in every direction. If you let your mind drift, you could imagine that you were a bird hovering above Pittsburgh, just trying to decide where to land. Tonight, I'd land on The Angel. Tomorrow, I'll land on the Butcher.

"Red, that was so beautiful what you just said. It's poetry with symbolism that Edgar Allen Poe would doff his hat to."

"Annie, I didn't realize that I was thinking out loud. You forget what I just said. Promise me you won't bring it up, especially tonight. The pain pills I took before we left must have caused me to hallucinate. Yeah, maybe I took LSD by mistake. Promise!" I asked, knowing Annie wouldn't reveal the ramblings of a recovering alcoholic. I have to get my mind and mouth back in sync. Loose lips sink shit or something like that.

The obsession with the replacement windows on the rear of the IG building and now this disconnected rambling must be a warning to me to stay off the suds. That must be it. I'm not completely dried out yet, but I'm in control, and my instincts are accurate.

While the others were pounding down adult beverages, I'd be getting hammered with the methadone of recovering alcoholics; O'Doul's near beer. I was gonna make it back all the way.

The valet parking was backed up and I was caught on the road with some asshole blowing his horn at me and giving me all the hand signals cause he couldn't get past me. That could get his face broken. I started to get out of the car and head back to the punk to adjust his attitude when the line in front of me moved. I followed it up to the entrance of the Angel. Now I'm torqued up and want to get into a fight. Annie knew it and held my hand tightly and calmly uttered, "Don't do it. Don't ruin the beautiful night for us. Have a drink. It's ok. I'm here."

"No booze. I don't need it. It's just these last two weeks have been intense and I'm still cleaning myself up. I need to settle this thing with the German and get on with finding the Strump murderer. I think I figured out what's up with the Germans. Two days after Hilda shows up at my office and hires me to find her husband's killer, these files show up at the company plant just as I show up asking questions about Horst's murder. These two old broads claim they had them all this time because no one asked them specifically for their personal records on Horst. The word spread that I picked them up even though I told the old broads not to say anything about their existence because they could have legal problems for withholding evidence. The next day, they pop up dead in the dumpster behind my office, and some German guys show up to get the files from me and then pop me."

"What's the problem with that sequence of events?" Annie asked.

I didn't figure it out until just now. "I think Hilda had the files in her possession since Horsts' murder. She and whoever else she brought in to investigate worked the documents over, looking for some clue that she and the Germans both wanted to find. For fifteen years, she's been reading and rereading them and coming up blank. The Germans that had an interest in them fifteen years ago, for some reason, got a renewed interest in Horst. What would have prompted that interest? Hilda? Maybe!"

"If Hilda had the files, why didn't she just turn them over to the Germans if they were squeezing her?"

"She couldn't because she's been denying that she had any documents from Horst since his death. My bet is she knows this gang of new Nazis, and if she suddenly came up with the goods after fifteen years of lying to them, she'd probably get whacked and maybe even the rest of what is left of her family."

"Why did she bring the two women from the factory into that danger?"

"She probably gave each of them a bag of money for the set-up and didn't figure the Krauts would want to squeeze them hoping they may have had something else that could be useful to them even though the old broads wouldn't know it if they did."

"If you're right, Red, the women would have told these Germans that Hilda set them up. Why would they kill them, and why didn't they go after Hilda and kill her?"

"My bet is they were going to nail her after they got the files from me. They probably slapped the two old women around so hard that they died. Could have been an unintentional consequence. These guys were pros but didn't realize that it didn't take much of a beating to kill sixty-year-old women. They fucked up.

Once one of the old ladies croaked, they had to kill the other one. They couldn't leave a witness. They didn't think a drunken ex-cop would pose a problem for them either. I fucked up their plan when I killed 'Fritz and Rinehart' and claimed Hans had the missing files."

"Hilda has plenty of money. Why didn't she just buy them off?"

"It's not about money to these Germans. Horst must have taken something from them that's much more valuable to them than money. It's an object or a something. If I can capture Hans alive, I'll get him to spill what he's been chasing after. I think the one other person that knows is Hilda. She may be harder to crack."

"Red, your detecting is brilliant. I don't believe anyone else in this city could have put all that together. Can we talk more after our dinner party?" Annie asked, showing an interest she hadn't displayed since I took the case. It looks like she just joined the team. And what a team it is. A recovering alcoholic: then there's my cousin that has all the wiring in his head screwed up; a one eyed over fifty-five fat guy ex-cop; an ex-soldier with no hands; a middle-aged black guy that hates whites; and now one normal woman… almost. I forgot Spooks, a homeless bum that wears long sleeve flannel shirts year-round.

I wondered for an instant if I was thinking out loud again as the kid that handed me a parking stub was looking at me with that dumb expression on his face; one that some people get when they want to say something to you but are afraid too.

"What is it, kid? You got something for me?"

"You're Red Canyon, right?" the kid asked and told me at the same time. "Mr. Ross said I should watch out for you and tell him when you get here. He asked you to please wait to be seated. He's going to take you to your table himself."

"Thanks, kid. You got something else you want to ask me?" The kid was sputtering when he spit out the message he was holding for me.

"Could I get your autograph?" he finally coughed up.

"Sure kid." I pulled a twenty out of my wallet, took out a pen from the inside pocket of my new suit signed it and handed it to him.

With a broad smile on his face, the kid thanked me and told me he'd take special care of my car tonight and never spend the twenty.

"Don't spend it kid, except on a good looking broad. It will be worth more than a Jackson if I get bumped off while I'm working on the Carson Street Caper. Take my word for it."

Annie gave me a surprised look after I gave that advice to the kid. "Are you trying to expand the Red Canyon following through that kid with that Carson Street Caper thing and that stuff about getting bumped off?"

"Yes, I am. Now, let's find Ross. The others will be showing up soon. I want to get seated at the table before anyone arrives, so we get the best view of the City."

"Are you going to tell me why you're having this dinner party tonight? Is this some kind of a celebration?"

"Maybe!" That was all I could say to Annie. I couldn't tell her anything about what went on at Wreckers junkyard in the early hours of the morning. Jimmy would probably spill it to Annie one day soon. She knows how to work him. She knows what buttons to push when it comes to Jimmy. The good thing is that she can never be sure if the information he gives up is accurate or if it is mixed with that reality that exists in the other dimension his mind often drifts to.

Benny Ross came over to greet Annie and me when we entered the Angel. Annie knew him from her other life when she worked in the financial market. I first met him four years ago when he and his other three partners reopened the restaurant. They purchased it from the bank that foreclosed on it. Annie said she was offered a piece of the place but declined. She had other investments at the time; me and the Gardens.

"Red, you're a celebrity of sorts. When the help found out about your reservation, they set up a raffle to see who would draw your table tonight. I'll try my best to see to it that you and your party are not bothered by any curious patrons in the restaurant."

He ushered us to the upper section of the dining room that had been added recently. Our table was at the point of the addition with nothing except windows any way you turned and nothing except air underneath. We were hovering over Mt Washington with the city lights spread out in front of us as far as you could see. It was the million-dollar view and right now I was the pilot of the hover craft that made the view possible tonight.

Benny sent over four bottles of Champaign, compliments of the house. It was easy for a shot and a beer guy like me to pass on it. Annie smiled at me as she lifted a glass of the Champaign the waiter served and took the first sip that signaled the beginning of the dinner party, but for some reason that conjured up the memory of the scene from the bar in Star Wars. Inside were strange looking characters that didn't match up with each other. They were from different parts of the galaxy, and each spoke their own distinct language that made it difficult to communicate. Last night, in a bar, I formulated a plan and communicated it to each member of my crew, and just as in the bar in Star Wars, they functioned as if they were each from some other place in the galaxy, and my cause was confused when they translated my words into their own distinct language. It fit because they didn't follow anything that I told them to do. And just as in Star Wars, in the end, everything worked out. Maybe...

While I was still into Star Wars, I saw Annie get up from the table to greet the first arrival. It was like intermission time at the movies. One Eye Eddie was walking toward me wearing a freshly pressed suit and shirt with a tie he must have picked up from the Good Will box. It was a couple of shades of white and as wide as a dinner napkin. The good thing about a white tie is it goes with any shirt or suit. The exception was the one he had on. While I'm thinking all this crap, I hear Annie telling Eddie how sharp he looks and how she especially liked his tie and how it certainly reflects Red's influence on him. She glanced over at me with that same half hidden smile on her face Eddie had showed to Wrecker a half day earlier. Then she asked him if I had given it to him as a gift for some special occasion like a birthday or maybe a funeral.

I looked at Eddie to see if he picked up on the last remark by Annie, but if he did, he didn't show it in his expression. One Eye just thanked her for the compliment, looked over at me and said, "Where's the waitress? I'm thirsty, and I need a fucking beer. It's open bar for us isn't it, Red?"

"Yeah, Eddie, it's open bar tonight, and I want you to look at the menu as if it's a buffet menu. You order anything you want off it and if you don't like the taste of it then order something else. You can order anything off the menu as often as you like. As a matter of fact, I'm going to order every appetizer on it to start. Don't worry about drinking too much, either. If you get bombed, I'll send you home in a cab and we'll get your car tomorrow."

I was going to offer that same message to the rest of my crew. That's what I'd call them from now on until I get a better name, my crew. They were my crew of soldiers today. They all put their lives on the line for me. Can any man do more for anyone than to offer his very life for another? That's what Eddie, Wrecker, Jimmy, and Billy did for me this day. I was going to make this a real party tonight for everyone. Maybe it will end with an in-house brawl. When Wrecker gets a load on, he wants to fight. I'm not going to say anything to Annie about my thoughts. I can hear her very words, "Don't you dare start any brawl! What's wrong with you? Grow up, Red!" Whoops! Here it comes.

"You know, Red, you were always immature, but I thought you would eventually grow up. Now, I think I finally figured out why you never did. You're missing the grow up chromosome." Annie said it with a smile in her eyes and an expression on her face I'd seen many times before.

I thought about what she had just said and realized she must be right. I can't help behaving like an immature teenager as she so often tells me. She's been telling me to grow up since the first day I met her. It's not my fault. I'm a fucking victim, the same as junkies' alcoholics and pedophiles claim. Annie wasn't serious, but the other victim groups are. Their claims are just bullshit. No one is born scum. They willingly join and jump onto the scum bandwagon. That's enough of this mental philosophic bullshit exercise.

I won't let any fight break out. I just want us all to have a memorable evening together. To that end, I asked Annie to get Ross to give us an extra full-time waiter at the table to keep the drinks flowing and food coming. Hilda can cover it.

I looked up and saw Jimmy being escorted to the table by Ross. Following behind, I saw Jackie and an unexpected guest, Hilda Strump. Billy was right behind her escorting some broad I didn't recognize. Now, only Wrecker was missing. He'd be here. Wrecker would never miss an opportunity to run up a tab on me.

They were all heading toward me with the usual greetings except for Hilda. She just nodded as she looked at me. It took two steps to reach her, grab her arm and lead her to a seat on my right. She reached for my hand and squeezed it the way you would when you're relieved to see someone. Maybe she's worried about me. That wouldn't fit her personality. I have her pegged as a tough old woman without much emotion.

"Mr. Canyon, I haven't seen you since you were shot. Are you almost recovered? Is there anything I can do to help your recovery?" Hilda was asking although my take is she's just making conversation.

I had an answer for her that I'd have to put on hold. This wasn't the place to tell her. I believe she set me up as a straw man. I wouldn't try to pin her down on why she's holding out on me. If she knew about the Germans, she should have told me. I could have been caught by surprise. Maybe she didn't figure out how bad these boys are.

"I understand from Jimmy that you had scheduled a meeting last evening with the person responsible for murdering Marie and Alice. I want that person brought to justice. Hire as many people as you need to track him down and close that terrible incident."

That was her way of telling me to kill him.

"My reason for being here tonight is to let you know that I am planning to be away for the next several weeks. I'm leaving Jackie an open checkbook for you. Please be judicious in the future, but money should not interfere with your judgment. She will inform you of your new position in the company. No questions now. Meet Jackie tomorrow if it's possible. At least call her."

"Hilda, you just dumped on me. How can you tell me not to ask questions about anything you just said to me?"

"I can assure you, Mr. Canyon, that I have tried to strengthen your position with me. I have adopted you, so to speak, as one of my family. You should consider your tasks as that of our families not as only a hired gun. Please see Jackie tomorrow. You should be pleased. Now, order me a shrimp cocktail and a taxi. I'll leave you to your business, our family business. Go visit with your people. I want to talk with Annie alone."

Hilda turned to Annie and started a conversation without missing a beat. I ordered a double shrimp cocktail and told the waiter to call a cab. What the fuck was Hilda talking about with her reference to 'our family' when she addressed me? Yeah, I know. Ask Jackie.

Jackie sat down across the table from me and asked me to see her later to arrange for us to meet at the factory tomorrow. She mentioned that she had news about the grand jury findings about the shooting on the Southside.

"Tomorrow, Red! Look at the envelope I put under your plate. It has a company credit card in it issued in your name. Use it tonight if you want. If not, I can use mine for the bill. Congratulations, Red."

Congratulations for what? I didn't know what these two were up to, but I know Hilda is a devious and cagy old lady. It will wait till tomorrow.

Everyone had ordered drinks except me. I was going to drink the near beer tonight. I had to have a sit down with Jackie in the morning and maybe later in the afternoon I'd have to make a closing time visit to the butcher shop in Germantown. When Billy finishes making copies of the files, I hope to have them mysteriously show up somewhere in the city, maybe the factory where they came from. That will get the Feds off my back, but not Hans. He'll figure out that I have copies of them, and he'll keep on coming until I stop him. Everything is tied together. Annie looked back at me and could see in my eyes that my mind had wandered someplace else.

"That's enough of business for tonight, Red. I want you to relax with your crew and so does Hilda, so knock it off." Annie scolded me even though she knew I would do what I wanted regardless of her protests.

The next time she rags on me I'm going to tell her to fix those fucked up windows in the back of her building. That will get her off my ass. Maybe…

The appetizers had arrived, and the party was on. We were still missing Wrecker, but not for long. I knew he was close without turning around to look. I could hear him asking Ross if those motherfuckers started without him and he wasn't speaking with his inside voice. I watched as Ross escorted Wrecker and his friend, or whatever, to their seats next to Eddie. I'd have to change that setup, or this party would be over in minutes.

Eddie was about to say something to Wrecker when I cut him off and loudly called him over to me. I needed to send him in the cab with Hilda back to her home and ask him to stay at her house tonight. I'd tell him I was concerned about Hans showing up there. That wasn't my reason and Eddie would know it, but he would do as I asked.

Ross was standing next to Hilda to escort her to the cab that had arrived. I explained my reasoning to Hilda for the bodyguard and she reluctantly agreed along with Eddie. Who knows, maybe old One Eye will get lucky tonight?

Now, the real reason I had to get rid of Eddie was the woman Wrecker brought to the party. She was, I guess, in her middle thirties, stood five six both ways and was topped off with platinum blonde hair. What was causing everyone to take a second look wasn't the hair. It was that she was white. That fucking Wrecker, with his constant insults about whites, had himself a white woman. Eddie would have hammered him to hell about his date. That's why I had to send him away. It would be better if I did it. I could see a grin on Jimmy's face and the look in Wrecker's eyes as he waited for the first jab. I was about to throw it when Annie grabbed and squeezed my hand tightly as she leaned close to me. "Red, don't you say a word about the fat assed white broad with Wrecker because if you do, I'll go home and that means no sex."

"I wasn't going to say anything about the Pillsbury dough girl with Wrecker. Honest. I was just going to ask Wrecker to introduce his companion to all of us." I knew Annie's warning was serious from her tone. I wasn't about to fuck up with Annie. It would have to wait for the next time Wrecker, Eddie, and I were together. Annie was right as she almost always is. I just wanted to give my boys a party tonight. I'll give Eddie an extra deuce for his cooperation tonight and promise him a shot at Wrecker the next time we are all together. Yeah, that's what I'll do.

It was time to learn the name of the woman Wrecker brought with him.

"Wrecker, introduce your lady to everyone," I said it without a hint of humor in my voice. It's a good thing I'm not drinking; otherwise, by now, I'd be hammering Wrecker one on one. I wouldn't embarrass his broad.

"This is my wife Clara and don't any of you motherfuckers start making any Clara-bell jokes." Clara stood up next to Wrecker and politely said hello to everyone. It's a good thing Annie nudged me in the right direction. It would have been unfair to openly pick on her just to harass Wrecker. Now, I had to ask myself when did I become fair? I got a million black and white jokes, and now I have a place to use them, but I wouldn't. Not tonight. Families are off limits. Once he made it clear that Clara was his wife, it ended any thought of hammering him tonight. I'd have to wait for him to show up with a white girlfriend sometime in the future.

I called Eddie to tell him that Clara was family and to come back in the cab after he delivered Hilda to her home.

"I'll pass." I heard him say and thought he must be pissed off at me.

"Hilda felt bad that I was missing dinner and asked me to have dinner with her tonight. I accepted."

"That's great, Eddie. Where's she taking you? It's probably to one of the five-star restaurants downtown."

"I'm not sure yet. She said something about comfort food and specially fried poultry." Eddie relayed to me in anticipation of being elegantly served poultry prepared by a world-famous chef in a setting of luxury.

Eddie would be back before the party ended if that crazy old broad was taking One Eye to the Colonels. Eddie would run through his vocabulary of expletives with Hilda before he returned.

I told Annie about my call, and she promptly announced it to the table. Everyone got a kick out of it, even Jackie. Wrecker looked over at me. "You should have sent me with the old lady. I'd a rather ate fried fucking chicken than the shit that's all over this table."

"Wrecker, shut the fuck up. Clara, can you knock the chip off his shoulder for tonight?" I asked, betting from her swagger that she could temper him a bit.

She looked at me confidently and said, "Sure, Red," as she tugged at his right ear and scolded him.

"Wrecker Johnson, you stop all the bullshit right now and enjoy the rest of the evening with your friends. You don't have many and you know you like these people, or you wouldn't have brought me here with you. SYFM! Shut your fucking mouth."

He listened, eased back in his chair, and took her advice, for now. His sarcasm didn't change. Clara just filed off the rough edges for the night. He'd go back to becoming the same asshole that he is by the time the evening ends.

Five hours and six grand later the party was over. I had Ross keep his parking attendants on the clock. Everyone had a cab to ride home in with one of the attendants following in their car. They would ride back in the cab to the restaurant. No DWIs tonight. I would drive Annie home.

The next time I have a party, if I'm still on the wagon, I'll have to smoke a rope to get high. It isn't much fun being sober when everyone is high. They all look and act stupid. I should have popped the oxy I have.

Eddie never came back to the restaurant. I'll find out in the morning if he liked the chicken. Who knows, maybe he tapped Hilda. I wouldn't put it past a guy who always wants to urinate in someone's face.

Billy and his date rode with me and Annie back to the Southside. Jimmy went with Jackie to her place. I was gonna ask Billy if he had some different settings for his bionic hands. He needed a mode that was different from choke, like maybe feel up or grope or something. If he didn't have an adjustment, the girl he was with is gonna have some awful sore boobs in the morning. I'll ask him tomorrow, or maybe I'll ask her too. I dropped them off at my house and said, "Good luck." Billy responded with, "Thanks."

"I wasn't talking to you, Billy; I was talking to your date."

They both stared at me with puzzled looks on their faces.

"Never mind!" I said, realizing that the humor only took place in my mind. Tomorrow, I'll let Billy in on it. He'll think it was funny.

Back at Annie's, I headed straight to bed to get a much-needed sleep. I had to be alert today if I decided to meet up with Freddie The Butcher. By the time Annie came out of the bathroom I was almost asleep… almost. I heard her walk over to my side of the bed and opened my eyes to see her standing next to me. When I saw how she was dressed for bed I knew that Morpheus would have to be put on hold.

## CHAPTER 30

BRIGHT SUNLIGHT and the smell of coffee brewing woke me up at six thirty. I was getting accustomed to waking up without a hangover. Annie was still in bed, so who was making coffee in the kitchen? I hope my mother didn't sneak back into town. I don't miss those lectures and I'd be able to get her off my ass by handing her a couple of grand. I could put it on my new company credit card. I wonder if she still takes Visa. At one time she ran credit cards when she sold that pink Cadillac product to women. Maybe I'm just overthinking, and Annie has one of those automatic coffee pots with a timer on it. Maybe me and my Glock will see.

I headed to the kitchen in my shorts and Glock.

"Don't shoot, and for Christ's sake, go put some fucking pants on!"

It wasn't my mother. How do I spell relief? It was One Eye Eddie. Somehow, he made it into the bar and then through two locked doors that led up to Annie's place.

"How'd you get in? Everything was locked up tight last night."

"I jimmied the lock on the backdoor to the bar. The doors to Annie's were both unlocked. You gotta tighten shit up around here, Red. Hans could a come in here and fucked you up."

Eddie was right. I let my guard down when I assumed someone else, Annie, locked up. I'll get a security guy over here to wire up the bar, Annie's place, and mine. My new company credit card is going to get a workout today.

"Eddie, what happened last night with Hilda and dinner?" almost hoping to hear that he jumped her.

"While we were in the cab, I was waiting for Hilda to tell the driver where she wanted to go. Finally, she tells him to jump off in Monroeville and stop at the KFC by the mall. Now, I'm thinking this old lady flipped out. Then she tells me she acquired a taste for my comfort food and hoped I'd indulge her tonight. She offered me five hundred to compensate me for missing the grand dinner you sponsored. I take the five bagger and tell her to order the twenty-four-piece bucket; I'm hungry."

"So how come you didn't show till six this morning?" Now, I had to ask him the big question, thinking that Eddie's been alone for the last couple of years since his wife left him, and he was getting ready to start raising sheep. "Did you bang her?"

"Hell no, I didn't bang her, Red! I ate some of the Kentucky T-bone with Hilda and then I left in a cab on my way to the IG. It was around midnight. I saw a hooker shopping on Twenty First and Carson. Since I had a fresh five hundred in my pocket, I went back to her place and partied till six. We got to talking and your name came up. The broad said she knew you and gave me a fucking discount."

"Funny, Eddie, very funny." I had to give him credit for that last comment. It was worthy of coming from a smart ass like me.

"I'll make a couple of calls before eight and get two retired shields to put eyes on the butcher shop in Germantown. Patty Logan and Al Sommers were both partners of mine at one time. They're always looking to make a buck."

I grabbed a cup of coffee and briefed Eddie on what I wanted in Germantown today.

"I want Hans, Eddie. Tell both our guys on stakeout to be on the lookout for a six-foot-tall pale skinned white guy wearing a foreign looking dark suit. He has light brown hair that's cut in a flat top. If they spot him going into the butcher shop, I want them to call you and then you can tell me. If they see him leave, I want a tail on him. You tell them to stay back from this guy because he's dangerous. He already smoked two senior citizens. When he lands somewhere, have them call us, and we'll meet up with them. I want this guy alive." The instructions I gave Eddie were clear and he would relay them to his old partners. He wouldn't want either one of them injured or dead, and neither did I.

I left One Eye in the kitchen and headed back to the bedroom to get ready for something. I wasn't sure what that something was going to be today, but if I get a hold of Hans, I'm going to send him to meet with Hitler after I let Wrecker play with him for a while. I need to know what he is after, and I can fit that together with the reason Horst was murdered when I discover what it was.

Eddie left me to go meet his old partners in Germantown. I'm now thinking that I'll keep tabs on the butcher for a couple of days before I make my move on him. Maybe Joey will come through with a tip on Hans if I wait a couple of days. Freddie will be expecting me today when he gets the message that Joey delivers to him. I'll let him sit unless Hans shows up at his shop.

Jimmy called me around eight thirty to ask me to let Billy into the bar so he could continue working in the office on the files. I set up an eleven o'clock meeting with Jackie to find out what Hilda and Jackie were talking about last night. I have Hilda pegged as a clever old lady who only plays blackjack with her own deck. Whatever Jackie must tell me about, no matter what it is, Hilda will be holding the house edge.

On my way out I stopped at the office to ask Billy if there was any way to speed up the copying process.

"Upgrade the equipment. This computer is a fossil. For less than three thousand I can get us up to speed."

"When Jimmy hooks up with you ask him to take you down the block and get you whatever you want. Don't worry about the price. Get the best."

I pulled out a handful of bills from my wallet and handed them to Billy. "This is for you. It's walking around money. You don't need cash at the store that Jimmy will take you to. Just sign for anything you want. If you don't find everything at that store, come back to the IG and see Annie. She'll give you cash, and you can go to the mall." With that said, I was out the door and on my way to Germantown to meet Eddie. Game on!

My driving suspension ended over the weekend. I could legally drive again. Sitting behind the wheel, I began thinking about who else could be holding out on me. I came up with Vinnie and Lerch, Hilda's brother, and of course Hilda and Jackie too. That old Dago Vinnie knows more than he told me. His warning about the suits was just to throw me a bone. In his mind, he satisfied an old debt to me for helping his homo son out of a jam. He figured the warning wouldn't make any difference since I'd been in the bottle for so long, the pros that would be coming after me would do me and that would be the end of the digging into the Horst murder case.

The way I see it the German and me are on two different tracks and we collided at the boxes of files. It's as if Horst got wacked before they got whatever he took from them. They're looking for the clue to find their pot of gold. That theory keeps coming up in my mind. Me, I'm looking for Horst's killer and maybe in the process finding out the secret that Vinnie is protecting and that would also mean the Italian mob is a player along with him.

The Italians are sitting it out until they see if Hans kills me. So, if I'm right and if I kill Hans then the Italian mob comes after me. If I'm wrong about this scenario then I've lost my identity. That makes me qualified to be a security guard at the mall. I'll kill Hans and then we'll see.

I headed into the traffic on Carson Street. In the morning and evening rush hours driving on the Southside was one big pain in the ass. When I leave the Southside, I feel like every place I head is up. It was kind of like being at the center of the South Pole. No matter which direction you stepped off the first step was always North. That's the Southside to me. Whichever direction I take, it's up.

I was going to what was left of Germantown. It wasn't bombed out like the country in the early 40's: it was abandoned. There were still a few of the authentic bakeries and butcher shops and a few solid German restaurants sprinkled in with the influx of Asians, Indians, and Hispanics. Most of the younger generations of German spirit had fled to suburbia. The age of the pure German population living in Germantown begins around fifty and ends at almost dead. The German Club is the magnate that draws the loyalists and the want to bees back into the old German part of the City which is now down to a twenty square block area. Going there is how they renew their heritage and pretend they're back in the homeland. They even have a Gestapo-like character, Freddie the Butcher, to add to the lure. I was sure I was on the right track to intercept Hans. Freddie would lead me to him. I'm not ready to become a mall cop just yet.

## CHAPTER 31

When I arrived in Germantown I knew exactly where to find Eddie; the closest doughnut digs to the butcher shop. I pulled into the lot at the first doughnut shop I saw and parked next to Eddie's car. I could see him sitting in a booth eating a box of doughnuts, drinking a coffee, and looking at a newspaper while he was waiting for me. He's still doing that cop thing. It took me less than a minute to join him in the booth.

"The boys are both on stake-out. I gave them the warning. What else have you got for me? I'm tired from entertaining that hooker last night and want to go home and get some sleep."

"Nothing that can't wait for now. I don't want to make a move on the butcher today unless I'm positive that Hans is inside at closing time. We don't want to risk creating any civilian casualties. Go home. Maybe you should consider dropping by your doctor and getting a shot of penicillin."

"You always have to be a smart ass don't you, Red? And for your information, I wore a bag."

"You may not believe it, but that wasn't a wisecrack. I just don't want anything to happen to you, Eddie."

"Thanks for your concern, Red. I'll be careful."

Before he split, he would tell his guys to call me till he's back on the line. I didn't want any new action today and almost hoped that Hans would stay away from the butcher shop. It was time to take my meeting with Jackie and find out what the hell Hilda has up her sleeve for me.

When I arrived at the factory, their parking lot was full except for the prime space assigned to Horst Strump. I guess Hilda kept a parking space with Horst's name on it for old time's sake. She's into that shrine stuff. It's sorta like the people who make these shrines on the highways where a member of their family was killed in an auto accident. The only problem with that move is that the family member that became roadkill doesn't appreciate the gesture. Screw that feel-good bullshit. I pulled into Horst's parking space.

Inside, the receptionist must have already had a call from the guard of the Horst parking shrine. She politely informed me that no one had ever parked in that spot since his absence, and I needed to move my car.

"Honey, call Jackie and tell her Red is here to see her. As for moving my car…No! And you don't have to worry about where I parked. Horst told me to use his spot until he gets back."

I was sure I had given her too much to process through her brain in the last thirty seconds. The expression on her face told the story. "Just get me Jackie, Honey, and relax. Oh, I take my coffee black."

I looked for the most comfortable chair in the reception area and didn't see one I liked so I planted my tail on the end of the receptionist's desk, much to her dislike. I was making myself a real pain in the ass because I didn't want to be here. I'll send the girl a box of candy. That ought to cover it.

Jackie showed up at the reception area and took me back to her office to discuss our business. First, she told me that the grand jury refused to indict me for the Carson Street kills. It seemed unlikely that the prosecutor would pursue the case any further. The Feds might go for that civil rights violation bullshit. That's the feel-good crowds' way to ignore the law of Double Jeopardy. Fuck them!

The next item she brought up was Hilda and her comment about me being in the family business. I was being appointed to the board of directors of Horst Enterprises LLC. It was a company owned by Hilda that managed several of her assets. I was to be paid one hundred twenty thousand per year plus a generous expense account. The company had offices on the third floor of the plant, and they were preparing an office for me as we spoke. I would have to attend a few board of directors' meetings. Also, the office was mine to use as I saw fit. It was more of an honorary position than an active one. She said that Hilda felt responsible for the near-death assault on me and wanted to see to it that I was financially rewarded… long term. The appointment was a lifetime contract that I would sign on for. More information would follow as needed. The whole point was that Hilda was paying me off for shooting myself in the leg. The credit card I was given was from the LLC and mine to use for any business pertaining to Hilda. Jackie would monitor it to keep things legal. She asked if I had any questions. I told her I'd get back to her as soon as I digested everything she just laid out.

Is Hilda setting me up for a fall? Before I sign on to her company Board, I'm going to do some checking around. Anne was in the corporate financial markets before she bought the bar. I'll turn this over to her and let her work it out with Jackie. She'll keep me clean. I told Jackie to send everything, such as contracts, to Annie. A shot in the leg is worth one hundred twenty thousand a year to Hilda. Lifetime payments? She's betting that my life won't last more than a couple of months pursuing this caper. So, her lifetime contract is a short-term policy in her mind. I'll just tell her to give me a lump sum of a million bucks instead of monthly conscience money. I could call her out. I'm not going to get knocked off, Hilda. Anyway, it's sweet… if it's legit.

I was heading back to the IG to begin going through all the piles of paperwork that Billy had copied. I wanted to review all the travel locations and the expenses on each trip. I was looking to see how many times he hit each city over the time span the files covered, along with anything that didn't fit within a grouping. Then, I'll have Jimmy and Billy scan the newspapers within a hundred-mile radius for the next seven days of any city he stopped at. I'd have them look for unsolved murders and unusual crimes as well as missing persons like wives, husbands, business partners, high profile people or crime figures. I'm playing a hunch. Horst was involved with Vinnie. That means anything is possible.

This guy could have been a stealth bomber. If he were, no one would pick him up on their radar… like law enforcement. He was a legit businessman traveling the States with a purpose, looking for new clients and servicing his existing business. Perfect cover. Who would ever peg a German optical salesman as an assassin for the Italians or some Nazi gang? I think I may be on to something. The better I get to know Horst the easier it will be for me to blow his cover. Without any other leads to work, that's where I'm going to take the investigation. Hilda's brother said Horst had a nasty side to him. That could have been the common bond between Vinnie Giganni and Horst Strump.

I hadn't heard from Eddie or his two watchdogs, so I assumed there was no action at Freddie's butcher shop. I needed the quiet time to get started digging. I wanted to dump the files right after they were copied so the Feds would back off me. I should put them at Hilda's home and then drop the Feds on her. Jackie could use the legal work and Hilda needed smacked down. She may be clever and rich, but she's not in my league. I don't want to blow my pension from her, I thought, so I'll eighty-six that plan.

I was back on the Southside and sitting in traffic on the twenty second street bridge. It was pretzel time. I cut out a dopey looking guy in a Mercedes and turned left on Carson aiming at the Southside Pretzel Shop. I double parked in front of the place in the middle of twenty third and ran into the store, grabbed my bag of pretzels, paid the clerk, and headed out the door.

Sliding back into my car I began eating a pretzel the way I did since I was first introduced to them. I break out the fat part at the bottom of the pretzel located between the two twisted arms. That was the fillet mignon of a pretzel. I started ripping that piece out of the other four pretzels as I was driving back to the IG. The rest of the bones of the pretzels I tossed back in the bag I'd give to Jimmy and Billy. If they ask what happened to the missing pieces, I'd tell them I got a discount cause they're missing parts.

I've been thinking about my soldier boys and what role they can play in this case and going forward in my detective agency. I had to keep them out of combat. Jimmy's' transmission could slip at any time, and it could cost him his life. Billy had the hands issue. I couldn't count on a choke out to end every problem he might encounter. He needed to be able to work a pistol. I didn't see that kind of mobility in his new hands. My phone was active again with inquiries on divorce matters, security issues and protection. The two of them could manage to return phone contacts and keep me filled in. There would be plenty of leg work on the Strump caper to keep them busy and off the front line until I fill the pipeline with divorce issues and security details. I would keep the two retired cops that Eddie brought on board and hire a couple more. Eddie's boys were street smart and had the kind of experience that I needed on this investigation. Their contacts in the police department would also be an asset.

I parked on Carson Street near my office, and I headed to see how it looked after the repairs. Annie had handled the fix up for me. The front window and shattered glass in both office doors were replaced and the place was painted and cleaned. The furniture was unchanged. My worn-out sofa was still intact and leaning against the wall where it always sat. Annie hadn't disposed of it. The blood-stained floors of the office were cleaned, but in my mind's eye I could still see the outline of my blood on the floor. If there were any blood spatters in the front office near the windows they too had been erased. I needed to thank Annie for taking care of the clean-up. Flowers! No jewelry.

I considered renting the office next to mine, but since it was vacant, I'll just use it until a new tenant shows up. That's where I'll dig into the thousands of pages of documents that I had copied. Once the Feds recover the files I drop on them, my bet is they'll get warrants to search my office, the IG, and my house. They will probably believe I held out on them. They'll take a shot, thinking that maybe they will get lucky and find something illegal, and they could hang on to me. If nothing else turns up, they will have at least put me on notice that I'm still up on their chalkboard. I'll warn Annie and Jimmy to clean up anything they don't want the Feds to see. I'd have to dump the computer Billy was using. It had too much data stored in it.

On my way across Carson Street there must have been a dozen people nodding to me and others greeting me by name. I recognized some of the faces. One local I recognized came up in my face and said, "Thanks for turning the lights back on here on the Southside, Red. The place has new energy since you hit the streets again. Don't go away." I guess I'm still a celebrity. After I lay out a few more dead bodies I'll be a superstar.

Back at the IG, Annie was waiting for me as I entered the bar. Spooks was sitting in his usual spot and talking to some of the regular afternoon drinkers. These were some of the street people that monitored the health of the Southside. If a new virus popped up, they would know it. They couldn't do anything about it, but they would recognize it. That's what Spooks was covering for me. I was looking for the Hans virus and when I isolate it, I'll cure it with the medicine from my Glock.

"Hi, Red. Is there something wrong with your phone? Jimmy has been calling you. He wanted to tell you that they finished the job you had them on. I'll let him tell you about it. Good news, huh?"

"I'm not turning my phone on. The Feds have it tapped and that means they have me tracked. I need to get a dozen of the phones that you buy minutes for, the throwaways. They can't track them. I want everyone to have one. We can use them until I'm sure the Feds are satisfied I didn't hold out on them, or they lose interest in me."

"Don't you think you're going a little over the top with this case? Does paranoia come with your sobriety? You're starting to see the bad guy's shadows everywhere and the Feds hiding behind them. When they get what they want, the files, they will have no reason to bother with you, will they?" Annie asked me with a puzzled expression on her face. She believed I was making the Horst murder into an all-out federal investigation. It is. That's why they're on my ass.

"Annie, this investigation is turning into something bigger than just a fifteen-year-old unsolved murder of a businessman. There are some powerful interests tied to this case that want me to stop the investigation and there are some others just trying to stop me. That includes the Feds. Hilda's opened her checkbook for me. She wants an answer and the money is no object. I'm going to get it for her."

"Call Jimmy!" She was annoyed.

There wasn't any need to call him. He and Billy were coming through the back entrance of the IG and heading for me. I motioned for them to grab a booth in the backroom where we could talk in private. It was empty this time of day.

"We finished copying the files," Jimmy said that with a smile in his voice. It was a proud smile. The kind you got on your face when you answered a hard question being asked in school by the teacher and the smart kids in the class along with the teacher never expected you to have the answer.

"How did you do that in so short a time? Did the upgrade in the computer make that happen?"

"No, Red. When we went to Bobby's store and told him what we needed he took us to a copying machine with a scanner that he said would do the job in a couple of hours. I bought it and he had it moved into his warehouse so we could knock it out in private. They're going to deliver the copier to the office tomorrow. What are you gonna do with the files now?"

"Good question. Maybe, let's leave them in a church in Germantown and call the Feds. Where are the copies and where are the originals?"

"The originals are in the trunk of your Caddy. The copies are in the empty office space next to yours. We installed a couple of new locks on the entrance door. The keys are in your glove box. Do you really want us to leave the originals in a Germantown church?"

"No, Jimmy. That was just my thinking out loud. I'll handle it from here. They might pop up in Germantown, but not in a church."

I wanted to turn up the heat on Freddie The Butcher. I could have Eddie drop the files in the dumpster he uses behind his store and then have Eddie call the Feds and the newspapers with their location. Finding them in his dumpster will put him front page and under suspicion as maybe an accomplice to murder; the murder of two old ladies. I could make that happen tonight.

The move would probably send Hans deeper underground. Freddie has a sweet deal going on in Germantown that he doesn't want fucked up. All that publicity would be bad for his businesses. With all the notoriety and the Feds taking a look at him, my bet is he pressures Hans to finish his business and get out of the city. Yeah, Freddie will go to Hans.

"You have anything else for me and Billy to do?"

"I need you to pick up a dozen of the prepaid phones with at least five hundred minutes on each of them. I want everyone to use them beginning tomorrow morning. Get a couple of new laptops for us with all the bells and whistles on them. You can use my credit card, my new company credit card. Get everything from Bobby's store if you can. If you two have some other plans, then just get me the phones. The laptops can wait a day."

"We can handle it. We don't have any plans till eight tonight."

I gave Jimmy my credit card and as I handed it to him, I thought this must be what it's like to be rich. You just buy anything you want without considering how you're going to pay for it. Now, if only I can make the big score and then stay alive to spend it. The blood money from Hilda and a half mil from bagging Horst's killers will get me a downtown address.

How do I handle Hans? I'm back to that same question. If I capture him alive, I could have Wrecker beat the information out of him as to what it is he's looking for and who he works for. Then I'd have to make him disappear. Wrecker can handle that for two grand. Maybe he becomes pig food. That way the Dagos will believe Hans is still out there following me and they won't make a move on me. If they know he's dead, then they step up to the plate and I'll have to deal with them if my hunch is right. I may have to throw a few fakes at myself to give the illusion to the Dagos that Hans is still in the game. Maybe…

This is Monday of week three into the investigation and I'm still flying blind on this case. If the files haven't turned up any leads to follow, then it's out on the streets retracing Horsts movements for the last fifteen years of his life and maybe even as far back as the early sixties.

Jimmy and Billy left for Bobby's store just as One Eye Eddie came in the back door and joined me in the booth. I could tell he was dressed in clean clothes. The blue shirt he was wearing still had the creases in it from the dry cleaner and his sport coat lost the gravy stains from the Greeks. He was old school and used Aqua Velva aftershave as his cologne. I think he uses it for mouth wash too. I used it myself until I retired. I may have downed a bottle or two on one of my benders when I ran out of booze.

"Red, what time do you want the guys to knock off today?"

"Have them hold till the butcher shop is closed and everyone is gone for the night. Then have them call us. Starting tomorrow, let's have them begin their watch every day at eight. They can knock off when the butcher shop closes and everyone leaves. Their only assignment is to tail Hans if he shows. Beginning tomorrow, I want three more men working eight-hour shifts with only one job: Follow Freddie wherever he goes and let us know when and where he lands. One of the places he stops will be where we find Hans. Can you come up with three more guys on this short notice?"

Eddie said he could handle it. He hung out in some clubs where a lot of the retired cops gathered. He knew the kind of guys I wanted. I wanted the ones that don't mind administering street justice. No Miranda bullshit.

"What are you paying these guys? They're going to ask me."

"Tell them three hundred a day plus expenses."

The two lookouts will be on the butcher shop till we show up later tonight. They were accustomed to doubling out when they were on the job. Eddie was free to hang out with me or do some business, like find me three more retired cops. I'm kicking into high gear now and expect the action to pick up. I told Eddie his options. He left to do the business. Working with me has given Eddie some new life. I could hear it in his baritone voice and see it in the jump in his walk. *Detecting* with me has given him a place where he can do what he does best. It's the action that's picked him up. I know it well.

I waved Annie over to the booth and asked her if she had time to make a call for me.

"Who do you want me to call and for what, Red?"

"I want you to call Andy Russell from the FBI and tell him I need to have a meeting with him here at the IG tonight at seven. No rain checks." I flipped his card to her from my wallet with his office number and his private number written on it.

"If he asks what it's about, what should I tell him?"

"Tell him it's about the missing files he wants."

That message would get him over here to me. What I really wanted from him was some inside info on Lefty Lotori the current head of the Italian crime family in the City. Vinnie was still a player in the mob, but not as powerful these days. Up until ten years ago, he called all the shots on the Southside and sat at the head of the table uptown. Today, he's a waiter at that same table. He doesn't have the juice he once had; now he just has arthritis.

The Feds usually have an ongoing wiretap on one of the mob bosses or some of the capos. I wanted Russell to give me some inside info that I could use to trade with Lotori if the time came. In return, I will get him the files by tomorrow morning and give him a German with connections to the gang that Hans belongs to. That lead may even turn up some info on domestic terrorism. It was just bullshit, but that was what it might take to get him to make the trade. He'd squawk about the fact I gave no notice to him for the meeting, but he'll show up. I'll remind him that he owes me the Intel on Hans and his organization.

I needed to have Jimmy or Billy stay close to Annie in case Hans or some other threat comes to the bar looking for me, like maybe a Dago. Jimmy is carrying and I'll leave a scatter gun for Billy. It could get messy if he has to use it, but at least he won't miss his target.

I keep coming back to Hans. Tomorrow, I'll have five guys sitting on Freddie the butcher, waiting for Hans to show. I gotta kill him… soon… and then the immediate threat to Annie goes away and I can move into fast forward on the Horst Strump caper. In the meantime, the files with the clues to solving this caper are sitting idle in the office next to mine.

"Red, now that we finished the paperwork what do you want me and Billy to do?" Jimmy asked me just as I was mentally making up their assignment.

"Cover Annie. Don't leave her out of your sight from the time she leaves her apartment in the morning until she returns to it. If I'm not with her, one of you is. The two of you can make up your own schedule. I'll tell her about her need to have protection."

"What are the orders if Hans shows up here?"

"Kill him and anyone else with him." I reconsidered the risk to Annie and had decided to kill Hans on site and take on the Italians. I could handle them. They're predictable; Hans isn't.

"I thought you wanted him alive."

"I did. The plans have changed. Kill him!"

I decided to go to the other source that knows what Hans is looking for… Hilda. I'll have to get her to open up. She fucked up dealing with Hans and his pals and that got two innocent old ladies killed. She knew these Krauts were in town and by not giving me a heads up she almost got me wacked too. When Hans turns up on a slab in the City morgue, there'll be a new set of Krauts coming after me. Eventually, even without her help, I'd learn what Hans was after when I take down the Krauts from the Homeland that show up in the City. I said goodbye to the boys and headed up to Annie's apartment.

# CHAPTER 32

When I got to her media room, I sat down and turned on the Pirate game. It would help me fall asleep. That was just the kind of TV show I needed. I popped a painkiller, and a few minutes later, Hilda came back into my mind. I knew her brother had no love for Horst, but I've recently picked up on this feeling that she didn't hire me to find his killer out of love. Maybe her shrines to Horst aren't shrines at all. Maybe they're just reminders to her that she has unfinished business he left behind. But why? I dropped off to sleep just long enough to have another one of those strange dreams.

I found myself in a big room holding onto someone with a hood over their head. Someone was talking… a woman's voice. I couldn't make out what she was saying. Next, I saw the outline of the woman pointing a gun at me and then firing it. That's when I woke up.

It must be the pain pills causing the dreams. I think I was dreaming in German. That's strange. Maybe it's time to pay a visit to the witch.

Annie came upstairs to tell me that Eddie was in the dining room with three men.

"He told me they're your new guys and to put all the drinks on your tab. You hired three more men today? Is it that dangerous out on the street?"

"The answer is yes, it's that dangerous out on the street. I need them for round-the-clock surveillance in Germantown. I'm closing in on Hans. When he's sent on his way, I'll enter the next phase of the operation and I need these men for the search team I'm putting together. I'll use them to street sweep every place Horst traveled to that we have a record of. They'll each bring me back a picture of Horst that they develop. Somewhere in those pictures is the answer to what his businesses were and why someone put a hit on him."

"You mean that by sending Hans away, you're going to kill him, don't you?"

"Leave it alone, Annie. You know I'm not going to answer that question. As always, there are some things you're better off not knowing."

"You mean like when we are going to get married."

I just stared at Annie after that remark. She could see I was irritated with it and her. It was about time to close her off before I said something that later tonight I'll regret.

"You don't believe Horst was killed during a robbery, do you? What else did you turn up that makes you think it was a pro that hit him?"

I thought about ignoring her question and heading to the dining room and then reconsidered; this is my Annie.

"The obvious clue was the slugs to the face. The account in the newspapers claimed his face was unrecognizable from the bullet wounds. The usual weapon of choice for a robber is a small caliber pistol. It's easy to hide in a pocket and at close range it is lethal. It would only take a couple of rounds of a large caliber bullet at close range to destroy a face. The parking space where the robbery took place is out in the open.

The nearest hiding place would have been a cluster of trees some thirty feet away from where he was parked. They're now fifteen years older than they were and wouldn't have given a lot of cover to a couple of thugs back then. That signals that he either knew the person or persons that killed him or he wasn't killed there. I have more work to do on the timeline. The newspaper account says he left his office for home sometime after six thirty. I need the coroner's report as to the time of death to see if they jive. When Han is out of the way I'll have two of my ex-cops dig up everything in the police files on the investigation, that's if any files still exist."

I followed Annie downstairs to the dining room to meet my new private eyes. Eddie had moved to a table in the back. One look at the four of them explained why. The booth would have been too crowded. It wasn't that they were all too heavy. They were just super-sized.

Annie headed to the barroom, and I grabbed a chair and pulled another table over so we could all have more space.

"These are our new guys. I told them all that you're good at recycling used cops and drunks and killing scum bags. The killing scum bag's part got them to sign on, Red. Meet Steve Francis, Sammy McCrery, and Jake Jackson."

I shook their hands as I walked around the table and welcomed them to the office annex.

"We all dig your office: A fucking bar. When Eddie told us you had a bar for your office, we all thought he was slinging bullshit," Steve said with a second from the other two new faces at the table.

"Is free booze part of the package?"

"Yeah! But not while you're working. We have more dead bodies piled up than you know about from the papers. I had to eat a slug myself. I don't want any of you getting killed. If you read the papers you know that a couple of the punks I iced were foreigners. They came from Germany on unfinished business. The case we're on has something to do with their unfinished business. There's one still out there. I call him Hans. Find him!"

"Eddie told us you took one in the ass."

"I took a slug in the upper leg," I shot back looking at Eddie hoping that remark and my tone would stop him from making any more shot in the ass references.

"You three start tomorrow as the shadow for Freddie The Butcher. I want eyes on him round the clock. I want to know any place he stops. You can work out your shifts with Eddie. One of his stops will be where the target is holed up."

"How do you want the punk delivered if one of us confronts him?"

"If you get that close to him you better kill him or he'll kill you. He's not going to let you take him. But what I want from you is to stay back and just get me the addresses where the butcher stops."

"Red, I thought you wanted Hans alive."

"Change of plans. That Kraut is too dangerous to fuck with anymore. I got another source that knows what he's after."

"You have a description of the guy. Does he have any distinct features or tattoos?" Jake asked.

"Eddie will fill you in on what we know. We don't have much, but he probably has a tattoo on the inside of one of his wrists. It appears to be a swastika with a trident driven through it. That's what the two in the morgue were wearing."

Looking at Eddie, I said, "From now on, you are second in command. If I go down, you finish the case for Hilda Strump. If any of you need anything, you can tell Eddie or me. All of you should take this case seriously. These aren't street punks we're dealing with. These are well trained professional assassins with an organization to back them up. There's also a finger pointing to powerful allies in some branches of law enforcement. Before this case is solved the Dagos may be on our asses too. Do you still want in?" I asked as I looked at each of them, searching to see any hesitation in their answer. If I detected that in any one of them I wouldn't bring him on board. A nod of the head gave me the answer as they raised their beers and drank a silent toast to the fate that awaited them.

"Thanks for the raise, Red." I heard Eddie call out to me as I sat down and considered my next order of business…the FBI.

"You're welcome, Eddie. That extra ten spot a week will help with your 'Viagra' bill."

"You always have to be a smart ass, don't you, Red?"

"Yeah, Eddie, I always do." I answered as the four of them raised their glasses for another toast.

"Where's your glass?" Steve asked.

"I gotta meeting at seven with the Feds. I need to be sharp. Later, if you guys are still around."

"With free booze on tap we ain't going anywhere." Jake announced as he looked around the table. "Any broads come in here?" was his next question.

I excused myself and told him to check with Eddie about the broads, grabbed Annie and headed across Carson Street to Max's café for a quick burger and fries. Max sat us in a rear booth and took the order. A glass of soda later, the food arrived. As we ate I wondered if the Feds would take a chance at blowing one of their investigations to make a deal for a quick resolution to the missing files. I'd trade them the intel they owe me on Hans and the files for the dope on Lotori. Information on Hans will have no value to me since I'm going to kill him. We finished eating and headed back to the IG. Max burned the check.

I asked Eddie to keep an eye on Annie and headed to my office for my meeting with the Feds. Annie would send Russell over. The new window in my office opened easily and the warm Southside air flowed through my lungs, injecting me with renewed strength. The air is different on the second floor. That's what I tell myself. I'm just like a superhero that has a secret to renewing his powers. The burned air from the J&L blast furnaces that towered over Twenty eighth street had been replaced with the smell of burning incense from the head shop below my window. It was mixed with the scent of yuppy and beer from a microbrewery down the block. Soot!

That's what the Southside needs again. Where did the clothes lines rigged on pulleys attached to every second and third floor window and strung out to the closest tele pole or neighbor's house go? Doesn't anyone dry their fucking clothes outside anymore? I felt a new energy in my office from the throwback memory of Steeltown and was confident I'd get what I wanted from the Feds and solve the Strump case.

I turned from the open window as I saw Russell crossing the street from the IG heading to me. He looked up and frowned when he saw me observing him weaving through the traffic. He was pissed at having to meet me tonight. Thirteen steps and ten paces later he opened my outer office door and entered. Even though the broken glass in the door had been replaced they didn't fix that god awful screeching sound it makes when it's opened. My alarm resets itself every time the hallway door was closed.

"It better be good!" Russell snapped as he pulled up a chair and sat down across from me. "Where are the files?"

"Where do you think they are? They're in the fucking trunk of my car. I don't know why you got such a shitty attitude with me. We're both on the same side, aren't we?"

"No, we're not on the same side. I'm going to lay it out to you again. This Strump case shows up as a black screen on the computer in my office. It has skull and crossbones on the screen and next to that image is a circle with an X through it and a picture of you inside the circle. That means that the highest places in the government want this case and your involvement in it ended. Give me the files and get lost for the next year."

"Fuck you and your bosses. Here's the bottom line. I want you to give me something you have on Sal Lotori that's current. You can skip the German info. You agree and I'll squeeze the city in the next twenty-four hours till the files drop out."

The expression on his face gave me my answer…no! It was time to sweeten the deal with the terrorist, Freddie the butcher. When I fed him that line he perked up. Could be a promotion in it for him if he found a terrorist right here in Pittsburgh.

"How would a gumshoe like you hook on to a terrorist?"

His interest level went up on the terrorist move. Maybe he was hooked. The chance to turn up a high value threat overrode his anger toward me. He was weighing his options. Give up something to me on Lotori and maybe risk blowing the case for him or tell me to fuck off.

"Hey, Russell, what do you know about a gumshoe? You're too young to be familiar with that term."

"You're right, Red. My knowledge comes from growing up sitting next to my grandfather watching old black and white detective movies from the forties and early fifties. You know, the ones with the old school dicks like Richard Diamond, Sam Spade, Mickey Spillane, Mr. and Mrs. North, and Boston Blackie to name a few. The first time we met I knew that I had run into a private eye that was a gumshoe throwback. Red, all you need is one of those Adam hats and a nineteen fifty black Chevy coupe to drive around in. You're black and white TV without a remote, Red," Russell said, but he didn't say it in an insulting manner.

It was almost like I detected admiration in his description of me.

"You forgot one more important detail: The gumshoes. I still wear rubber soled shoes from my days on the job, but I never wear a hat, Russell. Now, what about a deal?"

"Get me the files by tomorrow morning and I'll give you a piece of Lotori. Why do you want to fuck with him anyway? Do you think the mafia has their hands in the Strump homicide? Don't answer. I don't want to know. Just make sure that if you use anything I give you that it doesn't come back to me. I can't have my fingerprints on your business. Can I trust you, gumshoe?" He was staring into me to verify his instinct that I wouldn't implicate him.

"Deal, Russell. Keep your phone on tonight and call off the tail on me. Be ready to move when you get my call."

Our business was finished. Russell started out of my office then suddenly turned to face me.

"Pay up your accident insurance. There's a rumor that you are going to have a fatal one sometime after the files are recovered. You stirred up the dark side of a covert government agency. Whatever this guy Strump had on someone, they don't want it found. One other thing, gumshoe, Horst Strump didn't exist before nineteen sixty. Someone made him up."

Russell had just dropped a bomb on me. What he just told me caught me off guard. Not that line about some covert agency of the government setting me up for a hit, but the part about Horst Strump. If what Russell told me was true, then fruit stand Vinnie may have a bigger part in the case than I originally believed and so does Uncle Sam. I'll have to pay a visit to Vinnie tomorrow and maybe step on his grapes.

Russell had left me with another twist in the caper. I have to fit that information into the puzzle of Horst Strump. I wanted to pump him for more background on Strump and wished he had stayed long enough for me to absorb that new info. I heard the bottom door open again and footsteps on the stairs. Russell was coming back to tell me something else about Strump. I turned my chair to the open window to look across at the IG and saw Russell crossing Carson Street in that direction. Oh, shit!

My alarm went off, but before I could pull my gun out, someone was standing behind me, and it wasn't Russell.

"Good evening, Mr. Canyon. I thought it was time we met." A voice with a strong German accent announced.

With Russell walking down Carson Street and someone with a German accent standing behind me, I turned in my desk chair to greet the unexpected visitor.

"Hans! I've been looking for you ," I said as our eyes locked on each other's.

"That's what Wolf told me before I killed him," Hans announced without a change in his tone. I now had a close look at the man I called Hans. His expression and cold brown eyes told the story as we stared at each other. He had the advantage. The Glock in his right hand that was pointed at me gave it to him. How the hell did I get myself caught off guard again by Hans?

"Where are the files, Mr. Canyon?" Hans asked.

Hans was all business. It's just what I expected from this Nazi bastard. Ask a question about the files and then bang. I can see in his eyes that killing me outranks getting the files.

"They're in the trunk of my Caddy. Wait here and I'll get them for you," I answered as I was working on buying time till I could come up with a plan to stop Hans from pulling the trigger on me.

"You better be telling me the truth, Mr. Canyon. After I kill you and I find they're not in your car trunk, then I'll go and kill your girlfriend from the bar and that retarded relative of yours."

"Can't we all just get along, Hans?" I asked knowing my humor would miss this Nazi bastard. "Sit down and let's talk this thing out."

"No talk. I came to kill you. Get up and stand in front of the window. I'm going to send you to Hell through the same portal that you used for my brother."

I didn't have my vest on. The bullets from that Glock would go right through me with a force that, at this range, would propel me through the newly installed window in my office. I slowly moved from my chair and stood in front of the half-open window. Hans was six feet from me and about to act.

"Sorry, Hans, but you're going to be disappointed. The new glass in the window is bulletproof, and it won't shatter. Bounce a bullet off it and see for yourself." That was the best stall I could come up with. I needed to force Hans to make just one error that could give me a chance to kill him. Would he fire at the window and give me that split second to move at him?

"Move aside, Mr. Canyon. I'll see for myself," he said as I moved a step to my right while he moved close enough to the window to tap it with the barrel of his Glock.

That was the opening I needed. I rolled over his arm that controlled the gun and pulled him to me by the lapel of his suit coat and threw the both of us out the fucking window. If I could turn him under me as we were heading for the sidewalk some twenty feet below, his body would break the fall for me, and I might be able to walk or crawl away. If I couldn't make that move, then I'd be just like Humpty Dumpty and all the Kings horses and all the Kings men couldn't put me together again.

On my way out the window my life didn't flash before me and I didn't see any white lights at the end of any tunnel. What I did see was the sidewalk racing up to meet me. That meant I was on top of Hans. My instinct for survival was in charge of my movements. The sidewalk closed the distance and I went blank at the same moment.

# CHAPTER 33

Over at the IG, Annie was pouring a beer for a customer, and Eddie was slamming down shots with his new team.

The door to the IG burst open and an unfamiliar voice called out to Annie that someone had thrown Red out of his office window and he was on the sidewalk with his brains splattered all over it. Annie dropped the glass she had in her hand and raced to the door and down Carson Street to see if her worst nightmare had finally come true. She had envisioned this moment since high school when he told her he was gonna be a cop when he got out of the Army.

Eddie and his new soldiers heard the news at the same time as Annie. They were out of their chairs and following right behind her. Eddie too was wondering if it could be true. After a moment he convinced himself that it could not be. Nobody could throw Red out a window. They could ambush him or shoot him in the back, but never could they throw him out a window.

Two doors down from the IG, Eddie saw Annie leaning on a car and holding her head in her hands. He held her for a moment, then asked Steve to stay with her until he returned. He warned Steve to be on the lookout for the German or any other suspicious threat. She would be safe with Steve.

Eddie and his remaining two soldiers weaved through the stalled traffic on Carson Street that was caused by the spectators spilling out onto the street and onto the sidewalk in front of Reds' office. He pushed through the crowd while identifying himself as a police officer and moved forward anticipating the worst. And there it was.

He saw a pool of blood surrounding the head on the ground that was unrecognizable. It was twisted sideward with the neck stretched and a throat that looked collapsed. As he ran to the body, a new picture came into view. The mangled face that was pouring blood and brains onto the sidewalk wasn't Red's. There were two bodies on the ground that appeared to be locked in a death grip. The body on top had almost completely covered the one that owned the bloodied and smashed head.

"Everybody move the fuck back!" he called out to the crowd as Sammy and Jake began pushing them away as they scanned the crowd with their weapons in their hands.

"Red! Red! It's me, Eddie. I'm going to take care of you. If you hear me, try to move one of your feet," he said in a pleading, almost begging voice. If he could move his foot, then Eddie would know that he wasn't paralyzed.

There was no response from Red. Eddie had seen many injuries during his career from gunshots, auto wrecks, knife wounds, cracked skulls, but never one like this. He decided to act. The way he saw it, either Red was dead or needed immediate medical attention. Either way he was going to act. Red had to be moved off the other body.

He shifted over to the right side of the body and dropped to his knees, reached under the motionless body of Red, and rolled him over to cradle his body while trying to support his head. He could see that Red still had a clenched hand on the jacket lapel of the other body. Eddie called to Jake to come over and try to release the death grip Red had on the suit coat. As Eddie held the limp body of his friend, the most famous detective in the City, Annie and Steve had pushed their way through the crowd to view the tableau. Annie joined Eddie on the sidewalk and with tears streaming down her face, she called out to Red.

"Red! I know you can hear me. It's Annie, Red. Open your eyes, Red. Please!" Annie pleaded.

She looked over at Eddie and could see tears welling up in his eyes as he began rocking his buddy, Red, in his arms. They both knew they were helpless. Red's life was out of their grasp.

Sirens were getting louder as the distinct tune of police and ambulance mixed together in a song played countless times each week. It wasn't a popular melody. There was no admission price to the theatre of the streets or was there? Who would win the race to the headliner: Cops or medics?

Eddie watched as Red's eyelids slowly opened and his eyes rolled back. He had seen that same uncontrolled eye motion on some of the dead men who seemed to be looking for something to catch their soul before it left their body for the beyond. He wasn't going to allow Red's soul to fly on to that place, at least not without a fight. He had to do something to jolt Red back to the reality on the street so he spoke to Red with the only thing that came to his mind that might draw Red back to the Southside.

"Goddamn it, Red. I don't have any water or beer to pour on you to wash the fucking blood away like at Wrecker's," Eddie said, with a broken voice choked from emotion. Real men don't cry, but Eddie was close to breaking that covenant. Annie was now sobbing and softly repeating the words, "Red, you can't do this now." Over and over and over again.

And then it happened. Jake called out first. "He's breathing!"

Just then, Red reopened his eyes. They weren't focused as Annie and Eddie could see, but they were open, and he began breathing in short, quick breaths. Then he weakly spoke.

"Where's Annie," he asked in a soft and shaky voice that Eddie had never heard before or expected to hear from Red.

"I have your hand, Red. Eddie's holding on to you until the medics get here," Annie told him. "They'll patch you up at the hospital and then I'll bring you home."

Red could hear Jimmy's voice faintly telling everyone to get the fuck out of his way as he made a path to his cousin.

"Red, you ok?" Jimmy called out as he broke through the crowd.

"I feel like someone drove a concrete truck over me, Jimmy. My fucking head is killing me, and my left shoulder is on fire." Red managed to get out in a weak muffled voice.

"Eddie, did I get him? Is that fucking German bastard dead?" Red managed to sound out.

"You got him, Red. He's dead," Annie told him as his eyes closed and his body sagged in Eddie's arms.

"Red's not dead. He's just resting till he gets to the hospital," Eddie kept repeating. Then, in his loudest baritone voice, he proclaimed to the crowd, "Hey! Everybody, Red Canyon's not dead! Not Dead! He's not fucking dead!"

Eddie continued his chant until the medics took Red's limp and motionless body from him and gently set him on a stretcher. No body bag this time for Red. His destination was the emergency room at the Southside Hospital.

The body of Hans was tagged and loaded into a black body bag the coroner uses with a final destination of the morgue in the basement of the Southside Hospital.

The Carson Street Caper had claimed another life and Red Canyon had escaped the clutches of Mephistopheles again.

## CHAPTER 34

BEHIND THE PALE green curtain of stall three, a mix of colored blouses and blue scrubs continued their search for the injuries that brought Red back to SSH. A dislocated shoulder had been reset. Cuts were cleaned and glass fragments on his body were located and attended to. X-rays were scheduled to find and repair any broken parts of Red.

Police poured through the swinging double doors that separated the waiting room from the treatment area. Reporters followed with their cell phones and mini tape recorders, asking anyone they saw if they had any information about Red Canyon.

Annie and Eddie pushed their way through the dozens of mixed onlookers until they reached his bedside in spite of the protests of the medical personnel and police. Annie found his hand at the end of a taped port that was connected to four opaque bags of liquid hanging on what could be a coat tree. Annie and Eddie were being asked who let them in when an unexpected voice answered the protests.

"They're with me. They stay. The rest of you get out of here and someone get me my clothes," Red called out in his usual not too polite manner.

Annie began weeping: Not in sorrow, but in joy. It was as though someone turned the Red Canyon switch back on inside him. He was starting to sit up and pull off the connections to the lifeline that had been attached to him. Eddie went to him to help him sit up when Red gave his next order.

"Eddie, get me a fucking beer. I feel like a have a bad hangover and I need to back it down with a brew."

"As soon as we get back to the IG, Red, I'll even buy!" Eddie said with a smile in his voice.

Somehow, Red had shaken off the last two hours of his life and the trip from the second-floor window of his office to the pavement. The body that had been motionless less than a half hour before, now again energized, was catching up with the other parts of it.

The police had circled the bed and an unfamiliar detective was ordering everyone to leave the area and informing Red that he wasn't going anywhere.

A new voice then spoke out over the others as Annie and Eddie were about to react to the order just given.

"This man is in my custody. He is under Federal protection."

A Federal shield was being held over the heads of the others. Special agent Russell had arrived and decided to take over. The detective who had moments before declared his authority was now being told to stand down and not to interfere with the FBI. He ordered the entrance to be cleared and his car to be brought to the exit doors.

Russell came over to Red and asked him if he really wanted to do this, leave the hospital. Red nodded and just said, "IG". Everything else including the countless questions from the authorities would have to wait. Red would have his beer at the IG and then rest. He knew that Annie would take care of him. Annie always took care of him.

I took a quick survey of the clothes I put on for my exit from the hospital. Sam The Tailor, would be selling me another suit. This is the second one a German punk tore up for me.

I held on to Annie and Eddie as Russell and my guys cleared the way for me through the reporters, cops, curious onlookers and patients that lined the outdated emergency room facility. If I was going to keep using this place, I needed to talk Hilda into donating a remodel job. This emergency treatment area had its own emergency. It was one level above wheelchairs with wooden wheels and park bench seats.

Tonight, Russell's black Government Issue suburban would act as my limo instead of my hearse. Before I entered the SUV I decided to tell the crowd that I was going to the IG for a beer and that I'd give a statement at eleven.

In my mind I had planned for the rest of the night. I was going to set up shop in the dining room of the IG and bang down beer…a lot of beer. That was my first priority and then I'd wait for Jackie to show and tell me to give the no comment bullshit to the media. At eleven I was going to give the press a kick in the ass. Then I was going to pound beer and rethink this fucking caper. Somewhere between drunk and sober I'd find the answer; maybe not tonight, but soon. I had to. I was running out of suits. Suits!! Was Southside Vinnie warning me about my own suits?

The word had spread that I was heading to the IG. Reporters and the curious were waiting at both entrances to the bar. Eddie had arrived before me and had the back dining room emptied. I found my way to my usual booth. I had to tell Russell and Eddie along with the rest of my pack to hold back their questions for now. I could feel the painkillers wearing off and asked Annie to bring me an oxy lollipop and a draft. I almost felt like a character in a soap opera or maybe a reality show and I was waiting for the writers to hand me a script for the next episode. I would have to wait for that script since it hasn't been written, but I'm working on it.

"No drugs with alcohol. That's a lethal cocktail: one or the other," Annie reminded me.

"Beer…beer for everyone. Run me a tab Annie."

Everyone in the back room kept stealing glances at me waiting for me to give them some word about my condition. I had to let them see that I was on my game and ready to make it rain on the bad guys.

I slid out of the booth and stood up and looked around the room at everyone.

"I have a shoulder issue. It'll clear up in a couple of days. I want everyone back here at the IG tomorrow at ten. This thing ain't over with the Germans or the other interested parties. News at eleven and the tap is shut off at midnight. I want you all hangover free tomorrow."

With that business finished I raised my glass to salute the group and took my first taste of beer in weeks. Lent was over for me.

My cousin Jimmy was out in the bar and started shouting to me, "Red, have them flip the TV on to channel three. You're on it. They have a movie of you diving out your office window with that German guy. On the way down, he's trying to shoot you. You didn't say nothing about that."

I didn't remember hearing any gunshots, but there on the news a reporter was describing the scene that included the sound of gunfire. I need to get a copy of that action and have a lab dissect it. I don't think the shots were from Han's gun. I had to address everyone again.

"The Hans I killed didn't fire off any rounds on the way down. In the few seconds it took to hit the pavement he was struggling with me to get the top position. When they check his gun, they'll find out that it wasn't fired. There must be another Hans out there. Dark European suit, close cropped hair and fair skin. Find him. Eddie, get two men back to the butchers at seven. The rest of you back here at nine." The shit just hit the fan.

"Russell, get me a copy of the tape you guys have." His head snapped back quickly and turned toward me.

"Don't look so surprised that I know about your team in the second-floor apartment across from my office videoing the Red Canyon Story. I need it and you know why. There's another shooter out on the street. If your analysts comes up with a face and you share it with me, I won't need the video. Otherwise, I want the fucking tapes. Unless I get them tomorrow, I'll go public and tell the press the Feds are withholding evidence from a crime scene. There's no statute allowing the withholding of evidence where a death occurred."

I didn't know if anything I just quoted was true or not. If Russell's response wasn't to tell me to go fuck myself, then I wasn't blowing hot air.

"I'll see what I can do, but if I make it happen you have to assure me that it stays between you and the Department. No media. Are we clear?".

"Yeah, we're clear. Tomorrow. Now for some good news for you. I know the location of the files."

I called Jimmy over and quietly asked him to get me one of the

Pre-paid phones and log in the number. It was going to ride with Russell. The man with Eddie will call him and tell him the location of the drop. Eddie would take a second pre-paid phone and use it to make the calls then throw it in the river. Russell would be instructed to smash the rental phone on the pavement and kick it into the sewer close to the files. He would be told that he was being watched, and if he didn't follow that direction, the delivery boys would put a beating on him and take the files with them. He would have to leave his phone with me before he left so he couldn't get back up at the drop site. The first call would give him a bogus address in case he has a phone stashed in his ride. The second call would be made when he was close to where Eddie would leave the files.

I moved from the booth to the back of the dining room to talk with Eddie privately. When I told Eddie the plan he complained that it was too complicated just for turning over some files. "We ain't spies and he ain't Gold Finger."

It wasn't quite the right analogy, but I understood what he meant.

"Eddie, the Feds would tag me with spitting on the sidewalk if it could put me away. Russell would fail a lie detector test his department would give him if they thought I gave him the files and he didn't take me down for obstruction. That's why Russell must be blind on the turnover."

"You think the Company would squeeze their own guy that hard over those fuckin files?"

"Yes. They'll cross the line to get me to drop the Strump investigation. They may even try to whack me if they think I'm getting close to finding something

Strump buried underground that ties them to something illegal."

"Red, why don't you have your press conference out on the street in front of the IG? That will drag everyone interested in you out front. The alley will be clear. Have Russell leave his car keys and one of the boys will make the transfer somewhere on Sarah Street. It's dark out and we'll make sure it's clear before we make the switch. Just make sure you drag Russell outside with you."

"Do it your way, Eddie. Just keep it clean."

Eddie turned back to look at me as he was tapping Jake on the shoulder and raised his middle finger in my direction which I would take as a gesture of his confidence. Eddie had become very special to me in these last few weeks. I'd have to keep him close to me. I didn't want to let the City off the hook on his pension.

"Russell, give me your car keys and wait till after my news event. The files you've been after will be delivered."

"I warned you there was a bull's eye on your back. I've been instructed to drop you off the screen when I recover the files. That means your protection from the locals ends tomorrow at nine. That's when I'll make a statement that you are no longer a person of interest to the Bureau. My job is finished with you at that point. There will be other faccs you don't recognize replacing me. It's too late for you to get out of the quicksand you're standing in. You're a dead man, Red."

I needed some information from him before he pulled out. "What part of the government set Strump up in Pittsburgh?"

"Don't know and wouldn't tell you if I did. Believe me gumshoe, this is one case you won't live long enough to solve. Not only are the Germans coming after you, but rumor on the street is the Italians are shopping a contract on you or have a contract out on you. All I can tell you is that it didn't originate from here. Try looking west if it's true."

"When you get back to DC you can tell your bosses to buy stock in the body bag manufacturers. I like you Russell. Maybe you got too close to me and you know too much. You're like where I'm at. You don't know what you know too much of. You might want to consider a new career. Maybe as a Southsider."

"This assignment got my hands dirty. Tomorrow morning, they will be clean." But there was hesitation in his answer, and I sensed some doubt.

"Russell, you're like Pontius Pilot. He washed his hands and walked out on a deal, but they never came clean and it followed him till it did him in. Be careful of the suits."

"Red, you don't know what the fuck you're talking about. And what's that suit thing about."

"That's one of those things I know, but I don't know. Just like the thing about Horst Strump not existing before 1960. You know, but you don't know. Get it?" I said, trying to get him to consider that his future may be linked to me and the Strump case. His life could depend on it.

I drank a couple more beers and considered what I would say to the press. My approach would be; no statement. That way I could just keep saying no comment and the *advice of council* thing. They would get angry and frustrated. A few generic questions would pop up that I could answer. Fifteen minutes at most then pull the plug. That would be enough time for Eddie to transfer the files to Russell.

Wrecker showed up as the get-well party was breaking up. He said he saw on TV that I was buying. I could see the real purpose in his eyes. He wanted to know if I had the strength to continue on the case. He had his answer.

Sometime after midnight I went with Annie to her apartment. She called my mom and some of my relatives that called for me. I told my mom and the others that I was on the mend and to stay away from me until I finish the case I'm on. Annie told my folks that they should stay home and that I didn't need them around to distract me. She would keep them posted. I took aspirin and hit the bed. Tomorrow, I'll deal with the butcher and the Hans clones.

# CHAPTER 35

I WOULD HAVE to spend the night in a recliner next to the bed when I crashed. My shoulder wasn't bed ready just yet. My phone was inundated with texts and the voicemail was full. Everything was moving fast. Jackie called Annie and told her to watch for the doctor she hired to look after me. He makes house calls and we needed him to help block the cop's attempts to get to me. The IG would be my sanctuary for the next few days. I was grounded. I would use the time to find the clue in the boxes of Horsts' past. As the lights were going out for me one of those cartoon balloons appeared in my mind's eye with the caption of *OH! FUCK!* then nothing…

The next morning in the dining room I sat back in my booth across from Annie and three dozen doughnuts with three boxes of coffee she had delivered for the nine o'clock meeting in the bar. Everyone showed except the two shadows I had stationed at Freddie's butcher shop. With a coffee in my hand, I started what I had hoped would be the beginning or end of the Strump case.

"Eddie, I need you to send a couple of guys to city hall records division and then to the precincts that investigated Strumps' murder. What I really want to find out is which government agency leaned on city hall to back off the Strump case."

Jimmy came over and sat down next to me. I could see he was troubled.

"Tell me, Jimmy!"

"You been putting me on the back burner lately Red. You need me with you. No one can cover your back as good as me. We've been together since we were kids. You're the big brother. I know you think you're protecting me. Don't! These punks can't take us if we hang together. I don't go to my hiding place anymore. So don't worry. Red and Jimmy, that's how it's supposed to be."

Annie heard the conversation and stared at me, looking for some sign that I was turning Jimmy down. I wasn't.

I put my arm around my cousins' shoulder and pulled him close. "Jimmy, you're right. That's the way it's supposed to be. Now get your ass out of the booth and get me a coffee and two doughnuts."

Annie looked at me as she shook her head knowing that I have Jimmy covering my back. That called for a response from me. "Jelly." She would know the meaning.

Last night I decided to keep One Eye Eddie with me. I know I'm a target and my Southsiders become targets by association. They all got the warning from me today and a chance to walk.

Jimmy was sitting in front of the entrance to the dining room talking to a clean cut balding white guy wearing a suit. Another fucking suit. I thought for a minute I could be was looking at a suicide bomber wearing a vest full of TNT or C4.

"This guy says he's the doctor Jackie sent to take care of you for the next three days. He wants to come back and talk to you. I searched him. He's clean."

"I'm Doctor Simmons, and of course, you must be Red." He spoke in a whiney voice that didn't fit his size.

He went on to tell me that he had a hospital bed being delivered along with some other medical equipment. I told him I wouldn't be using the bed, and this wasn't the Southside Hospital annex.

"The bed is not for you. It's for me. I was told that you had an office in the back of the bar. That's where I'll set up. You see, Jackie instructed me to keep you under a medical watch for the next three days to give her time to handle the legal end."

"What's your first name?"

"Gerald."

"We'll call you Jerry. Let me give you the rules. You don't leave this room. You stay in the office with the door closed. If the cops show up, we'll bring you out to blow them off. If you need anything, including food and drink, you ask the guy with the iron hands. His name is Billy."

"Jackie asked me to examine you and make sure your injuries are treated. If you have any pain, I brought a bag full of happiness to make it go away".

"I don't need any juice from you and don't pass any of your happiness to anyone else. Got it?"

It seems that Jackie found a pill pusher she could buy for the next three days. Maybe he's her client. It didn't matter. He would be the roadblock I needed for now.

I gave Billy his new assignment and asked him to go get me a bag full of the files stored in the office next to mine. I was going to go up in Annie's apartment to take a trip through Strumps past.

Instead of heading across the street to my office he went into the office I was going to store the doc in and brought out a black bag and set it in front of me. It contained one of the new laptops he bought.

"Why don't you just use the laptop to look through the files? They're all in there along with a breakdown by category from travel to company charges and personal data as thin as it was."

"You mean you scanned them all into the computer after you made copies?"

"Hell no. The equipment we got from Bobby copied, scanned and sent them to the laptop in front of you."

"You sure you got everything on this laptop that's in those file boxes?"

"Positive."

I didn't need them anymore. Time to turn the over.

"Alright," Billy answered with a smile. It was the kind of smile that called for a 'good boy or nice job' or maybe some cash or maybe all of them. Yeah, all of them.

Billy sucked it up, the way I thanked him, but he turned down the money.

"Billy, since you don't want money, maybe you'd rather have some flowers," I said in the usual Red Canyon style that was sure to generate a response.

"Fuck you, Red. Now I'll take the money. How about a thousand?"

"How about a hundred?" I countered.

"Cheapo! I'll take it."

"Now, show me how to open the files."

Some changes had to be made to the dining room entrances. A curtain was strung across the bar entrance and all the back windows. Eddie had called Bobby to get him to send us a carpenter to install steel doors at the bar entrance. What other material would we use? Pittsburgh is still thought of as Steeltown to the diehards of the City.

Doctor Jerry came to bitch about his accommodations. He told me he wasn't happy.

"Jerry, you took this job because Jackie either is paying you big bucks or she got the goods on you. You have a bag full of fucking happiness, don't you? Get happy."

I called Billy over while Jerry was standing next to my booth. "You're in charge of Jerry. Get him anything he wants to drink or eat, but he stays in the office. If he gets out of hand, slap him around, then toss him out in the alley and have Jimmy call Jackie."

Looking at Jerry, I asked if he understood, pointed to the office, and then waited for my next problem to show up.

The next morning Russell finished his news conference at nine thirty and a minute later the cops were banging on the IG doors. Doctor Jerry met with them on the street and said I was resting and couldn't talk with anyone since he had me sedated. During the confrontation on the sidewalk Jackie showed up with four high priced criminal attorneys who along with her favorite judge blocked any attempt to get to me. The stall would work for now, but the DA would find one of his judges to override her judge. The other lawyers Jackie hired would then appeal to their judge, and so on and so on up the ladder until Friday.

The news media had the front and rear of the building painted with TV cameras. Because of the crowds, the cops had to set up barricades so people could walk by the IG on the sidewalk without going into the street. They closed the alley behind the bar. Only residents and deliveries could get through. They had me locked up inside the IG.

Jackie found Annie and told to her to have me stay inside the IG. It was my sanctuary, like a church, but with better booze than sacramental wine. She left two lawyers behind to deal with the city. The fucking barroom is getting crowded.

Upstairs in Annie's apartment I started looking at travel and expense records to see if there was any kind of pattern in this mess. Maybe somewhere Horst missed dotting an 'I' or crossing a 'T' that could give me the break in the case. I had browsed through about a quarter of the documents when One Eye Eddie showed up.

"Fruitstand Vinnie is downstairs. He says he wants to talk to you. His face is on channel three if you want to see him banging on the front door of the IG. You want me to send him up?"

"It's business. Right now, the IG backroom is my office. When I come down, I need you to clear the dining room out and lock the Doc in the office. When I get to my booth, bring Vinnie over to me, then go have a beer. I'll call if I need you."

"His son, fat ass Sal, is with him."

"Take him to the bar and get him whatever he wants. Don't let him in the back unless I tell you to send him. They may have just wacked themselves by showing up at my door with the City tuned in on live TV. His Dago gumbas are gonna figure he's selling them out."

"Didn't you want to put the squeeze on him?"

"Yeah, but I'm going to let him talk before I make a move. He may know if there is a price on me from his Dago godfathers. Unless he's here to fill the contract himself then he and Sal are hamburger."

"Red, you didn't say anything about any contract on you. When and who called it in and how big is it? If it's six figures, every punk on the street is going to try and collect on it."

"That's a couple of the questions I'm going to ask Vinnie. Russell told me he heard a rumor. Nothing for sure."

It took me longer to get to the dining room than usual because of my shoulder and leg injuries. I couldn't take a pain stopper. I had to be up for my meeting with Vinnie. For a moment I wondered if a contract on me would cause the Italians to be successful where the Germans failed. I needed to get to the family that's putting up the money for the contract. Money! Follow the money. It's always the same. Could that be the angle on Strump? Money!

The booth became too restrictive for me. I had a table moved to the far corner of the room with just two chairs. I could see the entire room from that spot. Vinnie could sit in front of me and I would sit with my back to the walls. It was the best place in the room for a private talk. I had Vinnie brought in.

# CHAPTER 36

I STARED at Vinnie as he sat down in front of me. He had the movement of a worn-out WW Two halftrack. "Where's the flowers, Vinnie? That's why you're here, isn't it? A wellness visit, right? So now you can see I'm ok. Do you want something from me, Vinnie?"

"I came to tell you a story?" He had a shaky old man's voice with that frog in his throat that some old guys get from swilling down too much booze over the years and smoking a warehouse full of stogies. He used to chew on and smoke those little Italian stogies. The stains on his lower lip was the visual proof.

"I can read my own stories, Vinnie, and I pick my own books. What else you got?"

"You ain't gonna read this story in no book. It ain't been published. I lived it. It's in my head." I saw fear in his bloodshot eyes.

"Red, you know I don't like you and I don't care if someone shoves a stick of dynamite up your ass. In case you don't know it, you and me are dead men and now my son Sal is on the same hit list. It's all about Strump. I told you when you grabbed that deal it was gonna get you killed. In the last three weeks they missed you twice. Now, I hear some of the big gumbas want to put you on their dance card. They won't miss tappin your shoulder when the music starts. Me and Sal are already hearin the music."

"I got a tip about maybe a hit being put out on me. Maybe you can tell me who's shopping me around. Is that the story you want to tell me?"

"No, Red. I got a proposition I'm gonna make you. I knew the business I was in and the risks. You walked on the other side of the street and knew you were a target cause you always looked to light the wick on the dynamite. But my son Sal is a fruit and vegetable stand man. He was the doorman for my office. Sal is clean. But the word is that 'cause he's my son, he goes too. The story I'm gonna tell you is all about this guy Strump. Maybe the missing pieces you're looking for are in my head. Just maybe you can put it all together and find the cave Strump buried his past in. If you can find it and lay it all out in the news the reason to pop us is removed, maybe. That's the only shot Sal has. As for me and you? That's why I'm here."

"Why don't you take your story to the FEDS? They could put you and Sal in a witness protection program. I know a Fed that looks to be on the level."

"They're in this thing too. Their hands are dirty. I told you about *the suits.* While you were falling toward the sidewalk, they had a shooter trying to pop you from the second-floor window across from your building."

If Vinnie was trying to get my attention the bomb he just threw, did it. What he just said fits with my own suspicion. I wanted Russell to get me the tapes the Feds have. There wouldn't be any evidence of the shooter on the street if what he said was true. If they killed me, they would have stuck with the Hans scenario and covered it up. I'm not too popular with the local police and they would support that story. Unless Russell has a tape showing a shooter on the street then Vinnie and me are both right. Now, he has my attention and just maybe he has something I can use.

"How do you know about the lookout post across from my office?"

"The building is owned by Cheech, my cousin, and the dumb bastard Feds came to me to get the go on it from him. They only wanted to rent for a month. I guess they figured you weren't going to be around much more than that. They must have believed that I wouldn't care what they were up to and I wouldn't warn you because of our history."

"Yeah, Vinnie, they were right about that, huh? But how can you tie the Feds to the shots that were fired?"

"I saw it myself. I saw you coming out the window."

"Why should I believe that you just happened to be walking by my office at that exact time?"

"I was coming to see you to have this talk with you."

"How did you know I was at my office at that time?"

"I called the bar and the guy that answered the phone told me where you were. He told me to hurry if I wanted to catch you. Did you tell him you was gonna bail out your window with a passenger? You think he was just being a smart ass with that *catch you* bullshit or did you tell him you was going flying?"

"You're on the clock. If you have something you want to tell me about Strump then spill it. I have some important people waiting to see me." I was letting Vinnie know he wasn't important to me although I was curious about what he had to say.

"There's only one thing I want. I want your word that you'll keep Sal standing if I go down. Your word."

Vinnie was almost pleading.

"First, let me hear what you got before I make any deals with you. Now, tell me about Strump."

I almost felt sorry for the old bastard. If he comes up with anything that helps me close the deal on Strump then I'll try to work something out. I didn't want to be the guardian of a burned-out old mob boss and his dough boy son.

"I'm going back to nineteen sixty, July. I had a beef with the Feds and was getting ready to cop a plea and do a ten timer for trafficking in intrastate stolen cigarettes and booze. They came to me early that year and told me I was their target in the City. They wanted to get the top bosses in the organization, and they wanted me to become their snitch. I told them to go fuck themselves.

It was after that they hit my warehouse with all the stolen goods I had stashed. That gave them all they needed to send me up. I decided to take the rap and haggle for the ten. Before it gets to court around the middle of July three Feds, the suits, walk into my store in the morning. I recognized one of them. Then the guy carrying the briefcase starts talking as he pushes all my numbers, slips off my desk and onto the floor and drops his briefcase there. When he began opening the case, I started to think maybe he got a piece in it with a silencer and he's closing me out. I'm sweatin.

Then he lays out a deal for me. He says this guy, Horst Strump, is a friend of the Director and I can solve all my problems if I help him. The Director would consider it I personal favor and for my co-operation I would have all charges dropped and I could keep all the things I had stored in my warehouse in Lawrenceville. However, I had two days to clean it out. One other thing, I was to sign over the deed to the building and make Mr. Strump feel comfortable in his new surroundings. There were rumors about the director that he was ac/dc. I figured this Strump guy must be one of his toys. The suit with the briefcase said I had one minute to give my answer and sign the transfer of the deed he was holding in my face.

I asked them what they meant by comfortable cause I ain't no fag. I was warned to be careful what I say. By comfortable, he explained that he is to have no trouble with any criminal factions in the City. No one bothers him or his business. I should see to that. If I followed the terms he laid out, it could be beneficial to have a friend with contacts in high places in the government. I signed the papers. That was how I came to know this guy called Horst Strump." Vinnie paused and looked at me for a reaction.

"That's nineteen sixty, Vinnie. You got over forty-four more years to cover, but I don't have that much time. Give me the Readers Digest version."

"I'll try to, Red, but some parts take time to explain. Just listen, goddamn it! You'll see."

I called Eddie over and told him to hold my calls for the rest of the day. I decided to take Vinnie up to Annie's media room where I could turn the camera on him and record his story just in case I want to replay any part of it. I wasn't going to tell Vinnie that I was recording. He might just be a bomb thrower. We'll see!

"So now I gotta wipe the nose of this punk who owns my building or the ac/dc vacuum cleaner from Washington sucks me up and empties me in a seven by nine in *Sing Sing*. Finally, Strump spoke. He said he didn't need me to protect him, just to show him around the town without any introductions. He wanted our deal to stay with us and told me he would find it a violation of his trust if I spread the word about what took place this morning.

He spoke in a monotone voice all the time, staring right at me. This guy had a slight build on a six one or two frame, brown close-cut hair and brown eyes that could burn holes through you. I seen a lot of bad guys, murderers, child killers, and hitmen, but nobody like this guy. Just the way he looked and how it felt nearby him I knew he was evil. I figure this guy was probably gonna live a long time cause the Devil probably didn't want the son of a bitch.

Just from the couple of sentences he spoke I started to wonder if I should reconsider the deal and take the time instead. I got my shit out of the warehouse and didn't hear from Strump for over two years. Seven o'clock one morning in September 1962, he comes in to see me. He says he wants to tell me some things about himself. He wants us to be friends and that requires trust and loyalty between us. I got no idea where he's going with this. I just know I don't want any part of this guy. He's a spook."

"So why didn't you tell him you weren't taking on any new friends? You had the *juice* back then."

"Red, believe me, you didn't blow this guy off."

He continued his story for the next two hours. He told me more about Horst than I would ever find in the fucking files. From what Vinnie just described to me, this guy was much too clever to leave anything behind that he didn't want found. I'd have to filter out the bullshit from the truth of his story. If everything he told me was accurate about this fucking guy, then he made the New Jersey "Iceman" look like a punk.

Now, I'll go back again to the files looking for that piece of information that could break this case. I was sure that he left a clue. This guy had an ego bigger than mine. I asked myself why he would leave a clue behind. The answer is obvious. He never expected anyone to find it, not his clue. He was much too clever, and if someone did stumble on it by accident, he probably figured that he would be dead by then, so it wouldn't matter. This guy knew he was too smart for everyone. If this guy was Einstein, then why didn't he leave a dead man letter when he got offed? All this shit I'm looking for would have been exposed after his death. Just another piece of the puzzle that's Horst Strump.

"Vinnie, you gave me a good story but nothing big enough for me to go to war with you. You got anything left?" I asked as I got up and headed to the steps.

"I got the name of the guys that wacked Strumps kid and the black kid from the hill and I got the proof. One of them is still alive."

If Vinnie was telling me the truth and he had the goods, then its war.

"Where's the proof and what's the name of the last one standing?"

"Come to my store tomorrow morning at seven and I'll turn everything over to you that proves what I just told you."

Fucking Vinnie maybe still throwing bombs. Tomorrow, I'll see.

Now, while I search for the answers to the Strump caper, I'm going to also have to add a war with the head of the Pittsburgh Outfit. I also needed a plan for Vinnie and Sal. They were waiting in the bar for my decision; help them or watch them get capped. When I returned to the dining room some of my guys were sitting around drinking beer and eating pizza. The Doc was pounding on the office door and begging for someone to let him out to 'take a pee.'

I had another issue that was hanging around in my mind that I had to act on. Sparks! "Anyone know how to tend bar?"

Anne was going to need someone to cover Sparks shift tomorrow. From the day I took on the Strump case he's been telling anyone that asked him where they could find me. I warned him not to give out that information, but he did it anyway. Either the Butcher or the *wops* got him in their pocket. I wasn't gonna cap him just put a beating on him then give him a day to get out of the City. Now Sparks has to go...

I sent Jimmy to check out his apartment. I knew he had a wife and a couple of kids. Maybe Jimmy could find out from his wife who he was working for beside Annie.

When he got back to me, all he found at his place was a bed in one room and a stuffed chair in the living room sitting across from a big screen TV. That was it for the furniture. The neighbor said his family moved out a week earlier. On his way back to the IG Jimmy saw Sparks coming out of Pizza Mans joint with a slice in his hand. That was a Lotori spot. That was all the information I needed. He's a rat.

Vinnie and Sal were still drinking wine when I sat down behind the table I was using as a desk. One Eye Eddie was sitting next to it, watching the two of them.

"What's the answer?"

"If you deliver tomorrow morning, we gotta deal. I'll get the backdoor, but you and Sal are out front. I call all the shots. You take them. What makes you think I'll be around long enough to make a difference?" I asked looking into their eyes.

"You got seven more fucking lives left here on the Southside; that's why."

"Sal, you agree with your old man? You going to go along with what I tell you to do even if he gets nailed?"

"What do you got in mind?"

Sal spoke with a strength in his voice I never heard before.

"Sal, you two have any hardware and can you both hit what you aim at?"

"I blow Lotori's face off if I get the shot," Sal answered.

Sal was stepping up, but I couldn't count on him. He was untested. Vinnie was another story. He'd kill without any hesitation.

"You need to do what I say. You don't take any action without coming to me first. That's the only way I come in. Agreed?"

They said a few words to each other in Italian, then stared at me for a few seconds before Vinnie offered his hand. It was done. I was now the new *boss*.

I didn't have the whole package together in my mind just yet, but I had enough to get Lotori's attention.

"You're gonna put a contract out on Lotori when I tell you to. You have to change the dynamics of this war. Tell me how many soldiers you have that you can count on. You're going to need at least a dozen to begin with. What you don't have… you buy. That means you need to come up with the cash to pay for the loyalty. That won't be much of a problem. The cash is right here on the Southside. It's in Lotori's book. You're going to take it over. Once you show you can defend the Southside against Lotori, the Southside bookies will all fall in line with the rest of his business on this side of the river. You have to make them fear you more than they fear him. This is a war you're fighting, and you don't have any prison camps. Get it?"

"I got maybe a dozen not including family that I trust and will back me." Vinnie answered.

"We get it. When does it start?"

"It already started. Dig up the box full of cash you buried in your backyard because you need some seed money. I'll send two of my guys with you as backup for now. You keep anybody I send with no questions asked. You got twenty-four hours to get me fifty grand to draw on for your payroll. Don't use any of your phones. Go buy some throwaways from Southside Bobby's store. That's the only phones you talk on from now on. Shop the contract out on the street when I say. Make it with a seven-figure payoff. It's an open *bounty* to anyone. You'll hear from me when it's time to make your first move against Lotori's producers."

"I ain't got that much in the backyard. How am I gonna pay up if some punk gets lucky and makes the hit?"

"Trust me. Isn't that our agreement? I make the calls and you carry it out. No fucking questions."

"It don't matter anyway. You fuck up, Red, and we all go down."

I had Eddie send two of our guys to baby sit Vinnie and Sal until I get everything worked out in my mind. Maybe I can save Sal. There needs to be a mob guy in charge on the Southside to fill the void that a hit on Lotori would create.

"You think you can pull it off?"

"No, but maybe one of them gets Lotori. They gotta kill Vinnie either way, but Sal, he's negotiable. Either way I'm kicking his ass off of the Southside. Chaos works in my favor. The fire that's set on the Southside will help keep the Feds and the City cops too busy putting it out to worry about me. A mob war like back in the forties will fit right in on the Southside."

"Red, you're fishing in a toilet. Why you helping these dagos?"

"I don't know for sure, but let's just say for now it's because they're Southsiders and I don't like that grease ball from the north side. Could be! Maybe!"

I took Jimmy and Eddie with me to Vinnie's for the seven a.m. meet. Billy and Steve had eyes on the place from midnight. I wasn't concerned over Vinnie, but I didn't want to walk into an ambush by Joe Lotori.

Steve stopped the three of us out front to tell me that there were four dagos inside. I sent him in to tell Vinnie to send his two gumbas outside before we entered. This was just a training exercise for the fruit stand pair. They had to get familiar with taking orders from me.

Vinnie called me into his back office and told me what he was going to turn over to me. It had to stay between the two of us until the last man involved was dead. He asked me for my promise no matter what I was about to discover. Then he placed a grey rusted steel box in front of me and opened it. It was Nagasaki and Hiroshima! I could see why he wanted my secrecy. I'd keep my word for now, but Hilda Strump and Wrecker Johnson will have the answer to the seventeen-year-old unsolved murders of their sons.

I had followed my leads to the same end on four occasions. They always led to the same person. The evidence was all circumstantial and I couldn't put the finger on anyone without that one piece of hard evidence. Vinnie just gave it to me, but Hilda would have to wait and so would Wrecker.

I had to move things along fast. I had Jimmy call Wrecker. I would offer him a chance to kill some white men. Italian white men. He wouldn't turn the offer down, especially if he could get paid to do it. Could be that he and Sal could partner up to run the Southside.

I was about to make my next move when Jimmy gave me a message from Jackie. She cut a deal to have me show up Monday at the Federal courthouse to answer questions on the two incidents with the Germans. I wasn't to talk to the press before the Q and A. The Feds and the police would begin pulling out within the hour. I should keep the doctor since he was paid till Monday. Don't kill anyone else till Tuesday.

Back at the IG I spent almost two hours reading the files on the computer when I found an entry in May

1984 under miscellaneous disbursements that I needed to check out. A five-thousand-dollar check was paid to the South Hills Eternal Light Cemetery. A week later it was reimbursed by Vincent Giganni with the notation it was for repayment of a loan made by Horst to Vinnie on behalf of the company. Back then Vinnie was heeled and didn't need to borrow money. May be a payoff? Could be Horst was making Vinnie buy his own dirt bed.

I was tired and in some pain. I popped a pill and found the bed.

My mind was still working on a plan for Vinnie G. Tomorrow, the fight for the Southside and Sal's life begins... as I get my shit together.

# CHAPTER 37

I WOKE up to the garbage man's song being played in the alley outside the back windows of Annie's bedroom. They were playing the *tin can alley* show on the tailgate of their GMC with the full and then emptied garbage cans. The pitch changed as cans were emptied into the mouth of the hump backed giant garbage truck. They seemed to dump them by size to squeeze out the proper tone for the same melody they played at each stop on their tour. One of the trio must have been new to the band. Two voices were constantly offering him some advice in the form of the often-used language of the garbage gang *players*; 'Not that way you dumb ass, or like this you stupid son of a bitch.' Just another early morning in the 18th Street alley on the Southside. I always like a good start to the day.

"Red, your breakfast is on the table," Jimmy called out. "One eye Eddie is snoring on the sofa."

Annie stayed at her mother's last night. She was getting pissed at me for taking over too much of her bar. Maybe I could change that today. I was going to ask Annie to find my landlord so I could take over the office next to mine along with the third floor. I'd keep the second floor for business and the third for a place for my guys to flop when they get a load on at the IG.

I had my breakfast and told Jimmy not to let anybody come up to the media room for the next hour. I was going to play back Vinnie's session with me and consider his description of Strump.

Vinnie told me Strump had spent from 1940 to 1945 in a concentration camp in Poland. He said his family was swept up by the Nazis from his home in Milano which was on Austrian border. They needed labor. During that period, he saw his father starved to death. His mother met her fate in an oven. He told Vinnie that experience made him what he was. He was nine at the time. Nobody knew he was Italian but Vinnie. At one point, he went on to tell Vinnie that Hilda was the only one he ever cared about.

Red, this guy confessed to killing his German adoptive parents in 1948. Horst told him they were former Nazis. He said the Germans quietly released him from prison in 1951. He lived in the streets like a savage is how he explained that experience. Then, he met the US Army. They passed him on to another government agency.

I could see from Vinnie's description of Strump how he could have been chiseled into a violent man. Everything fits. This guy had no moral compass. His one weakness was Hilda. She must have represented his dead mother to him. He never hurt her, according to her and her brother. I wondered now if he was a Two Faces of Eve candidate. Could be… Yeah, it just could be.

My court date was postponed by the DA and Uncle Sam. Jackie told them she had a witness to the shots being fired at me from inside the Carson Street outpost of the Feds. She said that closed out any open court appearance. I was free to pursue the Strump case.

The rest of the week I went over every piece of information in the files: Some areas two and three times. Then, I found my lead. I wanted to run it down myself, but I'd have to lose the tails waiting outside for me before I could make a move. It wouldn't be that hard. I'd run the rooftops just as I did as a kid, and I hope the drainpipe from the roof in the backyard of the flower store will hold me. I'm a Southsider and this is my playground. With all eyes on the front and rear entrances to the IG nobody would be looking for me to come out of the flower store wearing a baseball cap and carrying a box of flowers to a waiting delivery van.

I told Jimmy about how I wanted to breakout and asked him to check it out. Twenty minutes later I had my answer.

"You have to find another route. The downspout on the flower shop couldn't hold a squirrel. Why don't you take a ride to the Kroger supermarket and beat it out the back? I could pick you up while one eye Eddie stalls the tail in the parking lot. I'll borrow one of Bobbie's delivery vans. They won't be looking for it."

"Get the van and call me when you get behind Kroger's."

My gut tells me I finally found the clue that Horst left behind or overlooked.

An hour later I was on my way to the South Hills to visit a funeral home, The Eternal Light Funeral Home. It didn't take long to reach the place on Brownsville Road in Whitehall. Since I was a kid, I never liked these places. They all have morbid written all over them. Some are bigger than others, but you can spot them anywhere. If I squinted, I could see a grey cloud hanging over their roofs. In between layouts, when there were no flowers for cover, just the odor of death comes breathing through the basement walls to the outside.

I found their ad online that gave the owners name as John Bennett Sr. He claimed that he was serving the community for the last thirty-five years. That told me he was the guy I needed to talk to. He was there fifteen years ago.

The parking lot was almost empty when we arrived. They were either between stiffs or it was intermission. A somber faced salesman approached us and asked if we were making arrangements for a loved one. A few minutes later we were seated across from John Bennett Sr. I told him we wanted privacy and had the office door closed.

"I'm Red Canyon, John."

"I know who you are. Your face is all over the TV and in all the newspapers. Do you have someone you want to arrange for?"

"No, John, but maybe you can offer your services to the City. They may need you and some additional cold storage before I finish the case I'm on."

John developed a nervous twitch on his lower lip and sweat beads started to form on his forehead as I spoke. That's all it took to move him to the place I wanted him in. He'd talk.

"What do you want from me, Mr. Canyon?"

I got up from the chair I was sitting in and moved around his desk and cleared a place for me to sit. He was staring at the floor and the papers I just pushed off his desk to make room for me.

"Jimmy, go stand outside the door and don't let anyone in. John and I need some time alone ," I said as I continued to watch John's facial expressions.

"Strump!\! I want you to tell me all about the business you did with him. Everything… I know about the cremation and the property he bought from you. You fill me in on the details and don't fuck with me. I don't want to have to pay you another visit."

"Are you threatening me, Mr. Canyon?"

"Yeah, John, I am. You may be carrying the missing piece of the Strump case that I need. Maybe not. But you're going to tell me everything that went on between you and Strump fifteen years ago. I mean everything."

I grabbed his tie and adjusted the knot around his neck till he choked and signaled he had enough.

" I located the only file I had on Mr. Strump. The folder is on the floor where you dumped it. I expected the police to show up for it, not you. Mr. Strump came to see me twice. The first visit he arranged for his cremation. The second visit he convinced me to provide him with a twenty-thousand-dollar mausoleum for five thousand dollars. He told me it was a fair price and if I didn't agree, he'd kill me. My impression of him was that he was evil. He warned me that after his death, Vincent Giganni of the Southside would be watching me to make sure I maintained its security. That's all. We cremated him and gave the urn with his ashes to his wife."

"Did you see any other wounds on his body other than to his face?"

"No, because I didn't see his corps. We received it in a standard morgue body bag and cremated it according to his instructions. We never opened it."

"Wasn't that an unusual way to receive a body from the city morgue? You're telling me that you cremated a bag identified as Horst Strump without verifying its contents."

"Yes. We usually pick up the body and then prepare it for cremation. Mr. Strump knew how his remains would arrive from the City and instructed me do as I was told or suffer the consequences. I feared him even though he was dead."

"How do you know it was Strump you barbecued?"

"Mr. Strump had a hip replaced at some point in his life. The device is made of titanium and won't burn or melt during the cremation process. We offered the device to Mrs. Stump, and she took possession along with the ashes."

"What about the mausoleum? What did he tell you to do with it if he didn't have his ashes stored there?"

"After we built the structure, he had his own people install the steel door and a complicated tumbler locking system that we were never to open until June fifteenth 2025."

"How do you know about the locking system? Did you try to open it?" I asked, although I knew the answer. "Don't lie to me, John. Tell me how you know about the fucking locking mechanism."

"I had my groundskeeper examine it shortly after Mr. Strumps' demise. There are pictures of it in the folder on the floor. It's quite sophisticated. Some of the people in that business that I showed the pictures told me it was above the level of the average safe cracker."

"Was he ever on the grounds to see his tomb?"

"The caretaker reported to me that Mr. Strump was here twice before his death. That's the whole story, Mr. Canyon. Now, will you go?"

"Right after you and me ride out to Stump's place."

Ten minutes later, I was looking at a Strumps concrete ornate block house. It didn't look any different than the other dozen surrounding it except for the entry door. It was copper clad stainless steel. The copper had oxidized over the years and turned green. Parts of the outer layer were missing and the stainless steel was exposed. My guess was that vandals had tried to strip the copper off the door but didn't want to work hard enough to get it all. It had a square protruding cover with double locks shielding what I guessed was the vault like entry system. Later tonight we'll crack it, my way.

My business with John was done for now.

I would have to get into Strumps tomb to see if he left behind any of his legacy like the Egyptian kings. His arrogance and ego made me believe he did. I was sure now that I was closing in on the solution to Horst Strump. We'll see!

On the way back to the IG, I decided to have dinner at the Southside Steak House. Just me and Annie. I was clearing the back room of the IG today and shifting across Carson to my office. The Feds had closed down their spy parlor across the street from me. I moved in the open the rest of the day while one eye Eddie gets a safe cracker that can operate a backhoe to open up the Strump mausoleum and bring me the contents.

I said goodbye to John with the warning not to tell anyone I was there to see him, and that meant the cops and the news media. I told him there was someone in the city wiping out the people I contact.

"John, right now, I'm the only one who knows about your connection to Strump. If you want to keep it that way, then button up or I'll tell the press you have new information about the Strump murder. When the people trying to stop the Strump investigation find out, you'll be dead before the evening edition of the daily City rag hits the streets."

I looked over at John to see if he connected to the message. The hesitation in his voice gave me the answer.

"Mr. Canyon, do I need protection?"

"That's why I'm leaving Jimmy behind. He's your protection, but you won't need him after tomorrow night. That's when I break the case open in the press."

I exited Bobby's delivery van and headed back down Brownsville Road to the Southside. Jimmy would keep John from telling anyone about the Strump mausoleum until I retrieve all its contents.

Once most of Brownsville Road was paved with cobblestones and steel rails that carried red- and cream-colored *streetcars* as they were called in Pittsburgh and known as trolleys in Frisco. They wound their way up from the Southside to Carrick and back down the hill to the Southside. The 77/54 STREETCAR turned right and headed to the Qakland section of the City. The number 50 turned left on Carson and headed downtown. Occasionally a renegade would turn left on Beltzhoover Ave and dead end at a little-known car barn; where else but the Beltzhoover section. They all ran through the flats of the Mt Oliver hallway.

With cars parked on both sides of the street, it was barely wide enough for two-way traffic, and with buildings lined on both sides for blocks, it created a hallway of concrete and glass that had to get equal consideration to the tunnels of the City. The rest of the trip to the Southside was down the $18^{th}$ street slalom. How fast could a driver race down the hill past Pious Street to the cigarette billboard that marked the last turn before the railroad trestle and the Jane Street finish line on the Southside? From Jane Street, it was jam on the brakes, and I hope you could make a full stop at Sara Street to complete the race. Back then, the intersection of 18th Street Road and Sara St. had a reputation for accidents late at night. The judges of the contest were the cops if they were around. They awarded the points to the losers.

They were the unlucky competitors that were caught. To be a winner, you had to score zero points. I claimed that title more than once before I reached eighteen. The race wasn't NASCAR certified. You could enter a souped-up Chevy or a 1956 six-cylinder Dodge. After a heavy snow a sled would do. None of that 'every car the same' bullshit. Gravity kept the odds even. Over the years the course claimed some lives of drivers, passengers, and spectators and even dogs. There were no deer on that route. They all had moved to the suburbs years before. Today, the young punks do their racing on an Xbox.

My mind jumped back from my past to real time. I lived on the edge even then. But now I have to solve a Horst Strump anomaly. Why would he have a mausoleum to store his ashes when he chose to be cremated? If His mother was murdered in the crematories of Treblinka, as he told Vinnie, why would he choose the same end, a gas chamber? His mausoleum is the vessel that he chose to store his past, complete with a stainless-steel door with a bank vault locking mechanism. I believe he left his safe out in the open, daring anyone to find his past in it. For fifteen years, no one has… until now. We'll see…

# CHAPTER 38

I PARKED the van on 20$^{th}$ St. and walked back down Carson to the IG. It seemed that everyone on the Southside knew me. The broads smiled and others nodded or pointed. I kept walking. Occasionally, I'd pass one of the punks that belonged to the Lotori outfit. They greeted me with the bad eyes stare. I considered bashing in a few faces, but I'd have to take a raincheck.

When I arrived at the IG, Annie was waiting for me.

"We have to talk, Red," Annie said with urgency in her voice. "Vinnie G has been in the back waiting for you for hours. He says he is hiding and only you know what to do. He's bad for my business, so get him out of here. I need you to get your clients to wait in your office. Promise me you'll do it."

She was right about that. The people that know me, like Vinnie, come to the place that gives them the best shot at finding me, the IG. "I'll do what I can. I'll have to hire a secretary to sit in the office, handle phones and entertain visitors. Make sure you hire a young looker. Maybe you can do that for me?"

"Don't you mean young hooker, Red?" Annie smart assed me.

"That will work too. Just make sure she can answer a phone and make coffee."

I headed to Vinnie G in the back dining room. I could see why she was pissed off. Old Vinnie had dozed off and was cutting down all the trees in Sicily, judging from the volume of his staccato snorts. The back room was empty except for one eye Eddie. Vinnie was playing his old man medley of snore to an empty house. He was still wearing the dirty stained white apron he wears at his fruit and vegetable stand. I awoke him with a tug on his apron. The expression on his face when he looked up said scared.

"What do you want, Vinnie? Did you bring me the fifty grand you owe me? No pay, no play. Cupish?" I told him, hoping he didn't have the money so I could blow him off.

"I got your fucking cash for you." He reached under his apron and handed me a brown paper bag. I threw it on the table. "It's all there, Red. Sit the fuck down and hear me out. My time is running out with Lotori. He sent Pizzaman to the store to tell me I got two days left to make a deal or me and Sal is finished."

"I gotta plan. Come back and see me tonight at my office at midnight. I'll lay it out, but you gotta give me more on Strump or you can keep the bag," I told him. I had a hunch that the old Dago was holding out some more details on Strump. I didn't need his money and don't need the action right now. If he's holding anything else, he's gonna have to produce, or Sal and him make the obit column in the papers.

"I have something I was gonna leave you in my will. I'll lay it out to you at midnight tonight, but you have to promise not to use it till I'm dead. Then you tell me how you gonna take care of Sal."

"Midnight it is Vinnie. It better be good and not some bullshit you make up."

"I'm gonna give you the answers to some unsolved cases you been working on. When I'm dead you'll be front page," Vinnie assured me.

"I am front page. Don't you read the fucking papers?"

"You'll see. You'll see. Tonight," Vinnie said as he slid out of the booth and walked slowly to the rear entrance.

I had a plan for Vinnie. It called for him to go all in. Lotori and Vinnie walk together down the same path. The threat to Sal would travel with them. If Vinnie delivers the goods tonight the *business* would be over in two days or less.

My focus moved back to Strump and the cemetery.

I called Wrecker and gave him the order for equipment I'd need tonight. He said for five grand he could get everything to the job by nine.

I wasn't going to try to blow the front of the safe. I was going to have Wrecker demo the concrete block structure and load the safe into a trailer with Wreckers' yard as a final destination. He could use a modern safe cracker (a plasma cutter) to open it for me.

Annie brought me a ham sandwich and a beer, then began to scold me.

"You're going out again tonight aren't you, Red? You probably don't know it, but you're limping. You need to rest."

"Annie, tonight I think I can put all the pieces of the Strump case together if my instincts are right. Maybe I can also save Sal's ass and get rid of some of the garbage on both sides of the river."

It was Eddie's turn to chime in.

"I have Jake, Sammy and Billy on their way here. You said seven; ain't that right? We still gonna help the grease ball?"

"Yeah. Eddie. I got the cure for the Vinnie G and Lefty Lotori disease. I need you to find me a case of Dynamite and wireless detonators. You know like the phone call actifiers. I need it tonight by midnight. Steal the TNT and the cell phones. Get Billy to set up the detonators. None of this can be tied to us. Can you do it?" I knew the answer.

"I got fifty sticks stashed in my garage. We can rob Bobby's store tonight for the other shit. What you planning? You gonna blow up all the bridges from the Northside and Southside to keep these punks apart?"

"Something like that, Eddie. You'll be in on it, but don't break into Bobby's store. I'll call him and tell him to leave the back door open tonight. I need the entire set up ready by noon tomorrow. For now, I need you and the boys to drive to a funeral home out in Whitehall with me. Wrecker is meeting us there with the tools we need to do the job. When we get what we're after, we all follow Wrecker back to the Hill and his junkyard."

"Are we fucking robbing graves now, Red?"

"Something like that, Eddie. We may just be digging up the last missing piece to the Strump puzzle."

"Then what?"

"Then maybe, just maybe, we find out why the Government, some German mob, and the Italians all wanted me to stop my *dig* on Horst Strump."

"I hope you're right, and we can shake the Feds and the Krauts. You're still gonna have a hangover from Vinnie to deal with. What are you gonna do about the Lotori soldiers left on the Southside? Did you figure out how to handle them?"

"Sal's gonna kill all of them and make himself the new boss of the Southside. Lotori's' gang war will take all the blame. If no civilians get killed the City will look the other way. The rats in city hall will find the winner and set up a new deal. The Outfit in the city will get weaker and the corrupt politicians will become stronger by virtue of the gang war. They win as always."

"We gonna help fat ass Sal do the deed?"

"In a way. The fifty grand I got from Vinnie G is for private military contractors if he needs back up. These are the guys the CIA uses. Billy made the connection. They'll snuff the Italians from the Northside then disappear. We stay clean. We just make sure the horse we back in the race wins."

"Pretty fucking smart, Red. Can I pop a couple of the Dagos? Just let me do Pizzaman. OK."

"We only kill them if they make a move at us. The war will be over in two days anyway. Trust me. Our end is the dynamite. That's you, Eddie. I'm gonna let you blow up at least a dozen Dagos. I wasn't going to tell you till tomorrow but, I don't want you pushing to get into the fight. Stay away from Pizzaman and all the pizza joints on the Southside. From now on they're off limits. You pass that on to the rest of the crew. If anybody can't follow the quarantine, then pay them off. They're finished with me. No exceptions. I'm only talking a couple days. Make the calls now then get ready to travel."

Jimmy was going to convince John to come with him to the cemetery where the Strump mausoleum sat. It was a five-minute drive from the funeral home and right off Brownsville Road. He was responsible for maintaining the grounds and prepping the earth for the new arrivals. The ad says family owned and operated. I was sure he would handle any problems that could arise while we work. He fears me and wouldn't want to risk becoming a new arrival himself. Jimmy would explain it to him with a few well-placed punches in the gut.

When we arrived at the site, Wrecker was ripping off the top of the mausoleum with the clam bucket on his track hoe. When he saw me, he stopped and waved me over to the cab.

"Red, you told me this was a reinforced concrete block building surrounding a steel safe. Climb in here and look inside. No steel. Check that. It looks like there is a safe sitting in the middle of the floor. That son of a bitch is no more than two feet by two feet by four feet. Is that what you want?" Wrecker growled out in his junkyard voice.

"That's it. Load it up and let's get out of here."

It's not what I had pictured a man like Horst Strump would do. I expected the elaborate high security vault. I wonder what other surprises I'll find inside the safe. We'll see!

"Hey, Red, you still owe five grand. That was the deal. Right? I'm taking that fucking phony stainless-steel vault door with me. I get the salvage. Right?"

"Yeah, Wrecker. It's yours."

"I'll be out of here in twenty minutes, Red."

I turned when I heard Jimmy shouting to John to shut the fuck up or he'd have the claw fuck him up. That's the nickname they gave Billy Hands.

"You can't leave my cemetery with this mess. Tell your nigger to clean it up."

"John, he isn't my nigger. He's one of my crew and my friend. When I get what I came for we're leaving, and you can clean up. I'm going to send Jimmy and the machine operator with you to your office. You are going to pay him six thousand dollars. I was only going to charge you five grand, but now you must pay an extra thousand for calling that man a nigger. If you want, you can pay the five grand and skip the insult money. In that case I'll call him over and tell him you called him I Nigger. I know he'd rather have you than the thousand."

While John was considering his options, I motioned for Wrecker to join me.

"Why do I have to pay five thousand dollars anyway? You ordered the work."

"Because, John, that black man coming over here probably killed Horst Strump and you feared for your life when you dealt with Strump. Call to him, John. Use the name you used with me. Then you'll be on a slow boat to China in a scrapped Toyota."

"I'll give you money." John quietly said with sweat beginning to well up on his forehead.

"Wrecker, I want you to introduce yourself to John. Greet him just like you did to the white guy in your trailer."

"You sure, Red?" He asked with a wide grin on his face.

"I'm sure." And with that Wrecker hit John with a roundhouse left to the temple. John was going to have one hell of a headache if he wakes up.

"I pulled my punch. I thought you might have unfinished business with him, so I didn't kill him."

"You got any other Honkeys you want me to meet like that Cyclops motherfucker over there?"

"Just grab what we came for and go. I'll see you back at your yard. Leave the safe for me to open."

John was still lying on the ground where Wrecker placed him. He was breathing. This bum had me angry enough so that I was going to let One Eye Eddie finally urinate on someone.

"Eddie! Come over here. The guy Wrecker just punked ain't moving. I don't see any water around to throw in his face to get him up. Have any ideas?" I asked One Eye, knowing the answer. A grin was already forming on his face as he started to answer me.

"Red, I could piss in his face. That should wake him up."

Eddie offered his body fluid on every occasion I had an unconscious body needing revived. Today I would give the old pervert his chance to perform.

"I need him on his feet, and since I don't see any water around, you're on, Eddie." He now had my approval.

"Do you need privacy, or do you want an audience? I'm sure Wrecker would like to see if you're all talk."

"Bring him over. I'll wash his face too. Tell him to lay next to the guy on the ground." Eddie called.

As Eddie was about to prepare himself for the nasty deed, I heard loud groans from the crumpled body near me. John was coming to. I stopped Eddie's water show. I really wanted John to be super humiliated. It would have to wait. I would send Sammy and Jimmy to get the cash from the undertaker. I have a feeling John and I will cross paths again. Next time, John. Next time, I assured myself.

Wrecker had the safe loaded and we left for the Hill District and the ending to the Horst Strump story, maybe! It had to be there in the safe. I began to travel down Brownsville Road. Wrecker exited through the service gate in the back of the cemetery. Jimmy was with him for insurance. It was ten thirty and I needed a beer. Now, that's the Red Canyon I know.

As I passed the spot of the old Mt. Oliver Theater, I picked up a black caddy on my tail. I recognized the driver as one of the Italians who hangs out with Pizzaman. Looks like three of them in the car. I had to get rid of them. It's going to be like old times for me, racing down 18th St. Road. At the intersection of Beltzhoover and Brownsville, I slammed on the brakes, then immediately floored the van and began the downhill 18th Street slalom. The route was still as I remembered it. Some new faces on old homes and old faces on older homes. I hit sixty with the caddy two car lengths behind. The right turn was three hundred yards ahead as I jammed on the brakes to drop down to forty mph, then hit the gas on the turn just as I did when I was a kid. The gumbas didn't know the protocol on the first turn. I watched the caddy lose control as it slid through the curve and across the center of the roadway into the oncoming lane. I needed every bit of my knowledge of the raceway to maneuver the van and regain control.

The dagos slammed into three or four parked cars before rolling over and bouncing back across Brownsville Road and hitting three or four more parked cars before it came to a stop and then spun like a top on its crushed roof until it exploded.

"Jesus Christ, Red! Did you see that fucking wreck you just caused? Whoever was in that car is charcoal. What the fuck was that all about?" Eddie asked in his I don't believe you just did that shit.

"That was three of Lotori's crew. How the hell did they know where we were? There's a leak in the IG. Sparks must have overheard me on the phone with Wrecker. Eddie, Sparks has to go."

"Let's give him to Wrecker. He'll do him for nothing." One eye Eddie offered.

"We'll use him to help convince Lotori that a meet with Vinnie G will be to his advantage. He's their spy. Lotori doesn't know that we made the rat."

Eddie would go to Wreckers' yard and keep Jimmy company watching the safe, and Billy would go on his mission. Equipment for the remote detonation of fifty sticks of dynamite. I'll head there after my meeting with Vinnie G. I hoped he didn't have anything big to tell me so I can walk away from his problem. The three bums I toasted on Brownsville Road could be a gift from me and I'd hand him back his bag of cash.

I had to push my way through the crowd of gawkers standing around on the sidewalk in front of the IG. As I pushed through, I heard some broad telling her girlfriend, "I told you he'd be here. The woman that runs his bar is his girlfriend. That lucky bitch."

That last remark caused me to turn my attention to the broad behind the voice. She was a fat three on the scale with a full rack. These days, I only look and don't touch.

Inside the bar, Bruce, the backup bartender, was drawing a beer for me. The empty stool next to Annie was mine. They were the last two seats in the bar. I use the dining room wall to lean on from my stool. This was the Red Canyon annex. I had to shake a bunch of hands and refuse at least ten phone numbers handed to me by some of the good-looking women. Life just isn't fair. That's what I would say if I were a liberal, but I'm not. Annie was more important to me than a quick feel and a fast BJ. What I would tell these broads is not to give up. That's the American way.

"Where to now, Red? Oh, don't tell me cause I really don't care right now. However, if you're looking for a new case, the girl sitting alone in the last booth came here looking for you. She says she's the stepdaughter of the funeral director you beat up tonight. Better talk to her, no?"

If she came her to threaten me with the cops, I was going to tell her to fuck off. John wouldn't press charges anyway.

I addressed her at the booth. "What the fuck do you want with me? "I don't have time for you, and I do business at my office across the street starting at nine tomorrow morning."

"Aunt Mary's Locket. It's about my Aunt Mary's locket."

"Do I look like a fucking jeweler? I'm a private investigator. The Jeweler is down Carson Street on the next block."

"The locket was buried with my aunt twenty years ago by my stepfather. It showed up by chance for repair at the store where it was purchased. When I was listening to messages last week for the Home, I heard it. This morning, it was erased. When I brought it up to my stepfather, he just dismissed it as a mistake by the store."

"So, it was a mistake. Forget about it. I'm up to my socks in shit! I don't need any of yours."

With all I have to handle, I'm not going to waste time on someone's errant message. I started walking back to the stool.

"Don't you read the newspapers or watch the news? There was a jeweler murdered in a robbery attempt last night. It was the same one that called about Aunt Mary's locket. Do you think it's a coincidence? I don't. Will you help me? I can pay."

"God damn it!" I called out loud enough to turn all the heads in the bar. She hit my hot button. Murder and coincidence tied together. Another case with the past tied to the present. I'm hooked.

"Call my office phone and leave me a number where I can reach you. The next time we meet bring your check book. Don't tell anyone you've talked to me. Now, go home wherever that is and wait to hear from me. What's your name honey?"

"Rebecca Smith. My stepfather is John Bennett Sr., Mr. Canyon."

Back on the barstool, I cleared my head with an Iron City and prepared to meet with Vinnie G. In thirty-six hours, his case would be over and it would be up to Sal to control his own fate. I'd have a spot for Miss Smiths' caper; Aunt Mary's Locket… hmm. John Bennett Sr. Hmmmm…

Back at my office, I looked up and down Carson Street to see if I could spot any unwanted visitors. I had the street entrance door upgraded with a self-locking mechanism. No surprises by Hans number two, whoever the fuck he is.

Vinnie G buzzed me, and I let him in. Would he step up and do the plan and off himself?

"What do you have, Vinnie?" I asked hoping for his answer to be 'nothing'.

"Remember, not till after I'm dead, Red."

"Yeah, Vinnie. Not till you're dead."

"Here in this box is a piece of the past. I told you you'd be famous with what I just gave you. Open the fucking box."

Vinnie had placed an old Buster Brown shoe box on my desk. He was too dumb to make a pipe bomb to fit in it, but I pushed it back in front of him and told him to open it.

"You open it, Red. It ain't no bomb, but it will blow you away."

When I opened the box and looked at its contents I was blown away like Vinnie said. The first item I saw was the driver's license of Wrecker Johnsons' son. The only other item was a wallet. The wallet with the initials T.S. Trent Strump, Hilda Strumps' son. Both these items have been missing for over seventeen years. The police at the time assumed young Strumps killers took the wallet during the robbery then killed him. There was no ID found on Wreckers' kid or any cash or gold chains he was thought to be wearing. Only the killer of both these kids could have these items. Vinnie added another dimension to the Strump Caper. This case keeps going sideways. More questions, fuck!

"Where is the black kids' gold chains and the other jewelry he was wearing?"

"Sold 'em to a shyster who melts down hot gold."

"Why the black kid?"

"We dumped the Strump kid's car on the Hill and left the gun I used on him in the glove box. I figured a shine would have eyes on it and jack it and find the gun. The car was on the cop's hot sheet and I figured they'd bag him before he hit a chop shop. Wrecker's kid was just unlucky that day. He was a smart assed punk anyway. No great loss."

"What about the Strump kid?"

"He was clean. He had a couple of hundred in the wallet. That's it."

"Who else worked with you? I want a name and address."

"Winky Fazio. You should remember him, Red. You busted him once. You can find him waiting for you at St Catherine's Cemetery."

"I could believe you did Wrecker's kid, but you were too scared of Strump to put a hit on his kid."

"You're right about that. Strump himself ordered it. He said the kid was gay and he was tired of trying to straighten him out. He didn't want a kid of his staining his name. I told you this guy Strump was an evil son of a bitch. Remember your promise, Red."

"Yeah, Vinnie. What about Winky? Who did him?"

"Strump popped him two weeks after the hit. He never left any loose ends."

"Why didn't he kill you too, if he was cleaning up?"

"He thanked me for cleansing his family of a pervert. He didn't know that I pulled the trigger on his kid and I didn't tell him. As far as he knew, Winky was the trigger man. After that incident he treated me with respect, and we worked together up till the time he got it."

"Who popped him?"

"I told you he was an assassin. I think he popped Hoffa for the Feds. I got no proof, but he was connected to Hoover back in the sixties, and he hated Hoffa. He showed up after Hoffa disappeared with an FBI ID that looked official. He said he only would use it if he got caught doing the job. He told me he was like James Bond and had a license to kill. Like he needed one, that's it, Red. Now it's your turn to put up."

"Who did he work for? You were his control and handed out his targets to him. Right?"

"I rented him from coast to coast. I was the only one who knew his identity. Back then I was connected to the outfit in Chicago. Sam Giacanni and me grew up together in Chi. We made our bones together. I set up here on the Southside at a time when there was a vacuum. He backed me. Strump would call him on a safe phone to get the job. He set the price and gave me a taste. I never knew his targets. He always handled his deals through a phone number I would give him. I sent him up on a lot of calls from sixty-five to maybe ninety-five. I lost track."

"Why weren't you upfront when we first talked?"

"I held out just in case you tried to weasel out of our deal. I knew I had leverage with the shoe box and some other Strump details. I was right. You did mussel me for more shit on him or some inside stuff I might have. Right, Red?" The old bastard said, not looking for me to answer.

"Fuck you, Vinnie! I've known you for thirty years and how you operate. Do you think I didn't know you were holding out? You go all in on Friday at daybreak. Are you thinking about backing out? You know that you're the only chance your son has to live long enough to collect his Social Security. I'll tell you where it's to take place and then you set the meet with Lotori. You offer him cash and yourself.

I have a rat in the IG that works for Lotori. He'll drive you to the meet. Lotori will know you're alone. Your driver will tell him. You give yourself up and take Lotori with you. That's the plan. I'll help Sal take the Southside over. I have the soldiers to back him if he needs them. With Lotori gone and his top lieutenants gone, he can fill the void left on the Southside. The other bosses will be busy fighting over Lotori's turf. When Sal whacks a couple of his producers, the others on the Southside will fold. I'll be his godfather till the shit settles. Then I'm out. If you taught him the business, he'll prosper. Only you have that answer."

"When did you say we go? I ain't taking real cash to the meet am I?"

"No, you dumb Dago. There won't be any place to spend it where you two are going. I'll call you when everything is set. Now get the fuck out." I ended the conversation and switched my thoughts to the safe at Wrecker's junkyard. How do you open it without damaging the contents?

## CHAPTER 39

TWENTY MINUTES LATER, I was at the junkyard with Wrecker, Jimmy, and Eddie.

"Anybody got any ideas on how to open this safe?"

"Just turn the handle. The dumb motherfucker that left it forgot to lock it. Don't worry. Red. We didn't open it just in case there was a bomb inside waiting to explode in your face."

Strump wouldn't destroy his legacy. No chance of a bomb being inside. It was 2025 in his mind when this safe would be found and opened.

"Take the contents into Wrecker's trailer. I'll go through it there."

"You gonna stay all night? Just lock up when you leave. I'm going to my club. If you white boys want some black pussy come with me. Not you, Cyclops. You got your date with Marys' palm."

I began my search through Horst Strumps' autobiography. As I read, it began to explain why the Feds and the Italians wanted these files to stay buried. He had supported his confessions with pictures, dates, times, receipts, phone numbers, and names of his victims and the sponsors of the crime. I didn't count all the murders he carried out, but two famous targets stood out. One would blow the top off an old and rehashed crime. All the names he listed that were involved, from the crime bosses to the top FBI echelon, are named. Horst Strump did leave a bomb in his safe; One which I'll explode all over the news …and soon. I packed the files in the back of the van I was using and assigned Jimmy and One Eye Eddie to sit on them till they heard from me. I told them to keep the boxes sealed. I gave them a story about the old documents crumbling if they were handled improperly.

Strumps arrogance gave him away. He was so sure of himself that if he left the hidden past, he would never want found till 2025 in an open safe. I had found the last piece of the puzzle I needed to claim my prize for solving the Carson Street caper.

I shifted my thoughts to finishing the Lotori and Vinnie G situation. Tomorrow was Friday and *D* day for those two. The *D* stood for dead.

After a couple hours rest at Annie's, I was back on the street gathering everything I needed to end the hunt for the Strump murder case solution. The game would be over for the Italians, the German gang and the Feds by Friday night. The evening news would disclose their history with Strump.

It was almost dawn on *D* day as Jimmy and I watched the players gather on the floor of the quarry for their last scene. I had the cameras rolling. Vinnie had arrived first and had positioned his black limo at his mark on the stage. I arranged for Sparks to chauffer him for a fee. I knew Sparks would tell Lotori just what I wanted him to know. He would inform Lotori that Vinnie would be alone except for the two capos that were secured in the trunk. At one point, the scene called for Vinnie to open it so they could play their part and spray the Lotori gang with the contents of their automatic weapons. Vinnie would tell Sparks that information just as Lotori arrived with his supporting cast of Italians. This morning, he brought two cars full of extras for the final scene, just as I thought he would. The Italians were predictable.

From our position above the quarry on 18$^{th}$ street road we could see by Vinnie's hand gestures that he was explaining to Lotori that he had stored the cash he brought in the trunk of his car. His car keys were in his hands and he believed a push of the trunk opener would bring the end to himself and Lotori in the shootout that would follow.

Sparks, being in the Lotori camp, would tell him before Vinnie could open it. At that point, the script called for improv by all the main players.

Eleven of Lotori's gumbas stood behind him as Sparks nervously blurted out the secrete hidden in the trunk of Vinnie's car. Vinnie was sure that it was true. Earlier that morning, I convinced him that I put two shooters in his trunk, and I would see to it that everyone at the site would be dispatched, including him.

I was the director, and I called… Action! Sparks played his part and told Lotori of the surprise in the trunk, and Vinnie fumbled with his car keys, trying to open it. It wouldn't open. I took the batteries out of his clicker. Lotori had his weapon out and fired three shots into Vinnie for trying to set him up. He fell backward and crumpled to the ground, clutching the black trunk opener and pressing it again and again until the cloud of death took his last breath. Vinnie had done as he said he would for his son. He made the ultimate sacrifice to save his kid.

Lotori motioned to Sparks to get the keys from Vinnie's hand. He would use Sparks to shield his men while they moved into place to kill whoever came in the trunk. Sparks opened it and the end to the last act of the Southside Italian Theatre exploded.

I had made a change in the method I used to carry out the final scene. There was no elaborate kill box, just 40 sticks of dynamite in the trunk of Vinnie's bier that was set to explode when it was opened. The curtain came down and fourteen actors in the drama were now part of the past. The earth shook. Sidewalks cracked and windows were shattered. A cloud of smoke and flame rose into the air over the quarry. The flames were carrying the spirits of evil men to Hades. Maybe Vinnie got a pass for his last good deed.

The Orchestra of the Streets began playing. The call must have been put out to bring more street instruments than usual. I heard more multiple police sirens, fire engine horns and ambulance bleeps than I ever remember hearing at one time. The play was a success. I had matched Shakespeare's Tragedy scenes. My identity as the author would forever be left to speculation. It was time for me to write the next play. The actors have been invited and only need me to provide them with the scripts.

"Red, nobody's going to know who got blown apart for days. You cleaned up the Northside. Now what? You got any dynamite left?"

"Yeah, Jimmy. It's a different kind of explosive, I'm setting off later today."

Annie was contacting Hilda and Jackie to have them meet me at my office at seven tonight. I was going to take Jimmy and Steve with me to pick up a package in Washington, Pa., which was an hour's ride from the city.

The explosion at the quarry pushed the Brownsville Road car accident off the news. Some were talking about a terrorist attack. They hadn't gotten around to laying it at my doorstep yet.

"What the hell did you do this morning? The building shook from that explosion. Tell me it wasn't you, Red," Annie asked.

"I just put the rock quarry back in business. More economic recovery for the Southside, Annie."

"Is it over, Red?"

"Almost. I'm going out after we go to breakfast. I need you to make some calls for me."

I called Jake and told him to be in front of Max's at four and cause a distraction when he saw me arrive. He needed to draw attention to himself so I could get a package into my building without anyone noticing.

Everything was set. Hilda, Jackie, Annie, the package, and five of my guys would be at my office by seven. The Carson Street Caper would be over. I would end it where it began, right here in my office on Carson Street.

The package I brought from Washington was secured on the third floor of my building. I had everything I needed to begin the meeting in my office. Hilda, Annie and Jackie were seated across from my desk, looking out the windows at Carson Street.

"Hilda, I have the answers you hired me to find. No questions. Just listen."

I explained how I found the mausoleum and Horst's diaries telling his activities up till his murder. They didn't need to know how the Feds, the Italians and the Germans were tied to him. They could read it in the press and see it on the news tomorrow. I sent Jimmy to bring the package I picked up earlier to my office. Minutes later, Jimmy was pushing a man with a hood over his head to a spot in front of the window to the left of my desk. Everyone now had front row seats.

I stood and removed the hood. I gave them a look at an aged and balding figure that I introduced… as Horst Strump.

After the initial shock in the room, Hilda stood, said something in German to him, then pulled out a pistol and fired five shots into his body. It pushed him backward from the force of the bullets and sent him through my recently replaced front window. The sidewalk had become familiar with dead men falling from my office.

"God damn it, Hilda! Why?"

"Don't worry, Mr. Canyon. I will pay for the window and pay you for finding the killer of my husband."As I took the revolver from her as she quietly spoke to me. "He killed our son, Trent, didn't he?"

"Yes, he was responsible for your son's death." She didn't need to know that he didn't pull the trigger. He set it up. Same thing to me.

I didn't have to call the cops. The dead body lying on Carson Street had taken care of that. Hilda had killed the one man who had the answer to why the Germans were hunting for his diaries. Now, I'd have to capture one of them alive to get that answer.

COPS… COPS… COPS. Everywhere!

Jackie would take care of Hilda and the cops. The newspapers and TV probably will want me banned from Pittsburgh. When a certain reporter breaks the story, I'm giving him tonight I'm going to be famous or infamous. I didn't care either way. I had the proof. With the pieces of the puzzle, I picked up at Horsts' hideaway and the confession backed up by hard proof from his mausoleum. I was going to solve *one* famous old mystery and shine a light on another. I'd throw in the answer for two seventeen-year-old unsolved murders. Hilda has her answer, and before the night is over, Wrecker Johnson will have his.

I decided to give the story to Annie's cousin Nick. He's a Southside kid working for one of those weekly rags that spotlight the go to spots that are in the City. He sells ads and writes junk about the nightlife. That would all change tomorrow. He'd move up to a desk in the newsroom of one of the City's two daily garbage wrappers.

I moved the show to the IG.

Me and One Eye Eddie pushed our way through the mass of thrill seekers, reporters, and stringers from the out-of-town media. I was gonna shove a mike down the throat of one of the weasels trying to get a statement from me, but Eddie stopped me. The bar of the IG was packed out because Annie had closed off the dining room. This is where I planned to tell Annie and Eddie the postscript to the Carson Street Caper. It will blow Hilda right off the front page.

"Is it over, Red, really over?" Annie asked.

"Mostly, but for Horst's involvement with the Germans. Hilda buried the answer to that connection when she killed him. I think she holds a part of the answer. Will she give it up? She hasn't so far but we haven't sorted out all the boxes of Strumps history. We'll see!"

There was too much activity at the IG, back to my office.

The Carson Street Caper would now have its second ending right where it began. Annie, Eddie, and Jimmy sat and waited. I was sure that they each had their own ending for the Strump case.

"Can't this wait till tomorrow?"

"If any of you want to leave, then go before I lock all the doors. You can read about it and watch it on the news for the next month or so."

I sent Jimmy to the IG for a case of Iron and a bottle of vodka. The show would begin after a shot of vodka and a beer. My body was aching from the beating I've been giving it lately. It was a choice of booze or pharmacy. Bobby had boarded up the office window and the blinds were shut tight. No free admission tonight.

"The Strump case began to unravel when I made the connection with him, Vinnie and a funeral home."

The rest of the Strump caper would blow the top off the Washington D.C. fuck ups. The crime of the century was bungled by them and covered up by the FBI and the DOJ and I had the proof.

"Stop all the bullshit and tell us what you got."

"Okay, Eddie, hear it is. The Kennedy Assassination."

"Red, that case was solved over forty years ago."

"Yes, it was but it wasn't."

"You been drinking again, Red?"

"No, Eddie, they got the right shooter but the wrong target. It's all right here in Strumps memories. He was at the Book Depository in Dallas in the same room with Oswald. He had a contract to throw Oswald out the fucking window after he made the kill. Oswald was hired by Sam Giancana to kill Jackie Kennedy not President Kennedy. Giancana had a long affair with Phyllis McGuire of the McGuire Sisters. He proposed to her, but she wouldn't marry him."

"Why would he want to kill Jackie?"

"Anne, Jack Kennedy was a womanizer. He had an affair with Phyllis then passed her on to his brother Bobby. Sam warned Jack to stay away from her, but Jack was powerful and ignored Sam. Sam held back but when Jack passed Phyllis on to Bobby that put the wheels in motion."

"So whacking Jackie was payback for the hurt and humiliation Jack put on Phyllis McGuire. The bosses wouldn't let Sam hit Jack. They knew the shit would come down on all the crime families from Chicago to New York and any soft spots around the country that the Organization had. So, he settled for Jackie O. According to Strump the families were split on putting a hit on Jackie. Sam figured he had enough juice to go ahead because they abstained from a vote. That's when Jack Ruby came into play."

"Nice story, Red, but what do you have to prove it."

"I got it all, Eddie. No more Questions until I finish. You can all look at the photos and negatives of Oswald with the rifle looking out onto Main Street and Dailey Plaza. The plan was for Strump to push Oswald out the window after he took out Jackie Kennedy. He guessed Oswald decided to kill Jack. When Strump saw Kennedy down, he made his escape. Governor Connally was just collateral damage. He didn't want to take a chance he might be seen and get tied to the hit. He had pictures in his camera of Oswald firing the rifle and if he got picked up, he'd go down with Oswald. Let's take a break 'cause I need a drink."

"Is your Carson Street Caper going to end now, Red?"

"Yes and no, Anne. The Hilda Strump case is going to be closed. The Strump files have legs. We'll see!"

"You're throwing bombs, Red. Unless you have hard proof, you're going to blow yourself up."

"It's all here, Eddie. I've got boxes of files and albums of pictures of his targets. There's a dozen handwritten diaries with details of his kills with dates, times and places and the names of who commissioned the hits. The exception is the FBI. When Hoover died in 1972, his handlers continued use of the code name 'HOOVER' as if he was still in charge."

"If you got all that detail then you just solved a lot of open murders and missing persons cases. But how you gonna prove the Kennedy switch. What you got.

Strump has a recording of Giacanni spilling the hit. Strump was the shooter that took Sammy out. He was pissed because the hit in Dallas blew up. He figured Sammy double crossed him cause the real target was Jack and he was gonna give Sammy a pass if he could back up his story. Strump figured he'd give him something to prove the hit was really on Jackie. It's all in one of his Diaries and on the tape."

"So how did he break in the house with Sammy not hearing anything and why did he want to whack him anyway if he got paid for the hit he didn't make? That was a win… right?"

"Strump was already in the house and just waiting for the right time to show himself. Strump always completed a job. Giacanni broke that streak. He had to pay. By killing Sammy, in his mind, I guess he figured the contract was completed."

"So, what did Giacanni tell him?"

"He said he shopped the Outfit in New Orleans for an ambitious wannabee in Dallas. They gave him Jack Ruby. He was small time but would probably sign on if he was 'put up' to the Outfit. Sammy met him in a parking lot at the KC airport and set the job in motion. Ruby told him he had a hunter on his book that could make the shot. He would tell him the target the morning of the motorcade. That's when he called the Southside and hired Strump. When Strump didn't take out Oswald, Ruby had to do it. Ruby saw it as way to have his name written in history forever according to Sammy G. Oswald had to be silenced because he knew the real target and could give it up.

It was unlikely, but it was still a loose end. If Ruby could take out Oswald, he would forever be credited with killing the man who killed Jack Kennedy. That was his legacy. He wouldn't diminish it with an admission he hired a gang member that couldn't shoot straight."

"Hey, Red, you can't possibly have looked through all the stuff from Strump. Why you gonna give it up so easy. You know the Feds are gonna deep six the shit."

"You know Eddie, you're right. I got ahead of myself. I gotta take it underground. We need to make sure all the pieces fit before I go public. I got a perfect place to secure everything. We got the proof on the Kennedy hit but we need more back up on Strump out there proving his connections with the Organization."

"What now, Red?"

"We release the information on the Strump case. Our client hired us to find the killer of her husband. We found him living like a hermit outside Pittsburgh. He faked his death. Case solved. We don't reveal any information about Hilda's son or Wreckers son. If we do, it's gonna open us up to more questions. Our story is our client hired us for a job, and we completed it. That's our statement, and NO questions answered."

"What about all the other shit we been dealing with the Dagos and the Krauts. It ain't exactly a secret with all the bodies in the streets tied to you. Now you got the Quarry thing that's going to come your way and you're going to sit on the biggest story maybe in history."

"That's right, Eddie. You called the right play."

"Are we going on vacation now, Red, or are you gonna push that Aunt Mary's Lockett bullshit on us?"

"Bingo Eddie. This one involves John Bennett and the funeral home in Whitehall. Remember, he is tied to Horst Strump and Southside Dago Vinnie. This guy, Bennet, was too cool every time we drilled him. He's too laid back in his attitude. He's into something that must pay big and has mussel behind it. He didn't push back at us because he didn't want to expose his actions. Bennett is dangerous. We keep him on the screen and continue the surveillance. The dead jeweler tied to Aunt Mary's Lockett is his. His stepdaughter was to meet me for lunch at noon today. She didn't show. I sent Billy to her apartment to get her. It was tossed. She wasn't there."

"So, what are we to do with this missing broad and the Lockett bullshit?"

"FIND HER, Eddie! AND THEN FIND THE LOCKET..."

## ABOUT THE AUTHOR

Originally from the vibrant Southside of Pittsburgh, I grew up immersed in the colorful sights and sounds of Carson Street. From my third-floor cold-water flat, I observed life unfolding below, forging memories playing behind the pretzel shop on 23rd and Carson. After exploring different paths, including traveling across the United States and settling in New Jersey, I discovered my passion for storytelling later in life. Drawing from my rich and varied experiences, my novels blend fiction with real-life tales, offering readers a glimpse into my unique journey. Committed to the craft, I continue to write and share my stories with the world, embracing each page-turning adventure until the final curtain falls.

Printed in the USA
CPSIA information can be obtained
at www.ICGtesting.com
LVHW090007010624
R18216800001B/R182168PG781182LVX00002B/3

9 798869 275585